THE HUNTED

By

DAVID O'NEIL

W & B Publishers
USA

W & B Publishers

For information:
W & B Publishers
Post Office Box 193
Colfax, NC 27235
www.a-argusbooks.com

ISBN: 978-0-6159886-6-5
ISBN: 0-6159886-6-0

Book Cover designed by Dubya

Printed in the United States of America

Prologue

The two people crouched, watching the men digging a deep hole in the ground beside the assembled vehicles of the building contractor. The site had been abandoned temporarily by the contractor and the vehicles left standing there until needed for the next stage of the construction.

The watchers were already in place when the two cars arrived. The men digging were preparing their own graves.

The male watcher, Quin Gilmore, turned to his female companion, "Ready for action?"

Cassandra (Cass) Richards nodded and lifted the automatic rifle she was carrying a little nervously, and lined her sights on the bigger of the men supervising the digging.

"Ready when you are!" She said in a cultured drawl. Her cool manner concealed the turmoil of different emotions she was experiencing at that moment. She was about to kill a man. The fact that it was to save the life of another two or three lives—or more—did not make it easier at this point, though she conceded it might help in the future.

There were four men standing and two digging. Both diggers were now down about four feet, and one of the four men standing had drawn an automatic and was carefully cocking it.

Quin sighted his own rifle and said, "Now would be a good time, from left to right."

Immediately Cass's rifle spoke twice, then twice again. Quin was a fraction behind, and all four men who had been standing were down.

"Are you okay?" His words were concerned.

Cass lifted her head and looked into his eyes. "I'm fine, thanks." The thing was, as soon as the action started, she became completely cool, no more twitches or worries, just concentrate and shoot.

Quin could see that she had lost that apprehensive look which she had started out with.

"Good. Let's get away now. If those two don't take advantage of the situation they don't deserve the service we have performed.

They travelled back to the river in the panel van they had used to get to the scene earlier that evening.

Quin dropped the van off in the lock-up garage, one of twelve rented by individuals on the south side of the river. They returned to the retreat in the Jaguar waiting in the lock-up.

As he drove in it crossed Quin's mind that after five weeks, he was beginning to think of the retreat as his home. He glanced at Cass sitting quietly beside him. Pleased at how she had dropped into his life, and recently become his partner, a situation created by the threat posed to both their lives by the local crime boss.

He parked the car and followed Cass down to the living quarters they occupied.

Chapter one

The bunker

There was no sign of the people following him when he finally stopped running. He surveyed the area around him carefully, quartering the entire 360 degrees in one long slow circuit.

Then, and only then, did he allow himself to relax against the ruined building dominating the surrounding landscape. He found a seat on a block of stone which had once been part of the building behind him. His hand subconsciously traced the texture of the stone. It was almost slippery to his touch. Without thinking his hand roamed, following a line of smooth rock that traced a ruler straight groove across the rough stone.

Realizing that there was an anomaly here, he turned and looked at his seat. On closer examination it was not, as he had at first thought, a piece of fallen masonry. It was in a place where it had been intended to be, a part of the original structure.

He stood up, turning to examine it properly, now curious to find the line he had located. He realized that it was well-nigh invisible.

He studied the surrounding area carefully once more, senses tuned to any odd sound or noise that might indicate his pursuers had located him. Satisfied that he was still alone, he took out his knife and located the line.

He found he could enter the point in a narrow slot and run it to the wall against which it was set.

Getting increasingly curious he looked for, and found, a similar groove near the far end of the stone, about four feet away and parallel to the other slot. Dropping to his knees he studied the front face of the stone and found an expected additional slot two inches below the top. Tracing with his knife once more, he realized that he was looking at a lid of some sort. Four foot long, by two foot and two inches deep.

A little excited, he nevertheless stood and carefully surveyed the surrounding area. Satisfied once more that there was no one in sight, he returned his attention to the slab. Running his blade along the long slot once more, testing to see if there was a catch or pivot point. He sighed, as with a quiet click his blade encountered something. It moved under pressure, and the slab slid open with a gust of stale air revealing, in the starlight, a stairway down into the hill below.

He climbed onto the stair, made of stone apparently from the same source as the ruin. and peered at the mechanism operating the slab with the help of the light from his cell phone. He released the catch, and the slab closed once more over his head. He opened it again just to be sure he could. Then, with a last look around, he closed it and stepped down the stairs clear of the entrance. With the slab closed it was very dark. He looked round by the light of his cell phone, and only then made his way down the stairs.

At the foot of the stair was a small hallway with a door of formidable proportions. However beside the door was a switch-box. With a shrug and some trepidation the intruder pushed the switch down. He was rewarded with the murmur of an engine starting up, and a light glowed into being from a flush ceiling fitting. The dusty panel beside the door came to life and began flashing. He wiped it clean with his sleeve and read the instructions. Then he pressed the switch below the notice. The big door groaned and opened slowly. As the gap widened he saw a string of lights come on down the corridor revealed.

He recognized he had entered a purpose-built bunker, probably a relic of the cold-war of the 50/60's. He stepped through the door, stopped and looked at the accumulated dust around the door sill and hinges. Using his hands he brushed away the dirt as best he could, making sure the door would not jamb and trap him inside. He then turned and walked down the corridor.

The door closed, rather more smoothly than it had opened. There was apparently a sensor which triggered the door mechanism. He was aware of a breeze, a breath of fresher air as he walked. Subconsciously, he ticked another box, air conditioning.

There was an elevator. The corridor ended at a square room, still a little stale smelling but the air circulation was improving all the time. The fresh-smelling breeze he could feel was clearing the dead atmosphere of many years of disuse. There were seven destination buttons.

He pressed the up button to see what would happen. There was another tense moment ending in anti-climax. The doors swished open and without thinking he stepped into a very normal looking elevator. He pressed the single up-button. The cabin shot upward and stopped. A panel lit up. It said in red lights. 'Air – clear.' 'Radiation level, normal.' Doors open.'

The button turned green, and when pressed the doors slid open and revealed another stone-walled chamber. There was a green arrow faintly visible on the floor pointing toward a gap in the wall of what he now saw was a cave.

"Later!" He thought, and stepped back into the elevator.

The down button gave him a scare he would not forget. He felt the lift drop away from under him, grabbed the handrail and hung on. After what seemed an endless drop the ride slowed and the elevator came to rest. Still shocked, he watched the doors open to reveal a reception area, complete with carpeted floor and a reception desk, telephone and electric typewriter. Beyond the desk there was a wooden door.

It occurred to him that this was beginning to feel more like a Hilton hotel than an air raid shelter. He walked through the doorway. The layout was divided between working and living. There were four doors marked Suite 1-4, another marked Dormitory.

The work section comprised offices with standard office layout. All the records, paper, seemed to have been removed. Document cabinets stood empty except for the odd scrap of paper caught in a drawer or still in the waste paper basket from the evacuation of the place.

The kitchen and storerooms were something else. With power there was the possibility of preparing food if he had any. He needn't have worried. The store room was still stacked with dried and canned goods.

Quin Gilmore surveyed the place he had found. Obviously it had been abandoned for years. The dates on the packages of food indicated around 1986. 28 years ago.

For a few moments he just sat, thoughts, ideas, and questions. Then, "Enough," he said aloud, hearing his voice echoing slightly in the empty room. He opened a tin, tipped the contents into a saucepan and heated it on the electric stove.

He ate well and slept in a comfortable bed.

Finding the bathroom was easy. He stood in the shower with hot water streaming down his body considering plans for today. He saw his reflection in the big mirror. Six foot, fit and healthy, smooth muscled with wide shoulders and a slim waist. His dark hair looked black, while it was still wet at least. There were scars, a four inch scar on his right side where a knife had slid along the rib, another just below his left shoulder. That had been a bullet. The third was on his stomach. The Taliban bullet had shortened his intestine, and nearly his life.

First to do today is to explore thoroughly and discover what exactly he had stumbled into. He sat and finished his bowl of cereal, thinking the bunker was not, as he had first thought, a Government project. Or, if it had started out that way, someone had modified it at considerable expense.

He searched the suite he had used. In the centre drawer of the desk he found the schematics for the entire construction. It appeared it had been funded from a seemingly bottomless purse.

Attached to the document was a letter addressed to a Mr Robert Mitchell. The address was a Mayfair apartment, and the date was 1959.

The content was mystifying until he thought about the stories he had heard about the case of Kim Philby. Adding two and two on this occasion made four. It seemed that this bunker had been financed by funds from behind the Iron Curtain.

Above the accommodation were other rooms. The elevator buttons meant five floors upward. There was also a stairway which he decided to use rather than trust the elevator.

An armory occupied part of the second floor with several single rooms furnished as accommodation, he guessed for staff. Then fuel tanks on the next. Above that came more stores and equipment and a workshop for the maintenance of the shelter. There was a fully equipped gym on the fourth floor, while the top floor contained a garage. There was a motorcycle on a stand and a dark blue Jaguar saloon. The plate was C prefix which dated it 1986. It stood on blocks. The bench tools and drums of oil were obviously there for additional vehicles which had once occupied the roomy garage.

In the glove box of the Jaguar he found a list. The suites were for a named group of people. The upper rooms were for the staff who would protect and care for the listed people.

He recognized none of the names, though the place was obviously for people important to somebody, worth preserving at the time. The fact that the cold war had not grown hot and the relevant persons no longer interested meant that the bunker had probably been forgotten. From what he could see it would be unlikely there was any official record of the construction. The ground in which it had been constructed was a grassy scrub-covered hill, in fenced land with what looked like WD warning signs on the fences.

It seemed that he had found a useful bolt hole while he gathered his resources.

Seated in the front seat of the Jaguar, the mirror reflected his face, currently thoughtful blue eyes, regular features with the slightly crooked nose - not games, SAS training at Hereford.

He returned to his more detailed search looking specifically for other exits, those other than the main way in. There had to be some way of moving the vehicles in and out. He checked the garage once more, testing every button and lever in view, until he finally found what he was looking for.

Beside the vehicle lift used for servicing the cars was an extra unlabelled lever. When he moved it, stiff from lack of use, the back wall of the garage rose in the air to a point level with the ceiling. It revealed a passageway, wide and high enough for a high-top van.

Intrigued, he unracked the motorcycle. The tires held air but he topped them up anyway. There was a compressor which, judging from the gauge had started up as soon as the power had come on. He put the sump drain-plug in on the motorcycle engine and topped up with oil. Then, finally, he filled the petrol tank with fuel from the storage tank. There was a dry battery plugged in to a charger. The power had started it operating so, if it were chargeable, it should be useable. He fitted it and wheeled the bike into the centre of the garage. Putting it on its centre stand, he mounted, poised his foot on the kick start and threw his weight on the pedal.

The immediate roar of the motor startled him and he nearly fell off the machine. As he straightened up he looked at the name flash on the tank, Royal Enfield. It crossed his mind that the company was as dead as the owner of this place probably was.

The regular throb of the 500cc single cylinder engine was a reassurance, so he pushed it forward off the stand. The tires seemed okay. So letting the clutch in gingerly, he set off along the road through the hill. The headlight shone on the walls of what looked like a mine tunnel, braced with heavy timbers. There was another door after about 300 yards. He took the bike out of gear, propped it on its stand and examined the doorway. It was another power operated slab which, like the first door, opened upward in response to the turn of a switch in a glass enclosure on the wall to the right of the entry. He was beginning to believe that perhaps the bunker had been built onto one of the WW11 official bunkers, using the entry and exit routes already established with upgrades and modifications.

Before closing the door he located the external control; like the others the door closed after he crossed a sensor.

Continuing along the track at a gentle rate, he realized that he was now in a tunnel, part of an underground system. He turned the bike and rode back, studying the place where the tunnels joined.

He guessed that there would be some sort of door here as well. There was! It was open. He presumed that the last people to leave had been in a hurry. No one had used this tunnel for years, so no one had noticed it.

He found the control and was relieved to find that it still worked. He closed and opened the door once more, before he carried on to the outside world where darkness had fallen.

He switched off his lights and sat breathing the night air, looking at the huge dome of lights which was the town stretching away into the distance. He heard the person stumbling along the road beside the track he was sitting on.

Leaving the bike where it was, he strode over to the wall separating the road from the former rail-track.

The woman was panting and trying to run in heels, not designed for it. There were two men walking along laughing at her efforts to get away.

Instinctively, he called quietly to the woman, "Over here!"

Startled, she looked over at him. "Help me, please? They are not nice men. I think they have guns."

"Here!" He held his hand out and, taking hers, he helped her over the wall.

There were shouts from the men as they broke into a run.

He dragged the woman to the bike and mounted, kick-starting the engine. She climbed on behind him and they roared off toward the town.

The pursuers ran back to their car and turned to follow on the other side of the wall. The two ways parted. Going beneath a former underpass. the bike managed to outrun the car for long enough to lose it. They turned back along the track and roared back into the old tunnel. At the door he stopped and closed the entrance. At the second door he allowed the door to close itself. The woman looked on in astonishment. At the garage, they dismounted and when, the door was closed, she looked at her rescuer; the question hanging between them.

He held up his hand. "Wait. Let's get somewhere a little more civilized and you can tell me why those men were chasing you." He turned and waved her into the elevator.

He smiled to himself when she gasped as it dropped to the residence level.

Once in the lounge area, Quin went to the bar. He lifted a bottle in silent invitation and she nodded. He poured two glasses of the Hennessy.

He brought both glasses over and sat on the chair opposite her. As he sat back sipping the cognac he studied his companion. Healthy-looking brown hair, still tousled after the wild ride. Green or hazel eyes, she was nice looking rather than drop-dead. The mouth was generous, the gaze steady and unafraid. *Nice legs,* he thought as she relaxed back into her seat, her neatly-proportioned figure reflected a healthy life?

She was doing the same thing. As she sipped her drink she assessed her rescuer. A friendly face which was neither handsome nor ugly, but somewhere in-between, with blue eyes and a nice smile. She guessed six foot tall, well built, not bulky. Trained rather than pumped up. Quick thinking and, she decided, intelligent.

"My name is Cassandra Richards, Cass to my friends. I work for a talented inventor, who specializes in medical research into what is sometimes called truth drugs. It is of course a misnomer, as the current crop only release inhibition.

"Where do you live?"

"Oh, Kingston, beside the river. I was going home from work when the two men jumped me. I know my way about the town pretty well but they grabbed me and drove off to the place where you found me. I got the impression that they had been told to silence me, luckily they decided they would have some fun with me first. So, having discussed who would do what in front of me, we all got out of the car. I asked who would be going first and when they started arguing about it I managed to pull free and run."

The face of the man opposite gave little away, but he smiled. "I'm Tarquin Gilmore known as Quin to my friends. At present I am doing my best to interfere with the life and works of the most important villain in the area. Your two goons probably work for the same man, my current target. Why do they want to get rid of you?"

"I'm not sure. I have the feeling that they are after something my boss is working on, and I am in the way because the boss trusts me and my judgement." She looked around and took a sip of her drink. "Tell me. What is this place?"

Quin rose to his feet and fumbled with the row of switches. Panels round the walls suddenly flashed up like windows, with views of countryside and seascape. It gave the place the appearance of an above-ground living room. He turned and told her about his find, the discovery of the bunker he believed to have been constructed in the cold war, when the threat of a rain of atomic warheads seemed real.

"I guess the bunker, as it is now, was created based on an existing structure, an area shelter for the local admin, or defense forces. They had apparently used pre-existing caves for the installation. The current development was carried out by someone who took it over for personal use. It has obviously been abandoned, probably forgotten since 1980's, possibly after the fall of the Berlin Wall. It was left stocked with canned goods and dried foods, fuel and a power plant. When I entered the power came on, using standby diesel generators. Since then an alternate system kicked–in I suspect its hydro-electric since the standby systems are idle once more."

"Are you going to stay here? Won't the owners come to check it out?" Cass was curious though not apprehensive. There was something about this man which was reassuring, a competence that said he was operating within his comfort zone. In fact, she was beginning to think his comfort zone seemed to cover a lot of territory.

"After standing empty for over twenty years untouched and unloved, I do not anticipate any interference from past owners. I decided that for now, at least, it would make a good base until I get my enemies off my tail."

He grinned and shrugged. "In view of the fact that they seem to know where you live and work, I suggest you stay here tonight. Tomorrow I'll take you home and you can collect a few things. Tonight we can discuss what action we should take about the two goons who attacked you." Quin smiled at her. "Would you care to join me for dinner?"

Chapter two

One plus one make two

He produced Spam fritters with scrambled dried eggs and beans. To her surprise Cass found she was ravenous. She cleared her plate and a bowl of tinned fruit topped with evaporated milk to follow.

"There's nothing like the threat of rape and murder to perk up your appetite." Quin commented drily when they finished.

The coffee and creamer followed, and Cass sat back with a sigh. "That feels much better." She said with a smile, "Thank you, kind sir. As a dinner date that rated up there among the best in class."

Quin bowed his head in acknowledgement and joined her with his coffee.

As they sat making small talk the lady said, "While I do not really know you, I confess I feel safe here. I am not accustomed to being too close with others. I was brought up at arm's-length I suppose, after my parents died. I have a guardian, though I have only been in occasional touch for some years. I was good at skiing and I spent a lot of time training and competing in cross-country events. I had to stop when I was injured. Though I am now fully fit, there was no going back it seemed. So I did a Management Course and got a job. I moved to Kingston last month from Chiswick, to be nearer work. Now, who are you?"

Quin studied her for long enough to make her feel edgy. She had been shocked at her instant acceptance of him. It was not like her. She was normally wary of men she didn't know. However she had become aware that she really wanted to know this man better. Her life thus far had included one or two skirmishes with men; the last serious to the point of discussing living together. Then his wife had made her presence felt, a factor she had known nothing about. It had rather knocked her confidence.

"Tell me, please. Are you alone? Is there anyone else involved?"

Startled at her question, Quin said immediately. "No, I'm quite alone. I have no one to answer to, no ties now! Does it matter?"

"Oh, I'm sorry that sounded terrible and I did not mean it to. I seem to have had my share of shocks and disappointments lately and I just….." She stopped not sure how to go on.

The man sitting opposite her smiled sympathetically. "I know the feeling. Life can be like that sometimes. Perhaps I should explain. First, another?" He held his glass up.

When he returned he handed her a glass with a similar measure, the cognac golden and glowing in the warm light.

He began talking quietly. "I, like you, lost my parents when I was quite young. My father was killed in the break-up of Yugoslavia. He was a spook, M16, stationed at the consulate in Split. Mother remarried a drunken thug, and died after a session with my stepfather and his friends. Car ran into the river, all four drowned. It left my sister and me. It was 2000, I was eighteen by then. I looked after her. Luckily my mother was insured. We had enough to live on and the house was ours. I joined up when she went to university, I went to one or two odd places and finished up at Hereford with the SAS.

"Like you I became involved. With the unexplained absences that occurred because of my job, she found the idea of our association no longer acceptable and sought and found another, more settled person to share her life."

There was a tinge of bitterness in the words that made Cass feel closer to the man who had stepped into her life so dramatically. "I see," she said. "I think I've had enough for to-day. Would you mind.....?"

"Sorry, I was not thinking." He rose to his feet and held out his hand. She took it and he drew her to her feet. For an instant they were very close. There was a moments' hesitation, then the spell was broken and Quin said, "I'll show you your suite."

As they walked Quin said. "We will need to plan the program tomorrow, and all the other tomorrows, until we have lifted the threat to your life and limb, and incidentally mine."

Surprisingly, Cass slept through the entire night, no dreams, and no nightmares. She woke, startled at the strange surroundings, until she remembered where she was.

***

After using the en-suite bathroom shower she dressed in the clothes she had been wearing the previous day and found her way to the kitchen by following the scent of frying bacon.

Quin fed her, then over coffee spoke. "First things first. Can we establish your situation? Would you prefer to get a plane to the other side of the world perhaps, way out of reach of last night's two gentlemen?"

Cass looked at him intently. "Do I read you correctly? You intend to do something about those people, and their boss."

Quin nodded.

"Would you be able to use my help? I can cook, use a computer. I can fire a rifle but I am not a street fighter." Cass could hardly believe what she was saying. All she knew was there was a deep burning resentment inside that made her want to punish the men from last night. They had scared her more than she had ever been scared before. The matter of fact way they had discussed her rape and murder in front of her had made her furious.

"What experience have you had shooting?"

"I competed in Alpine biathlon ski events, shooting is one of the requirements."

"There is an armory here and I believe a firing range of sorts. Show me what you can do. I can teach you to use a sidearm, if you are willing to use one? The reason I mention it is that the people we are up against kill. To have a chance against them we would need to fight them with their own weapons."

Cass looked at him with astonishment. Could he be serious? He looked serious! She thought about what he said, and realized that it made sense. It was a case of 'put up' or 'shut up'.

She thought for just a moment more, and then looked up at Quin. "So where are these guns and things?"

"I'll take that as a yes then," Quin smiled thinly. "We'll take a look later. For the morning, perhaps you can think about what you need from home; money, contact with work, that sort of thing."

"You really want me to move in here?"

"If we are going to work together, I must know that you are safe. Your apartment is vulnerable. If you are wandering about in public, at work, or just staying with friends, you will be vulnerable, and you may put your friends in danger."

Cass realized that he was talking sense.

"I see what you mean. You are right. Let's take a look at these guns." Cass smiled as she rose to her feet, stretching to ease the kinks still with her from her yesterday's exertions, unaware of the effect she was having on Quin, who quickly turned and led off to the stairway up to the armory, before she had a chance to notice.

***

They drove in the Jaguar to a lock-up garage, one of a row of twelve rented out south of the river below Kingston-on-Thames. He took the pick-up truck from the lock-up and left the Jaguar which was still unlicensed, inside and out of sight.

There were several items that Cass needed to take from her apartment. She had a suitcase packed with clothes and her laptop computer and camera. Quin gathered her desktop computer into a box and removed the wireless modem. They vacated the apartment and Cass called at the bank to report her lost cards and collect cash. The cards had been left with her handbag in the car with her attackers from the night before. Her mobile phone had been smashed in the struggle when they abducted her. She discovered that the phone was damaged and tossed it into the river as they passed over the bridge. Quin picked up another 'pay as you go' for her while she was in the bank. She insisted on calling at the supermarket before they returned to the bunker. Quin's pick-up was loaded by the time he parked it in the garage.

They carried the goods into the elevator and descended to the living area. As they set up the computer Cass said "This has to be a waste of time. We get no signals here so we have in effect a word processor and adding machine."

Quin grinned. He walked through the open door to the reception desk and picked up the telephone sitting unnoticed on the desk. The buzz of the open line could be heard quite easily. "I believe this is pirated from what is probably a dedicated government line." He went to the box of extras he had bought, and passed over the cell phone bought for Cass. He plugged the wireless modem into the terminal of the office telephone, then he took out a modern button phone which he attached to the modem. "There we go, and my guess is that this line does not exist." With this enigmatic comment he returned to unloading the groceries and stacking them in the now operating fridge and freezer, and the cupboards in the kitchen.

By the time Cass had unpacked her personal gear in the suite she was using, it was time to join Quin for the training session he had insisted she undertake. She put on her training bra and leotard, sweatpants and top.

In the gym they started off with a series of stretches, only then did they start basic tuition in simple judo moves.

Watching as Cass practiced the pattern of moves he had selected, Quin said. "You are accustomed to training in a gym, and you have been trained in judo!" It was a statement not a question.

Cass smiled. "It's the pressure of modern life you know. If you work in town you have to train in a gym, just to keep up with the others. You choose your speciality and get on with it."

"What is your speciality?" Quin persisted.

"Boxing, mostly punch-ball and heavy bag, then sparring, with the occasional inter gym contest. But my trainer insisted I learned some basic judo before anything else. His point was that it was good basic stamina and flexibility training. The boxing came as I muscled up a bit."

"Where are you in all this?" Quin started sorting out gloves from a cabinet of gear by the wall.

"I've competed for the gym on a couple of occasions, lost once, won six times." Cass said wonderingly.

The pair of gloves flew at her. She caught them and slipped them on. It seemed that she was in for a lesson.

She was wrong. Quin asked her to show what she could do. He found the heavy bag in the cupboard and hung it from a ceiling hook.

Cass showed him how to brace the bag with his body. She limbered up with some shadow boxing before turning to the bag and slamming it with a straight left.

Quin was not quite ready. He thought he would finish up on the floor, but he managed to stay upright and retake his position. He was amazed at the power the comparatively slight woman put into her punches.

He called time after five minutes of relentless punching. "How long do you normally spend at the bag?" He asked.

"Normally three ten minute sessions." Cass said, breathing normally.

"If you get into a tussle with our friends again try punching them. I'll show you where to place your punches."

***

In the range she faced a target with the Walther PPK he had found for her.

Insisting that she learns to shoot from all angles, he was adamant that she relax when she had the gun in her hand. "Always stay aware that you have a loaded gun, but avoid tensing-up because it's there. Shooting a hand gun is all about keeping it in line with your forearm. When you fire, make it part of your lining up and pointing movement."

He loaded the magazine into his weapon and cocked it, put the safety on and stood with his back to the range. "Keep relaxed!" He said as he turned, gun coming up and fired, two shots almost blending into one.

Cass saw the target twitch, so she wound it back to the counter. The holes, one overlapping the other were just below the centre of the target. She looked at it stunned, then at him.

Quin looked at it, "I must have been distracted." He grinned. "It's the effect you have on me." He quipped.

Cass laughed with him. "Let's see if I suffer from the same problem." She did just what he did. Load, cock, and put the safety on. She turned her back and held the gun across her stomach, then she turned and fire twice.

The target twitched. Quin wound it back. The two bullet holes were about an inch apart on a level in the left hand corner of the 12"x12" target.

Cass looked disappointed.

Quin asked, "Have you ever fired a pistol before?"

"No! Isn't it obvious?" Cass said pointing at the target. "As you can see, I did mention it."

Quin shook his head. "I have never seen a novice do this before."

Still not understanding, Cass said, "I'm sorry. I will practice."

Quin said, "Now, rifle." He reached for an Armalite from the rack. Cass stopped him and took a Winchester .22 Hornet from the rack. Opening a box of the special cartridges, she loaded the interior magazine, cocked the action and set the safety. The 10 meter range was already set up with a target. Cass walked over with the rifle slung over her shoulders. When she reached the target, she unslung the gun. brought it to her shoulder and fired five shots, rapid fire. Then she stood back and racked the movement to show the magazine clear. Only then did she wind the target in.

Quin looked at the target with the centre blasted completely out. He nodded slowly. "You'll do." He said quietly.

Cass felt the warm glow those words gave her right through her body. She remonstrated with herself. "Steady. girl, you're getting carried away. You've only just met this man and you still know little about him."

Using the system of point and shoot, her hand-gun progress was rapid. A natural talent combined with a quick eye made her a formidable opponent for anyone.

Having decided that Quin was right about the dangers of trying to live openly when the mob was hunting you, Cass had accepted that for the moment at least, her best chance of survival was to stay in the retreat. Her own feeling in the matter at that point was, as she stated, to contribute to the fight against the local mob, and their personal enemy, Athol Patrick.

Cass and Quin's partnership was established on a strictly business basis. Quin had made no moves on her at all, and since the brief moments when she sensed his interest at their first encounter, he had shown nothing but respect for her as an equal.

She realized that he had checked up on her story. That made perfect sense. Now, apparently satisfied that she had been telling the truth, he had accepted her status., and had undertaken her training in the same serious manner that he applied to his own.

Chapter three

Where did they put the explosives

The first foray against the local mob was the result of a glimpse of one the men who had snatched Cass when she and Quin first met. They were returning from town with some things that they needed. When Cass pointed him out, Quin did not hesitate. He pulled over and as the man walked past he opened the door of the car slamming the man in the legs. As the man collapsed to the pavement he leapt out of the car ostensibly to help the man; he punched him on the jaw. The man collapsed completely, so he hoisted him into the car, draping him across the back seat. The man weakly tried to sit up but he lost interest when the barrel of the Walther caressed his cheek.

The information about the burial party was repaid with the opportunity to disappear. Apparently the threat to inform Athol Patrick that he had given information to Athol's enemies was enough to send him as far away as the open plane ticket would take him.

As Quin explained it did save them the trouble of having to either keep him prisoner, or kill him, with all the bother of getting rid of the body. The news about the burial party gave them their first opportunity to strike out at Cass's attackers and coincidentally Quin's enemy.

With the information he gave, Quin and Cass were able to set up their ambush.

***

The return to the retreat after their first foray to the construction site was anti-climax. Cass, realizing that she had killed people, was in a state of shock. Quin, aware of this and concerned for her, kept silent until they were inside once more.

Back in the lounge area they shared in the living quarters, Cass asked him about the men they had saved earlier that night.

Quin, who had been making coffee when she asked, finished what he was doing and passed her a steaming mug. "You did well tonight!" He said. Then "The men we saved probably are no better than the men we removed. I set up the situation to send a message. The rescue was a collateral bonus. The object tonight was to provoke reaction, mistakes, call it what you will. We declared war tonight. If it helps, did you notice that one of the men we hit was one of the two who was going to rape and kill you."

Cass nodded her head slowly. "I thought there was something familiar about him, but I was too wound up to think of anything but what I was doing." She looked at him, tears starting.

He reached out and pulled her close. He murmured into her hair. "There are no duels in the sun in this little war. Just like the old west, this is a kill or be killed situation. They will show no mercy, nor can we. Don't grieve for those men tonight. They have murdered before and were about to do so again. Their own so-called code does not include the words mercy, or forgiveness. Their boss ordered your death without hesitation. His contempt for the law is matched by his lack of interest in the lives of all the people he has had removed."

They stood locked together for several minutes until finally, Cass straightened up still firmly supported in his arms. "Now they will know we are out there."

"Exactly. They will need to start looking over their shoulder whenever they go out of doors. Their rivals will start probing weaknesses. The police will pick up on mistakes. For mistakes will come. All because we are suddenly on the scene and can strike without warning."

***

Athol Patrick was not happy, but then that was often the case. Never renowned for a sunny attitude toward life, today had been a particularly bad one. Those who knew him well steered clear of his office if they possibly could.

The news of the death of three of the men he considered his elite group had come from a story in the morning paper. The surviving member of the group of four was in hospital in intensive care.

Martin Goody was on the carpet in front of the boss and feeling unhappy. Athol looked at him through lowered brows. "They fucked up over the girl." He shook his head irritably. "What's her name?" He demanded.

"Cassandra Richards, boss. Her name was Cassandra Richards..."

"Whatever! Don't you fuck-up. Another fuck-up would be difficult to forgive."

"Okay, boss. No fuck-ups. Charlie will feel no pain."

Athol looked at Martin shaking his head. "Am I bothered? Get him out of harm's way! Dead would be good!"

***

Martin came into the room where the others were drinking coffee. They all looked up as he came through the door. He scanned the group, cold-eyed, calculating who and what he would need. He pointed at two of the men and a woman, jerked his thumb, turned out of the door and went through to the office he was using.

Sitting at the desk, he took his time studying all three before he spoke.

"Eton! I need you to play doctor. Alice, you will be visitor/girlfriend. Knuckles, you're the porter and security backup." He waved for them to sit down.

"We are going to see to Charlie." Goody said tersely.

"Are we going to get him out, Martin?" Eton asked.

Martin looked at him steadily. Eton squirmed in his chair.

"Did I ask you to speak?" Martin said.

"Sorry, boss!" Eton said.

Martin looked around at the others. "Anyone else need to say anything?"

The others shook their heads.

"Right. At the hospital. Eton in a white coat will be visiting Charlie in his professional capacity as doctor."

Turning to the woman, he said, "Alice, you will be either hospital visitor or girlfriend. So you will have to play it by ear, possibly to distract any copper at Charlie's bedside."

"Knuckles, you dress as a hospital porter. You may need to settle the copper, so that Eton can do his thing. We do not need to be identified, CCTV, staff etc."

"If it is easy to get him out we will. If it is not possible, then Charlie has to go. Has anyone any problem with that?"

Nobody spoke as Martin looked at them enquiringly. "I think it will be too complicated to actually get him out, or even if he could survive being moved. So I think we should forget the removal bit and accept that Charlie has to go." He sat back in his chair. "Suggestions, anyone?"

Alice looked up, "Embolism! Simple air-jab into an artery. 30 seconds in and out. A good chance of a 'natural causes' verdict if we are not sussed. If we all have needles anyone of us can do it, if that's the way it works out."

***

The dowdy brown-haired woman shuffled through the hospital seeking and eventually finding the corridor where the uniformed policeman sat at the door to a private room.

He was reading from an electronic book and did not look up when the woman shuffled past.

Alice reported to Martin who was seated in a van parked in the car park next door. "Lazy bastard was too busy reading to even look up when I went past." She was stripping off as she spoke. Martin looked on with interest as she took off everything but her bra and panties. He has not really looked at her that way before, but he decided that he would pay a little more attention when this little caper was over.

Alice dressed in her girlfriend outfit, and put a set of hospital scrubs in a tote bag.

Martin paid attention to the action.

She twirled around having finished dressing, she asked. "Will I do?"

Martin grinned wolfishly. "You'll do." His tone caused her to realize that she had caught his interest.

It had been her intention. It was why she had arranged the quick change in the van. *Later*, she thought. *When this job is over, perhaps?*

Eton had been sitting in the front seat impatient with the verbal sparring in the back. His background and accent was upper class but he preferred the uninhibited life he enjoyed on this side of the law. His nature responded to the fact that he could do anything in any way, provided he was in control. The backing of Athol gave him that control to an extent. His thoughts were, as always, how he could take over from Athol. Then he would let that stupid bitch, Alice, know what it was like to be properly used. The cruel smile was still on his face when they moved into action.

The actual removal of Charlie was enabled by the fortuitous accident in the corridor outside Charlie's room.

Both Eton and Alice were armed with the hypodermic syringes needed for the operation. Eton was disappointed. He became involved with a pure accident when he dashed around the corner into the corridor. He found himself clutching the patient who had been falling off the trolley he had encountered. The porter had collapsed, winded. The nurse who was with the patient sprawled, exhibiting to the policeman's astonished eyes her 'Victoria's secret' knickers suspenders and stockings. The officer was halfway down the corridor when Alice slipped into Charlie's room from the other direction. She administered the air-bubble as prescribed, and was out into the corridor once more before the nurse was back on her feet in the hands of the policeman.

Having deposited the patient back onto the trolley, Eton was a memory swiftly fading. Alice was neither seen nor heard throughout the entire incident.

The alarm started to sound before the policeman was back into his seat. The nurse he had rescued dashed into the room, leaving the porter to get the patient to her destination. When the team arrived the nurse was doing her best to keep the unfortunate Charlie alive. Not surprisingly, she failed.

***

At the retreat, the days passed slowly. Apart from the brief embrace when they returned from the shooting, they both kept their distance. Neither referred to it. The training sessions were continued and there was conversation. But everything stayed on low key for several days, as both of them became accustomed to being together, and for Cass at least to accept the way her life had turned around.

The return to normality came naturally as both started to relax with their gradual acceptance of the situation. They were chatting naturally when Quin pointed out to Cass why they had shot the four men. "Like the man who gave us the information, if we had held them up we would have needed to take them prisoner. Where could we have put them? Here, perhaps giving away the only advantage we have over the men dedicated to kill us both. Or tie them up with all the risks that would entail."

"Why?" Said Cass challengingly. "Are they trying to kill you?"

"I was in the army, wounded in Afghanistan, so I was invalided out. I had been involved in trouble with the Russians there. It was they who put a price on my head. It's still there. As far as Athol Patrick is concerned, I believe I was targeted for the reward to start with."

Quin considered for a moment. Then he continued slowly. "Athol Patrick married my sister three years ago. We had no idea that he was anything but a legitimate business man. My grandparents noticed that she was under some stress. This was after the honeymoon, perhaps six months after the wedding. Angie, my sister, let them know that she was pregnant, but that was the last time they heard from her. My grandparents had lived in Scotland for the last 20 years and they asked me to check up on Angie. So I went to see why she had stopped speaking to them. At the house I was told she refused to speak to me. I told the maid that I was her brother and we were good friends. The maid looked sympathetic, but she said the master had made it clear. No visitors!" He paused. "I learned about the funeral by chance. The directors always put a notice in the local paper in case any friends wish to send condolences. I called on the funeral parlor and managed to get a view of my sister's body before they closed the coffin. I had to break in." He paused again looking haunted. Then he carried on, "She looked gaunt, broken. There were needle tracks on her arms. I checked her death certificate from the parlor records. Overdose of heroin, signs of beating, origin unknown. She had been identified by Athol Patrick, her husband, who had reported her missing three months before. I had called at the house two months prior to her death. There had been no such report at that time.

"My grandparents came down for the funeral. There was a blazing row with Athol. When they left, they were threatening an investigation. On the way back, they were in an accident, so called. A truck smashed into them on the motorway north. They were killed instantly. The truck driver was never found. They said the truck had been stolen."

Cass said, "I'm so sorry. I had no idea. But it was important to me to know that there was a real reason for the vendetta against Athol Patrick and his men. I am an orphan. There is no one waiting for me. I like my boss, but this is his fight. The attack on me would have been written off as collateral damage, without doubt. Now they have committed themselves they cannot afford to let me survive. I would like to feel we are together in this fight."

Quin looked thoughtfully at Cass, nodding his agreement. Then he started to explain "What you do not know about me is that after I left the army I went to United States of America. That was four years ago. I was restless, sick at having to leave the services. I have a degree in electronics and I was lucky enough to become friends with a man who thought the world was too wide, so he invented an IT way to make it shrink. I financed him for three years. His invention made it big time, and he did not forget me. I was presented with a bunch of shares. I am pretty well off as a result."

Cass grinned. "Sounds as if your girlfriend should have stuck it out!"

Quin smiled. "It's a thought. Mind you, in fairness, I don't think I could have. I think the fact that I was away a lot was one of the attractions for me, a sort of series of honeymoons if you take my meaning.

"It is something that bothers me, my wealth I mean. In the event I am killed, it would all go to the Government. I have no one else now, everyone is gone. I would rather the Government did not get it. I spoke to my lawyer about it. He said I could leave it in trust for charity. He also suggested I got married. We had a good laugh over that one, as I was already in conflict with Athol and his men.

"Meeting you gave me an idea. Since you and I became partners, both free and unattached." He stopped and looked at her enquiringly.

She nodded her agreement, waiting wondering what he was going to say.

"I thought it might make sense if we get married." He held up his hand to stop any immediate response she might make. "Let me explain. First it legitimizes our partnership. We can dissolve it after this mess is cleared up, if we wish. You'll agree it is not the problem it once was. If something happens to me, as my wife you will inherit." He hesitated. "I am not suggesting that this be anything but a business arrangement. We can carry on just as we are. No pressure! Just think about it see how you feel and let me know. You don't have to reply now." He was turning away prepared for the refusal when he heard her say something.

"Yes."

"Pardon? What was that?" He turned in surprise.

"What I said was 'Yes'. I trust you and I will marry you, and we can take our chances. As your wife and partner, that is a deal I will happily make, with or without your claimed wealth, and you can write that into the contract if you wish."

Neither made any move or introduced any romantic element to the agreement. It was an emotional moment nonetheless.

She sat back, breathless, excited and apprehensive at the same time. It was difficult for her to believe that she had actually stepped so far out of character. It was a spur of the moment decision as she had not even hesitated to answer the offer. It was as if she had known he was going to propose.

It appeared he had hoped and planned for a wedding. He detailed the arrangements that he had thought about in the event she did accept his proposal. "I could apply for a special licence so that we could act quickly in the event. I will call my lawyer. The licence could be sent to his office. He is a close friend and would accompany us to Torquay for the wedding."

He smiled quietly and tipped Cass's chin up to look into her eyes. "I confess, when we first met, the idea of getting to know you better did occur to me for the future. Don't ask me why or how. I think I was aware of that before we reached the retreat. I certainly did not anticipate this now. When we left for the construction site, I rang Gerald Butler, just in case. I asked him to alter my will and of my intention to apply for the marriage licence then and there."

That night Cass thought about Quin's words. She thought about her response, realizing that they both seem to have reacted the same way. She slept the better for that thought.

***

It was two days later when they actually married. The small ceremony in Torquay was over with little fuss. Gerald Butler, the lawyer, returned immediately to London by train, having been instructed to look after Cass's apartment. They were still making their leisurely way back to Kingston and the retreat when the lawyer contacted them. The agent he had sent to clear and store Cass's bits and pieces found that the apartment had been trashed. They were collecting and recovering what they could, and arranging for the renting of the place.

Cass shrugged her shoulders and said philosophically, "It's a wrench to part with some of the things in my home, but life moves on. I have the feeling that Athol Patrick will regret making an enemy of Cassandra Richards." She turned to Quin. "I should have said Cassandra Gilmore. I won't make the same mistake again." She smiled, "It's taking a little getting used to I'm afraid. This might be a good time to discuss our next move."

Quin yawned. "I was thinking it was probably time for bed."

Cass looked at him sharply, questioningly.

He was smiling. "I just happen to be rather tired," he said. "So if you don't mind, I'll love you and leave you. Goodnight, Mrs Gilmore." He hesitated for a moment.

Cass held her breath as Quin continued, "I rather like the sound of that. I'll see you in the morning." He turned and went through to his suite, closing the door gently behind him.

She sat looking at the door thoughtfully. This was going to be difficult, much more difficult than she had anticipated. For a moment she had thought that Quin was going to suggest.... The odd thing was she was not sure what she would have done if he had.

***

The following morning Mrs Gilmore awoke to find a tray beside her bed with hot coffee and croissants still warm for her breakfast. There was a card on the tray that said, 'Good morning, Mrs Gilmore. Enjoy. I will be back in one hour.'

She stretched and sat up, reaching for the coffee and nibbling a croissant. *I could really get used to this,* she thought.

She looked at the other undisturbed side of her bed thoughtfully.

When Quin returned he had news. Cass was in the pistol range practicing left and right hand shooting. The man target was shot to ribbons.

Quin looked at it. "Did you miss at all?" He asked.

"Not as far as I know." Cass said. She stripped the Walther and reached for the cleaning kit.

Quin looked at the lithe figure and the smooth healthy skin of his new partner, wondering at the fact that he was married, and at the circumstances that had brought it about. He was still not completely sure whether he should feel happy or worried.

He turned to the kitchen to prepare food for lunch. There was the rustle of movement behind him and as he swung back he encountered Cass who slipped her arms around his neck and kissed him. "Thanks for the breakfast in bed." She was gone before he could react, seating herself with her gun-cleaning materials, a faint blush on her cheeks.

He shrugged. There was a tinge of color on his face as he departed for the kitchen.

Cass rubbed furiously at the metal parts of the Walther. What was she thinking of? A few days ago she hadn't known Quin. Now she was married to him, and she had just kissed him for the first time. She looked at the gun parts, the piece in her hand. It seemed a time for firsts. Never had she dreamed that she would be learning to casually shoot from all angles at a man target, and incidentally at a man.

Over lunch Quin gave the news he had forgotten about when he returned. "The fourth man we shot was wounded and in hospital under police guard. Somehow someone got to him and gave him an embolism. At first they thought it was natural causes. But then it seemed the pathologist noticed the needle mark in his arm which had not been there at the examination after the operation when he was brought in. The police have just released the information"

"Who would do that....ah yes, I see. Dead men tell no tales. That is what you are saying, isn't it?"

He nodded. "Exactly, and it demonstrates Athol's ruthlessness. I'm sure his men were shaking in their shoes at the time, in case he told them to do something impossible. They will all be too frightened to argue in case he kills them on the spot."

"So what is he up to now? Still looking for us?"

"Bet your life he is!"

"Well, let's find something to do that will make it harder for him. What operations does he have running that you know about?"

Quin looked up from his plate, "Why do you want to know?"

"Oh, come on, Quin. Even in the short time I've known you, I know that you will not settle for sitting waiting until the man forgets we exist. Even here is vulnerable, and if you think I'm going to grow old eating baked bloody beans you can think again. What are you planning and what will be my part?"

Chapter four

What comes next

There was a period of silence between them as both absorbed the fact that they would have to re-adjust their thinking. Now there were two people involved in lives that had not been preoccupied with a close 'other'.

Eventually Quin spoke, "Right! I suggest our next target is the simple reduction of the warehouse in Brentford where they distribute drugs for several of the other gangs in London that operate in conjunction with Athol Patrick. There is also a chop-shop where they process stolen cars. I think, if we sort one of the places out a bit, there could be serious repercussions for Athol.

"It will be necessary to use a little guile on this occasion. The warehouse in question is in normal everyday use as a legitimate delivery distribution depot. The processed dope arrives in sacks, each containing four 25-kilo bags in a paper-based sack, labelled corn flour. They are marked with a blue tag on the corner so that they can be identified and separated from the others."

"How many bags are we talking about?" Cass asked.

"Up to ten each time, from what I can gather." Quin volunteered.

"Doesn't seem a lot?" Cass sounded doubtful.

"Broken up that is £5000.00 per kilo that is £500.000.00 per bag. £5.000.000.00 for ten bags, on the street of course, from an investment here in London of maybe £50K."

"Ah! I see. So how do you suggest we do it?"

"I have seen it arrive twice. At least I think I saw it twice, the first by accident." He sat down next to Cass and faced her. "I must stress this could be very dangerous. When I was nearly caught on the day before we met, I was in the vicinity of the Steam Museum close to Kew Bridge. I spotted a familiar face at a distribution warehouse on the Brownfield site backing on to the river.

"A truck arrived while I was watching and I saw it downloading on to the loading dock. I was surprised at the time because it was after 10.00 at night. Two palettes being unloaded. That was it, just two palettes of sacks. I got in closer. It was not difficult. All the major lights were off at that time and the security lights gave more shadows than light. With the truck gone I watched the man check the sacks. Then he went into the warehouse, and returned with a hand fork lift. He checked the sacks again, then lifted one of the palettes and pushed it into the warehouse. I followed him. He was making so much racket with his trolley he would not have heard an elephant behind him.

"I hid while he went out for the other palette. Having brought it through, he closed the door. He then took the first palette to the rear of the warehouse and dropped off four sacks marked corn flour. The remaining ten were marked the same but all had a blue slip clipped to them.

"He then towed the blue-tagged sacks over to the corner beside the office. He left the trolley outside, went into the office, and made a phone call. He then locked up and left.

"Ninety minutes later people appeared and set up a trestle table. They slit the blue tagged bags and extracted the four bags inside, in the end there were forty 25-kilo bags stacked on the table. The buyers started arriving at 0200. The auction began and ran until all the bags were sold. The customers dispersed. The staff cleared up and left, taking the empty sacks with them. By 03.15 all was back to normal, ready for business in the morning."

Cass rose to her feet and put the kettle on. "What'll it be? Coffee?" She called.

Quin growled, "Coffee will do. So what do you think?"

Cass made the coffee and brought the mugs through. "I think we should be ready to go and upset these people. How about switching the labels and removing the dope?"

"I suppose we could use the van! But then what? Ten bags of dope, what do we do with it?" Quin said thoughtfully.

"We have room here," Cass suggested. "But no. that would be stupid and it would not remove the problem. It would just put it off. How about some quiet spot and a gallon of petrol? Maybe some deserted beach, where the wind would blow the smoke out to sea?"

"Let's think about that, see if we can come up with somewhere not too far away, meanwhile shall we say, Wednesday? That will give us two days to reconnoiter and prepare. I'll change the van numbers and see if I can find a couple of labels to confuse any witnesses." He referred to the magnetic name panels used for the swift labelling of vans. "British Water are using hire vehicles at the moment. I know where one parks overnight."

Cass noted the wicked grin when he mentioned this. "You are enjoying this, aren't you?"

"I'm just a big kid at heart," Quin said. "Seriously, I am delighted to be doing something that I know is right. So far, I have been surviving, longing to find something positive to do, but unable to think of anything that was not suicidal on my own. With you here it changed. Between us we can make a difference. Finding you, and this place, had made a real difference to everything."

Cass looked up as he stopped speaking and noticed as he turned away, that tinge of red had appeared once more. She opened her mouth to say something, but stopped herself, unwilling to precipitate things at this stage.

***

The two figures crouched down, waiting for the truck driver to lock up the tailgate and drive off. The warehouseman was inside collecting the trolley to move the two palettes inside. The two watchers waited as he collected the first palette. They followed him into the warehouse and hid behind one of the stacks of goods awaiting delivery. When the second palette was collected, Quin followed him to make sure that the location of the goods was still where he had first seen them. He need not have worried. Nothing had changed.

As the man left they swung into action. Cass left the warehouse by the side door and collected the van. She drove it to the loading dock. Quin was there when she reached it and between them they loaded the marked bags.

Cass removed the blue tags and took them into the warehouse where she attached them to ten innocent sacks of corn flour. Quin drew three small packs from his tote-bag and inserted them between the decoy sacks, carefully arranging the pressure switches before joining her with the trolley. They loaded the blue-tagged sacks onto the palette on the trolley and replaced it where it had been left.

As they left the building Cass asked the question that had been worrying her ever since they entered for the first time. "What about the alarm?"

Quin grinned. "Just like last time. Lazy bastard could not be bothered resetting the alarm when he was only away for just over an hour. Villains leave the place alone anyway. They know who it belongs to. With the doors locked, a casual would find entry difficult. Let's not wait to see the fun. I have a sea-side holiday in mind and time is a'wasting."

They departed the area before the first of the vehicles started to arrive at the warehouse.

***

The British Water van turned off the M25 onto the A12, heading for the Chelmsford and the Essex coast. The signage on the vehicle had disappeared before they reached Brentwood. They stopped for a pub lunch and Cass hired a car in Chelmsford.

Quin took the van to an old barn near the Ray sands on the North Sea shore. He walked back to the road and was collected by Cass in the hire car.

They were checked in at a pub with rooms as Mr and Mrs Hughes. Armed with the usual gear of the nature watcher they elicited no comment and little interest among the locals in the bar that night.

The twin beds in the room simplified matters that night. The location of their room was in the extension behind the main pub building. Apart from the privacy, they had the convenience of a separate entrance which allowed them to go out at 0200 to the barn where the van was hidden. Quin rolled it down to one of the creeks hemorrhaging the coastline, and between them they unloaded the sacks. Setting them on the shore below the tideline, Quin slashed the bags open with a long knife and poured the petrol over the bags, watching it soak into the contents.

A match did the rest. The fire was below the level of the field leading down to the sea. Though there was the flicker of the fire light visible from the road, it was not easy to see, and it could have been, as often happened, a bunch of youngsters enjoying a private party on the beach.

Back at the pub they climbed into their separate beds and crashed out.

They appeared for breakfast next morning nearer nine than eight o'clock. There was a certain amount of gentle humor poked at them based on the fact that Quin had mentioned that they were newly-weds. They were able to check the success of the burn when they walked the shore, binoculars in hand, watching for and identifying various forms of wild life.

The scene at the creek was interesting. A faint smell of petrol was still in the air, but of the drugs there was no sign. The tide had removed any debris that may have survived the blaze.

That night, tired, they acted the newly-wed part for the benefit of the landlord and the regulars even to the point of going early to bed.

The tension in the bedroom was apparent. Having taken turns in the en-suite bathroom, when Cass came into the room Quin was already in bed.

She looked at his apparently sleeping figure, shrugged, slipped off the nightdress she had brought specially, stood naked between the two beds for a moment. Then she switched off the light and climbed into Quin's bed, snuggling up beside him with a sigh as he turned to take her into his arms.

***

Once back in the retreat normal routine was resumed and Quin went on the prowl to find out what the situation was with Athol Patrick and his men. The word was that the search was on for the people who had ripped off the gang leader.

He returned with the news that the auction had involved an explosion which had killed both of the sack handlers and descended into a gunfight between the surviving warehouse men and the four bidders at the auction. A total of four killed and two injured. Athol himself was not present at the scene and this was read as a set-up by the other gangs.

"Where does this leave us? By the way, what was that all about? The explosions, I mean?" Cass asked.

Quin grinned. "I'm afraid that was me. You see, I found one or two bits and pieces here and put them together just to make things interesting. The sight of the sacks, stacked as they were, seemed an obvious place to try them out."

"I'm beginning to think you must have had a disturbed upbringing." Cass said with a smile.

"Me? No. I was a gentle child; unless I was upset, that is."

Quin produced a newspaper. "Gerald pointed this out. It could be a trap."

Quin put a paper down on the table. There was a piece underlined in red pencil.

Cass read the piece. Details regarding the whereabouts of Cassandra Richards are sought in relation to an unclaimed inheritance. She is last known to have been living in the Kingston area and is believed to be associated with Quin Gilmore also formerly living in the Richmond /Kingston area. The address of a solicitor's office was given.

The advert was in the weekly Kingston giveaway paper delivered virtually to every household in Kingston area.

Quin commented, "I have the impression that there will be a lot of people happy to help us collect the, so-called, inheritance. Unfortunately as far as I am aware this is just a ploy to find us."

Cass looked at the name of the solicitor given in the paper. Then looking up at Quin she said "Perhaps not!"

Quin turned to her eyebrow raised. "You have a reason for saying that, I presume?"

Cass blushed. "When I was in my teens I was befriended by an old friend of my mother's. He was a bachelor. I had the feeling that he and my mother had been closer before she met my father and married. He was a regular visitor at the house and got on well with my father. I guess he resigned himself to bachelorhood when he and mother split."

She sighed. "He was like an uncle to me, a favorite uncle. When my parents died I was fourteen and he was named my guardian in their will. He was also my godfather.

"He asked me if I would mind if he adopted me legally. I agreed, though I never took his name. He became my father, though I saw little of him. As far as I know he had no other relatives and always gave the impression that he was wealthy." She paused and Quin noticed that her eyes were wet, though no tears came. He said nothing but came and sat with her as she continued.

"He died nearly a year ago. There was a quiet funeral ceremony at the family graveyard on the Hampshire estate. The lawyer said that I was mentioned in the will but there were complications that would take time to clear up. He also mentioned that once the details were sorted out, the title would come to me as I was the legal next of kin. The title I have from Lord Emsley, my adoptive father is Lord of the Manor of Canonby. I suppose I am now the Lady of the Manor of Canonby, for whatever that means."

"It seems you will need to contact this lawyer, but it will be a risky business. If I can suggest it, perhaps Gerald can arrange something on a lawyer to lawyer basis?"

"Sounds good to me. Then we can have a private meeting and find out what is going on with Michael Emsley's estate. I expect very little, really. I am sure there will be death duties and all sorts of expenses before things are sorted out. Meanwhile your suggestion of involving Gerald makes sense. Let's get the show on the road."

***

There was a whole series of surprises awaiting the pair when the group got together at Gerald's office.

The executors of the will were a double-barrelled lawyers' practice from Kingston who had represented the Canonby estates for over 70 years. The death of the sole survivor of the original family had created turmoil in the practice, until the discovery of the presence of Cassandra Richards as the adoptive daughter of the Lord Emsley. The fact had been kept secret by the keeper of the Emsley estate account on the instruction of the deceased.

The denouement of the whole business was simplicity itself. Apart from the titles which passed as she had anticipated over the past year the lawyers had finally unwound the complications of an estate with investments the world over. Cass had, with the exception of individual gifts to estate servants, inherited the lot, with houses in several countries throughout the world and a bank account that appeared to contain half the wealth of the world. (Well maybe not quite that much) Cassandra Gilmore, nee Richards, Lady of the Manor at Canonby, was richer than most.

Her actions following the disclosure of what she regarded as an obscene amount of money was regarded by Quin with approval, Gerald with horror, and the double-barrelled lawyer with resignation. Retaining only the country estate, and two of the overseas properties plus a fraction of the inherited wealth, she gave the rest to charity, retaining Gerald and the double-barrelled lawyers between them to administer the disbursements from a trust, to which she had no access.

At the protest by Gerald, she pointed out the £20m-plus share income she had retained after all duties had been paid, was plenty to keep the estate in operation, and look after the two overseas properties she had retained. Her requirements, especially since her husband was already a multi-millionaire, were not that excessive.

***

Back at the retreat Quin spoke for the first time about the events of the morning. "Now you are a millionairess, what do you intend doing?"

"What have you in mind?" Cass turned on him. "Did you want to weasel out of our deal?"

Taken aback, Quin said, "Why no! I was just wondering whether things had changed for you. After all you are now independently well off. You can dash off anywhere in the world. Do what you like."

"And what do I do about Athol Patrick?"

Quin shrugged.

"We made a deal. As far as I am concerned I do not go back on my word. Nothing happens until that man is out of our hair. Is that still all right with you?"

"Of course bu…."

Cass chopped him off before he could finish. "That's settled then. Let us get on with the planning then shall we. I would really like to get my own life back under some sort of control."

Chapter five

Taking the lead

Athol Patrick was seriously upset, not only at the debacle at the warehouse, but also at the item he found in the newspaper that morning. It seemed that Robert Jordon had a problem keeping his mouth shut about his noble clientele. He had, through sheer attrition, managed to get into the fringe of the Vanity Fair set, by keeping the gossip section of the magazine tipped off about any juicy items of gossip about the beautiful people he came across. The note he had passed to his contact, with reference to the inheritance of the Emsley estate had found its way into the tabloid read regularly by Athol. The accompanying picture, though grainy, clearly identified Cassandra Richards, together with Quin Gilmore. Two people who were of particular interest to him.

Noting the bye-line to the article he spoke to the author of the article, and by twisting her arm, offered £500.00 for the information. He obtained the full details of Robert Jordon. He made an appointment to see Mr Jordon the next day.

For Robert Jordon the name Athol Patrick meant nothing. His reason for the appointment was to discuss an inheritance. At the appointed time the knock came at the door and his secretary, Anthea, announced the arrival of Mr Patrick. The decorative Anthea was not much of a secretary, but she was a spectacular bedmate, compensation for Jordon's pretty, home-counties wife, who regarded sex as a procurer of children rather than an entertainment to be enjoyed on a regular basis.

Athol followed the entertaining rear view of Anthea into the office of her boss and accepted the offer of coffee in the expectation of having a further opportunity to enjoy the view of the delicious Anthea.

The weather mentioned and coffee delivered, Athol got down to business. He thrust the newspaper report in front of the lawyer without further ado. Putting a finger on the picture he said, "What is this?"

Jordon looked at the picture and said, "Why, it is a picture of Canonby's," he said, wondering what this was all about.

"Where and when was this taken?"

"How should I know?" Jordon said indignantly.

"Since you were the source of this article I would think that was self-evident," Athol said, sitting back and lighting a cigarette.

"There is a no-smoking rule in this office." Jordon blustered.

Athol was getting impatient. "Is there a no shooting rule as well?" His question accompanied the production of the Walther PPK he took from his briefcase. He removed a silencer, screwing it onto the barrel while he spoke. "I will ask the question once more, and then you will reply. If you do not answer my questions truthfully and immediately, I will shoot you in the left knee. Subsequent mistakes will entail the right knee, then in turn the elbows left and right in that strict order. Have I made myself clear? Nod if you understand me."

Jordon was terrified. He felt the dampness spreading soaking his trousers around his groin. He nodded anxiously.

Axel stood and walked round the desk, gun held loosely in his hand. He noticed the spreading stain in Jordon's lap. "Tsk, tsk." He shook his head sadly. "Now, once more. What do you know about this?" Jordon explained about the inheritance, his words tumbling out anxious to please this mad man.

"You say that they don't live there on the estate?" Athol persisted and you have no idea where they live?"

"From what the other lawyer tells me he has no idea either. They communicate by phone."

Athol put the gun back into his case and produced a card. This he placed on the desk in front of the terrified man. "Anything you can find out about these two people will be of interest to me, and could actually bring an unexpected reward." He collected his case and left the office, stopping to ask Anthea if she would be free for lunch. Her effortless, but polite, rejection of the offer was a surprising disclosure of a facet of her nature he had not suspected.

Jordon stepped into his small dressing room en-suite which he utilised when staying overnight in London. He stripped to shower and stepped into the stall and felt the frission of cool air as he was joined by the curvaceous Anthea. As she moulded her curves against his back, she whispered, "That man is dangerous. I will take care of him if you wish."

Jordon didn't answer he just enjoyed the feeling of her hands as they roamed over his body.

***

Athol Patrick was annoyed. He had hoped for a lead in the search for the two elusive people that he had targeted. They knew far too much for his comfort.

The base used by Athol was a substantial office building in Brentford. The top floor was his apartment. Though there were other places owned and used by him this was his favorite, since it was on top of the financial and operating hub of his business.

The ground floor warehouse was already known to them. The damage suffered in the drug bust had been repaired. Still used as a storage and distribution area, the legitimate operation was operated as before, offering a certain amount of cover for what went on elsewhere in the building.

The second floor was the location of the planning and operation section of the organization. Here the team kept their armory and where the various deals were made for the importation of drugs tobacco and cigarettes, now once again becoming a marketable commodity. The chop shop, where vehicles were either repainted or restored, sometimes even dismantled for the spare parts, was in a different building. One of the buildings on the old gasworks site was used for the purpose, well separated from head office, if for no other reason than the boss did not want the noise created disturbing his sleep.

The man Athol Patrick sent to Canonby was not happy. He was a town person and he decided he really did not do country life. The boss should have used Eton for this sort of thing. He could have joined the set and got invited to the big house. So Willie Turner moved into the village pub and prepared to be bored for the next week or so. May Partridge returned to her job at the pub the second day Willie was there. Willie went down for breakfast that morning looking forward to the meal. Whatever else the food was well up the scale. When Willie saw May, the girl who brought it in, his entire outlook changed. Suddenly the country life started to take on interest

Back in Brentford the puzzled Athol Patrick continued sending out feelers, trying to locate the man and woman who were not only worth money. They had cost him money. He walked around the warehouse where the stolen cars were. It always pleased him to see the workshop full of cars. The only scene that pleased him more was seeing it empty, after all the stolen cars were sold.

The stolen car market was lucrative in this era of highly paid executives driving Lexus, Audi, and Mercedes. The exotic cars were becoming more common on the streets and the export market for Porsche, Ferrari, and Lamborghini was making the location and stealing of these cars a profitable business. The Range Rover was still always in demand for Middle Eastern countries, and despite the ever more sophisticated alarm systems, thefts of all these vehicles were still being regularly accomplished.

***

For Quin and Cass their next objective was to hit the Patrick organization at its most vulnerable point, and they had decided that the chop-shop was it.

Cass had quizzed Quin about the location, and how he had discovered it.

"It is known in the area by most of the people who live in the vicinity," Quin volunteered. "And before you ask, some of the police are aware of it. Why do they do nothing?" He rubbed his fingers and thumb together in the universal sign for money. "It pays well."

"So what is the plan?"

"You are sure you want to go through with this?" Quin asked.

Cass looked at him. "We made a deal to damage that man Athol Patrick. He had tried to have us both killed, for nothing really. I refuse to live my life with a target pinned to my back. Am I getting the message across? When I make a deal I stick to it!"

"Okay. I get the message. Tomorrow night, we will take the van. I'll sort out some whiz-bangs, and I'll find the stopcock for the water to the building. We do not want the sprinklers coming on and spoiling the nice fires before they have time to do their work. Get some practice with the pump shotgun, we will need the firepower. There are usually several men there at night, bringing vehicles in and taking others out."

Quin looked at Cass with a serious look on his face. "We wear armor tomorrow. Now I have found you I do not wish to lose you."

Cass looked at him with astonishment. She had not realized that his feelings were quite so intense. Though she said nothing, inside she felt a warm glow as her own growing affection for this mysterious man made itself felt.

***

They drew up in the van on the other side of the street and sat watching the roller shutter on the building rise and fall as vehicles came and went.

Quin pointed out the side door which was toward the rear of the building. "That is where we go in."

Cass reached behind her seat and took out the shotgun. Quin took the bag of gear and stepped out of the van. He disappeared around the rear of the building, returning almost immediately with a smile on his face. He said one word, "Water."

They made their way across the road to the small door in the side wall.

Quin knocked with a pattern of taps. And stood back Glock automatic in his hand up in line with the face of the man who opened the door. Quin put his finger to his lips. The man stepped back and Quin crowded him, following him inside the door. Cass closed the door quietly behind them. They were in a lobby. From the clatter it was obvious that the workshop was on the right, to the left was a sort of common room with three men sprawled around looking at magazines. There were coffee cups scattered around the room. Obviously nobody had bothered to clear them up. The masked figure of Cass stepped into the doorway and she cocked the gun. The noise drew the men's attention. "Weapons on the table!" Cass said with a growl. The men carefully lifted out weapons and placed them on the table. "You two, hands on heads and sit." To the third she said, "Drop your pants."

The man dropped his pants in a hurry. The ankle gun was immediately apparent. He took it out and placed in on the table with the others.

Cass made him sit with his pants round his ankles, and then looked at the other two. She waved the barrel of her gun. Both men retrieved their ankle holstered weapons and placed them on the table with the others. Cass threw a bunch of plasticuffs at the nearest man. He got the message and put them on both the others, He attached one of his own wrists and held out both hands and Cass laced up the other hand. She then checked all three to make sure they were tight. The guns went into her tote bag.

Quin stepped in with an aerosol can. He sprayed each of the men in the face with the contents.

Cass stood back as one by one they crashed to the floor. Whatever was in the spray knocked them out in a hurry. The scent of ether was in the air.

"Out! Quin said, and they left the room, closing the door behind them. At the far end of the corridor a door led into the glass walled office for the premises. The only occupant was slumped in a chair apparently asleep. Quin saw Cass look. "I had to hit him," he said. Through the glass it was possible to see the workshop, where several cars were undergoing work of some sort. The spray booths were off to one side. As they watched the roller front door opened, and a black Porsche drove in and stopped. The door rolled swiftly down. The driver left the car and walked to the office, where they stood watching the scene. The man entered, slamming the door behind him and turned toward them. He suddenly realized something was wrong. Cass lifted the shotgun into view. The moving hand of the man stopped in mid reach and he froze in place. Cass motioned down and he lay down on the floor on his face. Quin disarmed him and cuffed him. Then he dragged him through to the rest room with the others.

Turning, he said, "Now, we go!" Cass nodded and stepped through the door first gun up and ready. Quin ran to the nearest spray-booth and pressed a pack onto its side, he then put one on the Porsche, and others on some of the other cars being worked on. Somebody noticed him and shouted. Cass raised the shotgun and let fly at the Range Rover beside the outer door. The glass shattered in all directions, and the alarm started blaring to add to the confusion. Cass fired at some of the other vehicles in the workshop. Other alarms added to the noise. Then someone fired an automatic at the office and the glass smashed in the window.

Quin called, "Out now!" Cass turned and ran back through the office to the outer door. With the gun up she flung the door open. The man outside lifted his automatic. Cass fired. Her shot blew the man back sprawling into the road his gun flying from his hand. From inside the building came several thumps.

Quin ran down the road to the roller shutter and slapped a padlock into the tongue and hasp, locking it from the outside.

He heard the motor whine as it tried to open the door. The door jerked but the padlock held. He heard the shotgun go off again and ran back to join Cass at the side door. There were two men slumped at the door. Neither of them were moving. Another man ran from inside the building and the gun fired again. Quin called, "Time to go. Get the van started."

Cass ran to the van and jumped in, started the engine and rolled down to where Quin stood. He slid in through the passenger door. She drove off round the corner. They heard the explosion two streets away. Quin reported that the column of smoke rose high in the air where the building had been. As they crossed Kew Bridge the sound of sirens wailed.

***

Back in the retreat, the TV news showed the scene of devastation where only a small part of the walls remained of the building. The collateral damage to surrounding buildings had produced no casualties. They were all commercial premises and the night security people on duty were all inside the buildings and had survived without injury.

The devastated building revealed fourteen casualties all fatal except one. The survivor said he thought the paint store had caught fire.

Cass put the shotgun down and sank onto the settee, pulling her hood from her head. Her hair clung to her head, sweaty from the exertions of the evening. The flak-jacket followed and she sat for the moment, the tee shirt clinging to her sweaty body. Quin walked in and tore off his hood and unhooked his flak-jacket. The TV was blurting on about the explosion. He reached out and shut it off. Looking at Cass, he realized that she was reacting to the events of the evening, He hauled her to her feet and with his arm round her took her through to the showers. He kicked off his shoes and stepped out of his pants, and underclothes. Then turned and stripped Cass's clothes off.

He turned the shower on and stood, holding Cass close as the water beat down on them.

Chapter six

Another option

Athol Patrick was incandescent. He strode back and forth in his apartment in front of Martin Goody, who was looking distinctly uncomfortable.

The fact that Athol and Martin had been out at a night-club when the chopping shop was destroyed meant nothing to Athol. He needed to blame someone and Martin was the only one handy.

After ten minutes of blistering comment and invective, Athol cooled off enough to begin talking sense once more. "I suppose I have that bloody pair to thank for this mess?"

He swung round on Martin. "I want them stopped! Do you understand, no arguments, no excuses. Terminated. Obliterated. Killed. Easy or nasty. I do not care as long as they are dead, dead, dead!"

Martin stood there as the spittle from his boss spattered his face. Athol's flushed distorted features were within inches of his own sweating face.

"Yes, Boss!"

***

In the entrance hall to the upper floors of the building, Cass stumbled. Her mini-skirt flirted as she tripped over her own feet, giving a glimpse of her white panties to the security man at the reception desk. She clutched the counter, leaning over to make sure that he got a good unobstructed view of her breasts down the gaping top of her blouse.

The guard grinned. "What can I do for you then, miss?" He was thinking that she was obviously drunk and available.

"Gotta pee!" She said, slurring her words.

"Right this way, miss." The guard opened the security door beside the desk and took her arm, leading her to the ladies' room beside the elevator complex. He pushed the door open and helped her through. "I can manage." She said and tottered toward the first cubicle. The guard stood and watched her through the door. The sound of her relieving herself went on and on. Finally the door opened, and the guard stepped forward unbuttoning his shirt, ready to exact payment for services rendered.

He looked down at his exposed abdomen. There was an astonished look on his face as he saw the fist strike. It was just a small fist, but it caused him to empty his lungs in one explosive gust. It was the fist of the drunken girl. His body lost its ability to remain upright. He was falling, desperately trying to get air into his lungs. Then he was looking up, seeing the short skirt and the white panties he had intended removing. It was wrong, all wrong. The clout was with the small cosh and it ended his immediate suffering and puzzlement. He.....

Cass stepped over the recumbent figure, disgusted at the whole charade, realizing that Quin had been right.

"Expect trash to act like trash. Play the drunk and he will try to take advantage. He will wait until you have used the john. Then he will attempt to rape you. After all you are vulnerable, being drunk. Just remember. If he suspects anything he will kill you after he has raped you anyway."

Cass shuddered as she left the rest room, her gun in her hand by her side. As she walked to the desk, Quin appeared and another man came out of the men's room still zipping his pants.

Cass turned to face him. "Bad luck," she said, and shot him, the silenced weapon making little noise. Without waiting for him to fall she stepped to the desk and pressed the door release, allowing Quin to come through.

He turned and looked at the security screens. The office and working complex was busy with several men and women shuffling paper. In the supervisor's office there was an interview going on, from appearances. The man behind the desk was watching the woman opposite him unbuttoning her blouse. The screen went blank at that moment, as the man realized he be being recorded.

Quin shrugged. He was interested in the top floor, but none of the cameras was active anywhere, apart from the outer door of the apartment.

"Top floor! It has to be. Let's go."

The pair walked over to the elevators and entered the first car. Quin pressed to the button for the top floor and checked the magazine of his automatic. The suppressor on the barrel made the gun a little unbalanced, but nothing he couldn't handle.

The doors opened and they stepped out. Too late Cass noticed the camera over the door. She hit it with the butt of her own gun. The glass shattered depositing a scatter of tiny shards on the carpet.

Quin tried the door. When he realized that the door was not locked, he waved Cass to the other side of the door. He stepped behind the door frame on his side then crouching he shoved the door wide open.

The crash of the gunfire from within punched holes in the cabin of the still-open elevator. Had he been still standing at the door the shots would have riddled him.

He put his hands to his ears, pushing in earplugs, watching as Cass copied him. Then with eyes tight shut he rolled the flash/bang grenade through the door.

It went off. Quin swung through the door, gun up. Closely followed by Cass, he went through to the lounge of the apartment. Martin Goode was up. His gun was spitting bullets. Athol Patrick was lying on the floor, blood leaking from his ears. But he also was armed and the gun he held was pecking plaster from the corner of the wall which Quin was sheltering behind. Both stopped firing and the unnaturally loud voice of Athol called to Martin Goody. "What is happening?"

"I've caught up with you." Quin answered.

"Who the fuck are you?" Athol came back.

"Your former brother-in-law. I have come to repay you for murdering my sister." Quin called.

His voice brought a hail of bullets from the two men.

The firing stopped and Quin aware that the men downstairs would be with them fast. He prepared to go in. Cass beat him to it. Standing, she stepped round into the lounge and shot Martin Goody in the forehead.

Athol called out triumphantly, "Got you bitch!" His gun rose to shoot.

Quin's two shots broke both Athol's shoulders, and the gun fell from his hand. He cried out in shock at the impact of the bullets.

Cass called out to Quin, swung round and shot through the open front door. There was a cry followed by a gurgle as the first two men on the scene met Cass's fire.

Athol looked at Quin. Quin looked back. "For my sister." He dragged Athol to the window, the wounded man screaming from the pain of his shattered shoulders.

"Over here, Cass," he called. Cass put fire through the front door again and ran over to him. There was a fire escape that ran from the roof above to the ground below.

"Go up!" Quin called. Cass climbed out of the window and climbed to the roof. Quin dragged Athol out onto the plat-

The Hunted/O'Neil

form after her. Turning to the sobbing man he said, "Remember on the way down. This need not have happened." Then he dropped the wounded man letting him fall over the rim of the platform, to the ground several stories below. Once on the roof he dropped a grenade onto the fire escape platform. The explosion came as they crossed to the far side of the building. There, another ladder led straight down the side of the building to the ground below.

Cass was already halfway down when she heard the second grenade go off on the roof of the block. Quin appeared above her and started to slide down the ladder. Cass slid the last few feet to the ground and waited for Quin to arrive with a flourish beside her. They ran to the rear of the building. Guns and masks out of sight once more, they walked hand in hand down the street, just a pair of lovers. Men appeared from the side door of the ground floor warehouse. Guns concealed, they searched for the fugitives, scattering and looking without knowing who they were seeking.

Quin whispered to Cass, "They are hoping we'll give ourselves away."

Nobody bothered with the two young people who wandered down to the Jaguar parked further down the road. They climbed in and drove off sedately, leaving the headquarters of Athol Patrick's empire in turmoil.

***

Willie Turner, still cooling his heels at Canonby, put the phone down looking worried. There was no answer from Martin Goody, and the boss was not answering his cell. As a last resort he rang Eton.

The cultured voice of Eton answered, "What do you want, Willie?"

"What's happening? I can't get through to Martin or the boss."

- 57 -

"You're calling the wrong numbers, sonny. Unless you've got the code for hell, you'll never get through!" The chuckle that followed at this witticism was not amusing. It sent shivers up Willie's spine.

"So the business has shut up shop?" Willie ventured.

"Absolutely. Brentford has gone. The boss swan-dived out of his window and Martin Goody took a couple to his chest. I guess the posh totty and her partner tidied up matters properly."

"What now?" Willie was getting seriously worried. "Are we looking to even the score?"

"For what? Athol fucking Patrick, and his bum boy, Goody? Do yourself a favor. Get lost. The game is getting serious. Get your head down and find a number to keep eating. Wherever you are, don't come back here. Bloody Russians are taking over." The phone went dead.

Willie Turner, 22 years old, faced the fact that he was out of a job. He had cash, and a debit card for some company he had never heard of. Working out that with the boss dead, the card would get stopped, he moved fast. In Winchester he went to the ATM, cleaned the card with his hankie and inserted it. The number was written down for him. He punched it in. The balance shown was substantial, so he drew out the maximum, £500.00.

He hit three more banks before they caught up with the card and stopped it. With £2000.00 in his pocket he destroyed the card, got back in his car, and returned to Canonby.

In the hotel he paid his bill. Then he spoke to May Partridge. "I need a place to stay and a job. Anything going around here?"

May looked at him. "What did you have in mind?"

"I've had enough of the smoke. I like this place." He looked at May. She looked back at him. "I think I would like to stay around here. Have you any suggestions that might be helpful?"

"You might try Canonby. They are pretty good employers, I'm told."

Willie thanked her and jumped in feet first. "Would like to go out for a meal or something. I don't know the area very well. I could do with a guide?" He smiled hopefully.

"Ask me when you've got a job." May Partridge said. "We'll talk again.

***

The careful closure of the retreat was a matter taken seriously by both of them. The updating of supplies was undertaken quietly and without any publicity. By the time they moved out to the country house, the retreat was mothballed with currently up-to-date equipment and stocks.

Neither had any illusions that there might be a need of the place as a bomb shelter. What they did was a reaction to the events that had led to their marriage, and survival of the attempts of Athol Patrick to eliminate them.

Having moved to Canonby House, they promptly arranged to depart on an extended holiday on Quin's boat, a sixty foot ketch, lying in Valetta harbour, where she had been undergoing a refit under the supervision of Charlie Smith.

Having informed Charlie by email, Quin and Cass departed from Bournemouth by Air Malta for Valetta.

Just one week after the demise of Athol Patrick, Quin proudly led his wife Cass onto the deck of *Centaur*. Turning to Cass, feeling the slight movement of the deck beneath his feet, Quin said, "Well, what do you think?"

Cass looked up the tall mainmast, and breathed, "She is beautiful."

Quin grinned and swept her up in his arms and carried her down the three steps into the saloon. "Welcome to our new home for a month or six, Mrs Gilmore."

Charlie's girlfriend Jill's smiling face appeared around the door forward. "Shall I open the champagne now?"

***

Within 30 minutes they were clearing the harbour mouth, with the panorama of the ancient city spread out over the rising ground behind them. Once clear, Charlie set course for the Suez Canal.

Charlie and Jill were two extrovert dropouts. At least that was the way they put it. In fact Charlie was a former Marine Commando. He had encountered Jill long after leaving the service for the sake of his marriage. As he put it, he had not adapted well to civilian life and his wife had been unused to having him around for a large part of the time. She had departed with the estate agent who had found their house for them. For Charlie it was a blessed relief. He admitted he had been ready to leave himself by that time. He had bought *Centaur* sight unseen after a session of draw poker that had lasted for six days. He paid one dollar for the papers, unaware that she was undergoing a refit. The settlement of the losses of the former owner had still resulted in Charlie coming off well ahead of the game.

Jill Mather had been on terminal leave from the Israeli army. Seeing Charlie walking along the other side of the quay in Valetta had been fortuitous. Two muggers, laid on by the loser in the game, mistakenly thought that they had a clear field to dispose of Charlie. Their disregard of the pretty girl, who was the only other person around at the time, was in fact a fatal mistake for one of them at least.

She spotted them trailing the blond-haired Charlie and realized that they were not there to help him. So she wandered over to the other side of the quay in time to call a warning to Charlie.

When she called out, one of the muggers turned toward her and swung a fist holding a short club at her face. Jill smiled and kicked him in the knee.

The man collapsed to the ground in agony. Charlie spun round and straight-armed the second thug in the chest, stopping him in his tracks.

Jill's man screamed at her and pulled a revolver from his pocket. Her switch kick took him in the throat. He flew back over the edge of the quay into the blue waters of the harbour. When he surfaced he was not moving, but neither Jill nor Charlie showed any interest. Sadly, nor did his erstwhile partner in crime, who was still trying to recover from his cracked ribs.

Jill and Charlie looked at each other. "Hi! Thanks for the heads-up." Charlie said.

Jill said, "As if you needed it."

"It's the thought that counts!" Charlie said quietly. "Do you think you could get to like me?"

"I'm just beginning to work on that." Jill's reply was equally quiet. "Where are we headed?"

"I'm going to the boat I've recently acquired just down the quay. My name is Charlie."

"I'm Jill. Lead on."

The boat was well on the way to complete refit, but the bill was more than Charlie could ever afford to pay.

Quin had seen the for-sale card one day as he was passing. The rest is history. Charlie and Jill agreed to look after things in return for living on the boat, and keeping it in condition to sail at any time.

With her refit completed, Charlie had been able to discover what exactly had been included in the fitting out ordered by the previous owner. The man was either paranoid to a degree, or had serious problems with a lot of dedicated killers. Concealed behind the beautifully crafted wood panels in the saloon was an armory, that included shoulder-fired missiles and RPGs. The Gatling gun seemed to Charlie to be a little excessive. However he approved of the Armalite rifles and the H&K smgs. His curiosity was aroused by the presence of the AK74. While the latest model of the AK47 was an efficient gun, among the rest of the armament it seemed out of place. Jill suggested that the previous owner may have been a Russian. "You know how sentimental Russians can be."

Cass was an experienced sailor and, since she loved the boat as soon as she saw it, it was a considerable relief to Quin.

"How about Charlie and Jill?" Quin asked, "What do you think about them?"

"People who can cook like that and smile when you make a bad joke! They have to be good for us. Tell me how did you get them?"

"They came with the boat. By the way, both are lethal, trained killers." Quin admitted.

Cass sat up sharply, the question on her lips.

Quin kissed it away. "Charlie was RM Commando, and Jill, Israeli Army, Special Forces. As I said, they are trained killers. Both of them! And they can cook, too." Quin grinned as he completed the explanation. Then he snuggled down under the blankets, "Get some sleep. You're on watch at 0400."

***

They entered the Suez Canal a lazy two days later.

There is a lot to be said for the sheer need to slow down that is imposed on people who sail boats. They cannot dictate speed or exact direction. The wind, weather, and set of the sails arbitrate all things when at sea under sail. The transit of the Canal is in fact an enforced study of the passing of a series of sandy banks with the occasional interference of the odd straggly palm tree, camel or human figure. Accompanied by the monotonous beat of the engine, the ordeal of the transit was largely mitigated by the efforts of the crew to entertain, with virtuoso performances on the guitar by Charlie, supported by extraordinary culinary productions by Jill.

Cass commented, "If for no other reason, the trip through the canal, dodging the freighters and containerships, watching for hijacks, makes the journey a trial. The diversions provided by our talented crew took the load off big time."

The arrival at Suez at the juncture with the Red Sea was a relief. It gave them the chance to provision for the next stage of their voyage through the Red Sea and Indian Ocean.

The Red Sea has long been the playground of the holiday skin divers, but it was also beginning to gain a reputation for the contact area for many of the pirate groups of the Horn of Africa. It has to be said that while most of the actual pirating operations are carried out in the seas south of there, the Red Sea has begun to suffer from the attentions of the East African pirates. In addition, many of the targets are selected by watchers in advance for ambush further south where assistance is non-existent. The early selection of targets is one of the reasons why the odd Q-ship operations fail. The spy system has been successful so far in identifying the Q-ships and warning the pirates accordingly.

The ketch, *Centaur,* was a target selected as an alternate if a freighter did not perform as anticipated. Circumstances placed both craft within the area at the same time.

Cass was watching the helm as they approached the freighter, *Matlock,* sailing under a Panamanian flag. From the deck of the ketch the massive shape of the big ship loomed large between the *Centaur* and the far distant African coast. Cass tacked to windward and, having changed course away from the freighter, had to change course once more due to the vagaries of the wind.

Approaching the big ship once more, the radio blared and Jill picked up the TBS phone to answer it.

The others all came up at her call. "The freighter has advised that a high-speed rib is approaching from the direction of the African Coast. It is unidentified but they believe it may be pirates."

Quin started the engine and took over the wheel. "Charlie, break out the RPG and one of the shoulder-fired missile launchers.

The Mayday call from the freighter suddenly came through the radio.

"Switch that damn thing off. There is no-one near enough to do anything anyway." Quin said.

"If it's alright with you lot, I intend on giving the pirates a bellyache." He looked the question at the others.

Then, satisfied they were with him, he pushed the throttle fully forward and made for the slab-side of the freighter now only 100 metres away. He turned aft to pass behind the ship which was now slowing under the demand of the pirate craft.

The pirate rib came into view as they rounded the stern of the freighter.

The explosion of a missile striking the hull of the *Matlock* reverberated, it blew a hole in the side of the ship between two of the upper deck portholes. It scared seabirds catching a ride on top of the cranes on the cargo deck. Their screams of protest followed their rise in the air to circle the scene below. Before the pirate craft could close the freighter, *Centaur* came into view around the ship's stern.

As they surged around the stern of the slowing freighter, Jill raised the Armalite and shot one of the men standing in the slowing rib. Charlie lifted the RPG. He almost casually fired a shot at the rib.

The grenade hit the water about two metres ahead of the pirate. The reaction was instant. The rib turned away from the freighter and started to run for the coast.

The gunner in the rib, balancing, lifted his RPG aiming at the ketch.

Jill, offhand, shot him with the Armalite. "This pulls a little to the left!" She called calmly.

The RPG tipped forward and fired into the waves beside the rib, as the shooter and his weapon toppled into the sea.

Charlie looked at Quin. Quin nodded. Lifting his rocket propelled grenade launcher, Charlie fired. The rib jinked and the shot hit the side tube. The racing boat sagged to one side and Jill opened up with the Armalite, firing rapid shots into the surviving pirates. Two stood and opened up with AK47s but they were bouncing around and the shots went everywhere.

Charlie fired again. The rib disintegrated, flinging men into the sea.

Quin turned the ketch to run alongside the freighter. The skipper called them with a megaphone. "Whoever you are, I thank you. You have saved my ship."

Quin called to the Captain, "Do you know how they knew you would be here? We are over 50 miles offshore?"

The Captain called back, "I can only think someone, somewhere, is profiting from passing information to these people. As you say it is too far for them to come just looking. I have informed my Head Office. They might come up with something."

Chapter seven

New beginnings

They parted company, the ketch now back on course for the Seychelles, the freighter en route to Madagascar. Neither made any attempt to rescue the few men struggling in the sea.

Quin and Cass sat nursing their drinks. They had been discussing the events of the day. Cass brought up the discussion that had started when the news of her inheritance had been announced.

"So you see, Quin, I really do not want to go back to the sort of job I was doing at that time, and though I think I could enjoy being the lady of the manor, I have doubts about its keeping me interested for the immediate future. The action we have seen over the past weeks has convinced me that I want to continue making a difference." Cass sat back with her gin and tonic in her hand as they discussing their future plans.

Quin shook his head slowly. "Have you any idea how lucky you and me, how lucky we both have been over that time. Being a noble crime-fighter is all very good in comic books. It's nothing like real life. If you get shot, coming back for the next episode is more difficult than it looks. It hurts. There isn't some guy to draw the next episode with the bullet wounds all healed, no convalescence, no nothing." He looked at Cass questions in his eyes.

Cass reacted sharply ."OK! I get the message. If you don't want to know, you can drop me off at the Seychelles. I can fly home from there.

"Just what the devil are you talking about, Cass? There is no way I am breaking up this partnership. Hell. I told you before. Having found you I will not lose you. If you are set on giving it a try, I'm in. but we have got to set some ground rules. Anything we take on we finish."

Cass nodded.

"We only go in guns blazing if it is absolutely necessary?"

"Okay, I see the sense in that."

"And finally, no executions!"

A slower nod at this as Cass though about the implications of what Quin was saying.

"That's it for now. We can increase the envelope later if we need to. Meanwhile we stick to the rules. The first rule is enjoy the holiday. We can start looking around when we get home. Agreed?"

"Agreed."

Charlie and Jill joined them, the ketch sailing the self-steering set, and an open ocean all around.

Cass looked at Quin. "Now, how about clueing us in on the reason this whole business began? I understand where we are now, but I have to know why this all started?"

Quin looked guilty. For the first time since she had met him he looked lost. Cass wondered whether she had opened a subject that was seriously painful to her newly acquired partner.

As she waited for his answer she studied him with serious almost impersonal eyes. Just about six foot, smooth muscled, with his dark brown, cropped hair. If it were longer, with his even tan he would look like any other beach-bum surfer on the Malibu shore. As he lifted his head to face her she took in the level eyes, slightly crooked nose, but otherwise regular features. Not handsome, but there was a warmth about it that attracted her, and she suspected, other women.

She snapped out of her daydream as he finally spoke. In a retrained carefully measured tone Quin explained.

"As you already know, I am an ex-soldier. It was my chosen career and as a young man, I intended spending my life in the service.

I did pretty well, I qualified to join the SAS, and there I was commissioned from the ranks. In my job I helped select targets and planned operations, as well as taking part in the actual jobs.

It was in Afghanistan. I was working with the Yanks on special operations. You may recall the mad scramble to find and kill Bin Laden?" He raised his eyebrow enquiringly.

Cass nodded, saying nothing.

"Well, in that particular operation, we encountered an anomaly." He paused and looked at her searchingly, wondering. Then making up his mind he carried on.

"You are aware that, prior to the Allies entering Afghanistan, the Soviets had taken a real beating there?"

At her nod, he resumed. "Whilst we expected to come across Russian equipment, for example the AK47, known crudely as the arsehole gun because everybody had one. What we did not expect was to find Russian casualties after a raid on a known Taliban site. Nor did we expect to be betrayed by our own men. Betrayals that cost heavily in men and equipment and damaged the trust between the Allied forces involved.

"As you may guess some of our men had shady careers which had led to their enlistment in the army as a way of avoiding retribution, and/or imprisonment. Campbell McNeish was about as Scottish as a leek. He was an odd secretive man, built like a truck, and known as 'Crush'. He was rumoured to have wrestled a bull during an operation in Argentina, and won. He was my cover man. When we went into action we always paired up.

"We were waiting to emplane for a re-location to another base for a special operation, sitting around as usual drinking tea and sweating, cursing the Air Force for being late as usual. That was a joke. It was normally the other way round. But, there you are, that's the army for you.

"Anyway Crush leaned across and helped himself to a cigarette from the box on the table. As he lit up he said, "I don't like this one, Boss."

"I laughed at him and said something like, 'When did you like any operation we are assigned to?'

"He was serious. He looked at me carefully, then sucked his cigarette, spurted smoke from nose and mouth and said without pausing, "This is a killer job!"

I smiled "They all are, Crush. You know that."

"Not like this one, Boss! This is a set-up, like 'Carmine'."

"I really started to take interest at that point. 'Carmine' had been a disaster, an operation where we had information that Bin Laden was sheltering in a village, isolated in a valley in the foothills in the Hindu Kush. The information had come from impeccable sources, so we had been told. "

"'How? Why? Where did you get this idea that it's a set-up'?"

"Crush looked uncomfortable. 'I was approached.'

"'You are my cover, my partner! What is this all about? We have soldiered together for the past six months. You saved my life, and I saved yours. What do you know about this and, more important, how did you know?'

"Crush looked oddly desperate. But he made up his mind and started to tell me.

"You can guess the sort of thing up to a point, mean streets, low income, street gangs, then more serious stuff, grown-up gangs, with weapons. All the heroes were villains, and the code of silence was an honorable bond between the lawless."

Quin stopped and accepted a chilled beer from Charlie. Jill had joined the group and was listening attentively with the others. Quin beckoned them in to hear what he had to say. Realizing that what he was saying affected them all.

Taking a drink appreciatively he went on with the story. "So Crush got out. He drove trucks, travelled about the country. Finally he joined the army. He had come home!

"Working with Special Ops he found his gangster skills useful. He also found that his background was catching him up. One of his former associates was working at HQ, in admin. The recognition was mutual but that was about it at the time.

"It was on the last leave break that the first rumors came along the grapevine. Big money to be made for a little side line work for a nameless operator. Crush had been approached by his former colleague, now in HQ admin.

"All that would be needed would be a small service now and then. His retirement pension would be assured. The money on offer was more than Crush had dreamed of. Like winning a lottery!

"He was tempted, so he bargained for an up-front payment to guarantee he would not be gypped. To his surprise $50,000 was paid into his bank account at home. A note from his admin contact just said: 'retainer 5k pm.'

"He realized how serious it was when he spoke to his admin contact before the Carmine incident. Crush was not in on the planning for Carmine. It was conducted by their opposite ops group. He was in Camp Bastion HQ mess when his contact mentioned there was going to be a big foul-up. By then Crush's bank account was swelling by $5k per month. His contact told him that he had told his bosses that Crush had put the word in for the operation.

"When Carmine went belly-up, with heavy casualties, Crush had received $100k bonus, for doing nothing, courtesy of his contact.

"Seriously worried by now, Crush had considered speaking to me, but was worried about the bank account and the possibility of being blamed for Carmine. At their last meeting the contact spoke of the operation Crush would be involved in. When Crush mentioned that he was taking part in the operation, he was told to keep his head down and, when he was captured, shout out 'Hamid' and he would be protected.

"'I can't let you and the lads get slaughtered in a trap. I took the money because I knew if I didn't someone else would. I had some idea of doing what I'm doing now. But the timing never seemed right, and I was growing richer by the month.'

"Who is the man in HQ?" I asked.

"'The man they found mugged and robbed before we left the base.' Crush said quietly. 'By the way, I found this in the next street. The killer must have dropped it.'

"He passed over a leather billfold with cards and papers stuffed into it. No money!

"I took a look at the Cyrillic characters on the first card I withdrew. I believed him.

I looked him in the eye. 'That's it, then. 'All for one?'

"He grinned, 'And one for all!'

"Looks like plan 'C', then."

"He looked puzzled. 'Plan 'C'?'

"'No plan. Open early. Gather up quietly. Then call in the carpet sweepers!' I activated my mike, 'Last minute brief, team leaders on me now!'

"With the team leaders gathered, I briefed them for an early drop. 'I'll fix the driver. But this is to be a silent, sneaky, infiltrate and kill. Remember Carmine!'

"The British and American team leaders nodded grimly.

"'Watch out for Mercs. I believe there are ex-Spetsnaz in the area. If there are it will be no pushover.' The C130 landed, engines muttering through the mufflers.

"My American oppo hung back as the others left. 'What's up?'

"'I think we sprang a leak, okay?'

"'You got it!' He left and joined his team and we Boarded the plane.

"Crush survived that op and he was contacted by the dead admin's controller. Between M16, the CIA and Crush we played the game for two more months.

"I led the raid on the control group HQ. It was a luxury house in Northern Pakistan, owned by a Russian oligarch, so-called. He was actually Russian Mafia.

"We went in without telling anyone official on either side of the border. Just agents and my Special Ops group. The boss man was dressed as a servant. He was the only one with soft unmarked hands. All the women avoided contact with him. He talked his head off, betraying his comrades unhesitatingly after a promise of resettlement in USA. He fell off the sidewalk in Mobile, Alabama, and died."

"Crush left the service, quietly, discreetly, apparently undetected by the Allies.

"I was wounded, and I discovered that I had been targeted as the cause of the clean-up in that operation. Now, wherever the Russians have a foothold in the underworld, I am a target of opportunity, with a price on my head. That's my motivation, folks. Them or me."

Cass looked at Charlie and Jill. "Your choice, folks. We can drop you off at the first port of call complete with airline fare home, if you would rather?"

Charlie and Jill exchanged looks. Jill said, "And if we don't want to leave?"

Quin said, "You will be part of the team. 'All for.....'"

"Please no! Not that Musketeer's bit. We couldn't bear it." Cass and Jill said in unison. The tension of the moment dissolved in laughter.

"Athol Patrick, was he on the Russian's payroll?"

"No! In fact I guess he was just an opportunist. He must have thought he had an easy target with the prospect of a nice reward at the end of it." Quin smiled grimly. "They were just a bunch of amateurs who were meddling out of their depth in this game." He went on to explain. "When crooks step out of their straightforward area of villainy, they should recruit expertise rather than just assume they can cope with the demands of the new work with their existing crew. That was Athol's mistake, undertaking a specialized hit with thugs."

"Where do we go from here?" Cass asked the question, but thought she knew the answer already.

"We're on holiday. Let's all get to know each other properly." Quin looked around the group. "How does that sound?"

***

The hill above the retreat was now carpeted with a wildflower meadow. The stonework from the old building had been artfully rearranged into a 'folly ruin' blending into the landscape. The land purchased covered the entire footprint of the retreat, including the short length of now disused rail tunnel.

They had considered building a house on the site but, with the Sussex property and the alternate identity it provided, there seemed to be a case for keeping living and surviving apart.

Charlie and Jill settled in the ample accommodation at Canonby without causing a ripple. The staff at the house accepted the return of what they called the family with relief at the re-establishment of full occupancy once more.

For the few weeks after they returned from the cruise, the refurbishment of the retreat, the landscaping and the re-adjustment to a more static existence took up all their time, Charlie and Jill spent time in London, where they occupied the apartment that Cass had purchased to replace her compromised former home. Though Athol was out of business, the gap in the ranks had been filled and it was always possible that the replacement gang might take up where Athol had left off.

Charlie had already commented that the modern trend was for cooperation between the gangs on certain aspects of their villainy, drugs, prostitution etc. On this basis it would never do to become complacent about security. The increasingly intrusive presence of the Russians was making itself felt more and more in the London gang scene and skirmishes between gangs were becoming more focussed on the monopolising of the market in specific areas.

Quin Gilmore swiftly became known on the estate. His quiet presence was felt where problems arose. It swiftly became known that he would listen and help with the problems that arose. Cass had been reassured by the way he slotted in to the life of the small world within the boundaries of Canonby.

No title was conferred on Quin through his marriage to Cass, though he answered to Lord T when he was in the chair at estate meetings.

In the turmoil of the big city, Jill found that the eternal conflicts between the villains and the law-abiding continued as before. It was not long before the pattern of activity began to present itself.

As suspected, the replacement of Athol and his people was soon accomplished, however with the added presence of a particularly savage element of violence, introduced through the presence of a small group of imported East–European men of indeterminate origins.

The arrival of the new group caused a stir, and a rapid re-grouping of allegiances. According to Charlie's information, "Most of the gangs are tooling-up and keeping quiet. The city is holding its breath waiting for 'the other shoe to drop.' According to the grapevine, the first message received was the bodies of the two top dogs in the drug business. Both were found by their families, tortured and stuffed with their own product. They had been placed in their own houses while the families were away."

Charlie paused. Jill said, "Nothing said in public, no police involved, though I did hear that the mother of Alfie Furlong, one of the pair, was screaming for revenge. Alfie's brother, Bert, has taken over. Not a lot known about him, but I suspect he has more brains than the rest of the gang put together."

Cass looked at the others. She smiled. "Where is the nearest phone box when you need one. Mind you, I always thought the underpants outside the tights looked uncomfortable."

Charlie was the first to see the joke and laughed. "Superman could be useful in the circumstances."

Quin looked thoughtful. "If what you say is true, I think we should consider a little preventative therapy. Perhaps stopping the supply route in France, or wherever else drugs come from. Certainly, if the new boys are taking over the supply business, they must get it in somewhere, and it must come over the sea at some point!"

"Or under!" Cass added.

"Under, of course. First we need a little more information. Do we have any idea where the product will be imported from?"

Jill said, "Now there are no de-facto borders, there seems little point in them doing anything but despatching the stuff direct to a Channel port."

Charlie grinned and put his foot in it, "I think we had probably worked that out."

Jill froze him with a glance and continued, "My point is that the chances of on-shipping to UK direct are pretty high, since there is no way the customs can examine every single container of goods coming in from the ostensibly open border between France, Belgium and Holland, and UK. Our best bet, therefore, would be for us to work from the delivery point backwards."

Charlie had the grace to flush at the realisation that he had jumped the gun. Jill looked over at him and, seeing his discomfort, said "Gotcha!" She pointed her finger at him and fired her imaginary pistol.

The others exchanged looks. "Sounds like sense to me." Cass said. "We'll need watchers."

Quin commented, "It will be interesting to find out if all the containers come from a single shipper and point of origin. If they don't, where they meet en-route, or are they all sent individually by separate routes. Before we go any further, are Athol's successors using the same warehouse in Brentford?"

Jill volunteered the news that the current operator in place was in fact using Athol's warehouse. "Apparently, with the demise of Athol Patrick, the new man who took over is Lucas Arnold, equally as poisonous as Athol Patrick, if not worse." Jill sounded serious.

"Sounds like a job for the new guys on the block!" Cass grinned. "That is, if Superman is not available."

Charlie and Jill looked at the seated figure of Quin, who was studying the plans they had made before of the warehouse setup in Brentford.

Cass giggled. That started the other two off, all three were laughing as Quin looked up. "What?" He said, looking from one to the other. None of them could answer for laughing.

Quin shrugged and returned to his studies.

When the noise died down he leaned forward, placing the plan on the table. "If you can manage it, gather round and I'll explain how we can go about this exercise."

The giggles over, Quin began to point out the various details on the diagram.

"We can use the walk-in entrance. It's here beside the telephone box. He pointed to the place on the diagram and then stood back as Cass said, "The telephone box?" And burst into laughter once more with the other two, as visions of the quick-change by Superman in the nearest telephone box rose without bidding in her mind's eye.

Quin looked at the three laughing people. He said drily. "Perhaps when you have got over your hilarity, we will be able to make some preparation for the excursion we are supposed to be planning."

He turned back to the plan in front of him as the other three stopped laughing, and composed themselves to listen to the rather more serious business of the forthcoming operation.

***

The black transit van drew up in the street parallel to the warehouse targeted for that night. There was no activity apparent, all the local buildings were silent and the only light was provided by the lights at each end of the street. The light located at the middle of the street was not working.

Having drawn up at the darkest point between the two lamps there was no further movement for some time.

Eventually the rear door opened quietly and a dark figure dropped to the ground followed by a second. The two figures melted into the darkness of the entrance to the factory next to the parked van.

After five additional minutes of inactivity, the front doors of the van opened. Two figures got out and closed the doors. The driver locked the vehicle and, arm in arm, the pair walked down the street and turned at the end toward the lights of Brentford High Street.

Charlie and Jill crossed the yard of the factory backing onto the warehouse they were targeting. At the wall which separated the two buildings, there was a place where the outline of a gateway which had once existed when the two buildings were once under single ownership. The yard they were occupying had been empty since the owners of the building had ceased trading several months before. This was the third time the pair had been at the building site. The result of their efforts was the skeletal appearance of the brickwork within the archway framing the former connecting doors.

Over the past days they had removed the mortar from all the brickwork on their side of the arch. There was only a single skin of bricks remaining precariously in place.

Charlie rested the sledgehammer against the wall and relaxed. Jill took a bar of chocolate from her pocket and passed a piece over to her companion. Both were dressed in black overalls over Kevlar vests. They both had gun-belts with holster for their automatics and a pouch for the tazer each carried. In addition, in a back pack Charlie carried the H&K smg with spare magazines.

Jill looked at her partner fondly. She had been alone for a long time when she had bumped into Charlie. As a lieutenant in the Israeli forces she had spent time on both sides of the Arab border and as a result had little time for personal affairs.

Her fiancé had soon grown tired of waiting for his absentee partner and departed to find another, more available, mate. The connection with Charlie had been instinctive and immediate. When they met, she could not believe how, in that moment, her life had changed. She had looked at him and known. It seemed he was equally stricken. Neither had hesitated in agreeing to be together.

Jill looked at her watch. "Any moment now, Charlie."

Charlie picked up the hammer. "Ready, love?"

"As ever." Jill grinned, a little tightly.

The alarm next door went off. Charlie swung the sledgehammer at the weakened wall. For a moment he was stunned by the effect, as the entire section of wall collapsed in a cloud of dust, allowing the light from within the warehouse to shine across the yard of the neighbouring building.

The pair jumped through the opened portal into the warehouse.

They stepped through into what had once been the office part of the car chopping shop. The rebuilt area of the ruined workshop was now to their left. They were in a room that was covered in white dust. A desk and chair occupied one side of what was obviously an office. The important thing was there was no one in there.

Jill went to the door, while Charlie stood back to cover any problem outside when Jill opened it. She looked at Charlie, who nodded, gun up ready.

Opening the door quietly, the outer room was exposed. At the far end there was activity, as three men with weapons crouched watching the entrance to the building. About the floor were stacks of goods of various sorts. Two other men appeared from a room on the outer wall of the building. Both were armed with smgs. Jill slipped out of the door behind the two new people. Followed by Charlie, she tapped the near man on the shoulder. He started in shock at the unexpected touch. His companion turned round to see what was happening and found Charlie's gun in his face. Both passed over their smgs carefully and were secured by Jill with the ubiquitous plastic cuffs, and handy duct-tape to prevent them calling out. The sound of gunfire at the door of the building indicated that the diversion was working. So Jill and Charlie, keeping low, got on with the setting of charges to destroy the contents of the warehouse section of the building. The room that the two prisoners had vacated appeared to be used to repackage things. It contained a considerable quantity of drugs. They made sure that there was a charge dedicated to that room in particular.

There was no time to examine the mezzanine floor so they made sure the charges were sufficient to bring the floor down. The noise from the front of the building increased with the addition of the clatter of an AK47. From the sound of things reinforcements had arrived. Charlie looked at Jill, eyebrow raised. Jill shrugged. "Shall we?"

They turned and made their way to the sound of firing at the front end of building. They came across three men lying behind a barricade shooting at an unseen target near the front door. Jill snapped a shot at the nearest man. He jerked and dropped his gun, swearing as the blood coursed down his arm. His nearest companion swung round, shooting as he turned. Charlie shot him and a bullet took him in the head. The third man realized something was wrong, put his gun down and raised his hands.

Charlie called out, "Quin, Cass, all clear here."

Quin answered, "There's a van coming. If you are finished I suggest we leave now."

"We're gone." Charlie called. He took the gun from the survivor and drove him in front of them to the hole in the wall. Jill and Charlie climbed through leaving the prisoner behind.

"Your lucky night, sunshine. They left him standing as they crossed the yard and stepped into the street where the van had pulled up to collect them. As they climbed into the van Charlie pressed the remote control he carried in his hand. The van was moving but the sound followed them, as did a shower of dust and rubble from the exploding building behind them.

"Did you cover the territory?" Quin asked.

"I think so." Charlie answered, "We left enough to take out the mezzanine floor while we were at it."

Cass said, "The van should have been in time to get the full benefit of that lot."

"Shall we stop for a drink on the way home?" Jill asked.

"We are not really dressed for it." Cass said.

"In the case at the back!" Quin said.

"My husband thinks ahead." Cass said with a smile.

They stopped at the 'Barge Aground' at Kew and enjoyed a drink while the fire engines howled further up the river Thames at Brentford. The four made a fine group, brown-haired Cass, blond Jill and the two men, fair-haired Charlie, and the dark-haired Quin. They drew eyes from many of the other customers of both sexes.

They drove back to Sussex that night and enjoyed the hospitality of the big house for a quiet celebration of the elimination of another piece in the jigsaw that made up the pattern of the Mob in London.

Chapter eight

Signs of recognition

It has to be said that Quin Gilmore would be happy to have a quiet life. It had always been others who had caused his need for retaliation, and the real reason that he had begun his campaign of attrition against the Moscow Mafia and the London mob. They had been at the estate for nearly one full month and everyone was falling into the routine that went with living the country house life.

The news came like a douche of cold water, bringing the team up short with a jolt.

At breakfast the papers arrived in time to be studied while the morning glow of the awakening day combined with the relaxed feel of having nothing scheduled, no forgotten tasks to be undertaken.

Cass was casually scanning the small items of gossip in her favorite tabloid when her eye caught the item at the foot of the page.

She read it out to the others, "How about this, guys? It says here that able bodies are needed in tune." She smiled and looked up at the others. "What do you think that means?"

Charlie grinned, and Jill smiled and said "Someone is having a joke. Sounds like one of those 'in' things."

Only Quin didn't smile.

Noticing, Cass said "What is it, Quin? It means something doesn't it?"

Quin nodded slowly. "Sorry, guys. All bets are off. I need to get to town in a hurry. You stock up and hit the retreat fast. This is not good news. Cass, use the van. Charlie and Jill, hire another each. Do a collection run, for canned food, of all sorts. Cass, you know what we have in freezer space. Concentrate on that only. Fill everything food wise." He rose to his feet. "Someone, somewhere, has started the ball rolling. I don't yet know the target, but whatever and wherever it is means global trouble. We have today to prepare. If we can do anything about it, we will be better placed in the retreat than here. It's a warning, and we have at most twenty-four hours to do something. First we prepare, only then we act, if we can. I'll keep you posted, and we'll meet later today with the full story. We'll make plans then." He looked round the table. "Good luck all. I'll be at the retreat by 1300."

He kissed Cass. "Later" he said, and went.

They heard the roar of the Jaguar as it took off in a hurry.

For a moment the others sat stunned by the effect of that past five minutes.

Charlie said, "What?...." then leapt to his feet. "Hire vans, the man said. Let's get to it."

Cass was on her feet moving to the room, first to change clothes and then grab the ready bag with the personal weapons and ammo for both herself and Quin. "Arm yourselves," she called after the others!

"I'm on it!" Jill shouted back. "See you later!"

The three split into their various directions. Cass was on the phone already to the freezer center in the local town, having invented a gala day to explain her large order for collection in forty minutes. Rather than take an empty van north, she would take and dump a load from here, and top up locally from Kingston when she assessed how much space was available.

***

After a morning of complete pandemonium, the three shattered people were seated round coffee and doughnuts following their hectic activities, still mystified over the reason for the panic.

Quin appeared and collected a cup of coffee. He sat down tiredly.

"All of you are wondering what this is all about, I suppose."

He sipped his coffee and then began to explain, "For some years, I was employed by HMG before I got diverted by personal matters and resigned. The job I had/have is one that nobody once involved can actually resign from. So, in effect, I was given leave of absence on certain conditions. The main one being that, in event of a National Emergency, I would be immediately reinstated and return to active status. The newspaper entry was used as a recall signal. It means that there is time but there is a problem." He paused and looked at the three attentive faces. "You all are probably aware that there are certain key people in the world that are always under someone's surveillance. It does happen on occasion that one or two drop out of sight. Normally it is pretty innocent, a diversion when on holiday or something like that. However when the explanation is not forthcoming, or the person does not reappear, the red flags go up elsewhere. All the other persons under focus are subject to increased security."

"Sorry to interrupt, Quin. But what and why is there this panic?"

"As I mentioned before there are always some people under surveillance at all times. They are key people in certain positions who often are only significant in conjunction with others. What I am saying is that their presence is innocent in itself. But when they are linked with certain others they form part of a dangerous whole. A good example to consider is an atomic bomb. It is composed of components, if all the components are not collected together and linked in sequence it becomes a, not very good, traditional bomb. Correctly linked, it is devastating.

"That is what I am saying about the people who have started disappearing. Two have gone. Neither has critical information; without the other three people what they know is tantalisingly useless.

"An attempt was foiled to take number three. Happily it was prevented by accident. They grabbed the wrong person. There was relief all round. However, it was pointed out to be unfortunate for the abducted man whose life ended with a bullet in the back of his head."

There was a gasp of horror from Cass. "Just to prevent him identifying anyone, or indicating where he had been taken?"

"Precisely! To stop him from talking! It's an illustration of how ruthless these people are, and how highly they rate the importance of getting hold of the components of the chain. So I can almost hear the questions you have before you start. What does the chain add up to?"

He stopped and drank some coffee for a few seconds before he continued. "Think doomsday weapons, perhaps, a virus? He looked around the group.

Cass said, "You have something really nasty in mind, haven't you?"

"Oh, boy. I do not think I'm going to like this." Charlie said.

Jill said quietly, "For Pete's sake, Quin. Put us out of our misery."

"It's wipe-out of all animal life, from mouse to elephant, passing through man on the way, leaving vegetation and insect life in charge. Will that be enough?"

There was a silence following this statement, that was eloquent in itself. Cass finally said it. "So, what's the worst that can happen? We can all die, that's what you're saying. So folks, if you'll pardon me mentioning it, we are all going to die anyway. What we are discussing is when it is going to happen. Are we are going to allow someone, other than whatever deity we believe in, to dictate that particular moment. My vote is, let's terminate the sucker before he terminates everyone. What do you say to that? Just one more question, Quin. If this is such a devastating virus, weapon, call it what you will, why did they not just destroy the research and leave it at that. Keeping the formulae keeps the prospect alive?"

"The final chip, I am told, contains the antidote." Quin sounded bitter.

"You mean somebody decided that there may be a scenario where the weapon would be deployed, and only a selected group protected?" Cass said wonderingly. The others sat there appalled at the implications as Quin nodded.

"How about we start with the person who made that decision?" Charlie looked serious.

"Sounds most reasonable to me." Jill said quietly, her face still showing nothing.

"Dead and gone, I'm afraid." Quin looked at the others and continued. "I only learned what I know when the people concerned panicked. The four original creators died in a plane crash. An accident we were told. Remember though that this retreat was prepared for a selected few to survive Armageddon. That was the mind-set at the time. Remember that when you think of the situation we now face. If I think there is a chance of someone like that getting hold of the abomination we are discussing, I would have no hesitation deleting them."

"What makes you think that these chips are the only record of this process? From what you say about the sort of people who were in control, I find it unbelievable that there is no back-up tucked away somewhere."

"That idea is haunting me at this moment. I can confirm that the four who were killed in the plane crash included the scientists who made the original discovery. I am also aware that one set of formula was destroyed. I was told that another was lost in the crash. The copy used to create the micro-chips was allegedly destroyed at the time. I suspect that there is still another hidden away somewhere. That may well be the next task. The immediate problem is locating and eliminating the micro-chips we know exist, agreed?"

"I'm with you! Count me in!" Charlie contributed. Jill nodded also.

Cass said, "So where do we start?"

"With the next item on the agenda," Quin said quietly. "If I can find the next link in the chain, we cover the place and the person, and hope to catch anyone trying to snatch them. Does that sound a plan?"

The others nodded in agreement.

Quin rose to his feet. "Charlie, with me. I've no suggestions for you ladies, though I do think a shopping trip might be an answer. To pass the time, I mean."

"What do we know about the next link as you put it?" Cass said quietly, "Have you a line to follow."

"All I know is that the man is a civil servant, and that he was attending the conference in Vienna in 1998, as an aide to the British Delegation. Of the group that made up the delegation, a total of 26 people, five were given the memory chip. The three known are the ones we are aware of, two dead, one under wraps. The other two are unidentified, and they were both given new identities. They had the chip installed while they were unconscious. None of them is aware that they have the chip with the definitive sections of the equation. All were given new identities and new jobs. We need to identify and locate two out of the seventeen staff at the EO1 level, who have a new name and job.

"Needle in haystack time, folks. So let's get to it"

Chapter nine

Threading the needle

Finding someone who does not wish to be found is never easy. If they have a changed identity it becomes doubly difficult. In this case there was a routine which had worked in the past. It required time and patience.

Searching out the location of their last known workplace was fairly simple. From there, the difficult part began. This was especially difficult because they were not the only people looking.

Quin supplied the original identification and location of their places of work. From there the trail went cold.

Jill made the first break-through. The man she was searching for had been transferred to the Agriculture and Fisheries department in the month after the conference. He had never appeared on the staff list after the transfer. When she questioned the fact with the Civil Service Association, they were themselves mystified. While at their offices she did get the up-to-date details of all transfers on and about the date.

Having deleted all the female transfers and those of people widely divergent as far as age was concerned, she had reduced the list to seventeen. Of these, nine had turned out to be either Jamaican or Indian, leaving eight candidates, always assuming the person in question had remained in the civil service. Quin had suggested that they probably would have. To narrow the search ever further they decided to start off with the people unattached at that time, on the basis that there would be less complication over changing name and details of a single person, than a married or partnered person.

Three qualified and Jill called Cass to help with the sorting out of the finalists.

***

Newbury was not a huge town. Andrew Card had settled there without any qualms about the alteration in life style it had entailed. From the rented apartment he had first occupied, he had since bought a converted river barge moored on the Kennet and Avon Canal. Near enough to the High Street to have easy access to the shopping and entertainment, he had soon fallen into the easy routine of life on the canal. He made friends with his neighbours and over the past fourteen years had adopted his new identity almost seamlessly.

He was a solitary person and, though he had friends of both sexes, he had never felt the need to share his life with another. The houseboat reflected his way of life with every neat nook and crevice. Even the weekly replacement of the vase of flowers was part of the pattern of living he had fallen into.

He was reflecting with a glass of wine on the after deck of his home when he realized he was under observation. Allowing his eyes to drift about the area idly, he took in the presence of the small man with the reluctant dog.

He was a stranger to Andrew who had become pretty much established enough to know who came and went along the towpath. The dog was obviously not keen on his walker and spent more time trying to get loose than the normal combination of person and pet that Andrew was used to. With his senses heightened, he also questioned the casual clothes that the man wore and seemed too new. They looked as if they had just been taken out of their plastic bags to replace the more formal clothes which would have suited the man more comfortably.

The man in question cursed the antics of the dog which he could have well done without. "Take the dog. It will look more natural on the towpath. People always walk their dogs along by the canal."

Martin Hood was not convinced. Nor was he convincing and aware of it. He stood out in his own mind like the proverbial 'sore thumb.'

He would not have been re-assured to know that others were of the same opinion. Andrew was in fact thoroughly suspicious and for the first time in years wondered if his identity change was something to do with the watcher.

There was a number he had been told to ring in the event of disclosure. He was loath to use it without something more than suspicion to go by.

Jill slid quietly into the dinghy where Cass waited at the oars. "There's a watcher on the towpath with a stupid dog. I think our man has it sussed, but he is playing it cool for the moment."

"Well, let's go then." Cass pushed off and started gently stroking the boat through over the dark waters of the canal. She passed under the town bridge, where the scent of the cooking from the pork butcher's shop by the bridge reminded her that she was really quite hungry.

As they approached Andrew in his house boat, Cass caught a crab and lost an oar. It floated toward Andrew as he sat with his glass of wine now half empty. He made a half-hearted effort to get up and grab the oar but Cass called out, "It's okay. Don't bother. I can get it." She demonstrated by adroitly hooking the oar with the boat hook, and pulling it alongside the dinghy. Retrieving the oar she called out to Andrew, "Thank you for the offer of help. Chivalry is not dead."

He waved and sat back while Cass rowed further along the canal. The two women stopped beside the grassy bank and had tea from a flask, and sandwiches from Marks and Spencer. Then they sculled gently back along the canal, retracing their route.

Andrew called out to them as they approached, "Care for a glass of wine, ladies?"

Jill said, "Perhaps a little later. We should return the dinghy."

Andrew smiled. "I'll be here." He returned to his contemplation of the scene, noticing that the little man with the recalcitrant dog had disappeared.

Jill hopped ashore just round the bend, instinct made her suspect there might be problems for their putative host. Cass rowed a little further to a point where she could tie the dinghy, and climbed ashore to join Jill. "What's wrong, Jill?"

"Don't really know. I just have this feeling..." She trailed off as she looked at the quiet peaceful scene. "Oh, ho, visitors! Across the green the little man with the dog had been joined by two others. The dog had been released and it was running off toward the town.

"Let's get in quick." She rounded the bend in the towpath with Cass in train. They approached Andrew with a chatter and laughter. The three men stopped abruptly. Cass noticed they turned and made off towards the town.

***

The wine session with Andrew was lively and productive for the two women. The questions that they idly passed back and forth were loaded, aiming at getting him to slip-up over his past history.

The fact that he had it down pat made Cass immediately suspicious. She was aware that she would have difficulty in having such a clear memory for events of thirty years ago. To recall, as Andrew was demonstrating, took serious memory training or practice. Most would not bother!

Looking at Jill she lifted an eyebrow. Jill nodded and her hand passed over the drink in front of Andrew.

He nodded off three minutes later. Jill ran along to the dinghy and rowed it to the houseboat. While Cass packed a bag, Jill manoeuvred Andrew into the dinghy.

Cass joined them in the boat and, reaching under the seat, switched on the electric motor. They silently moved back under the road bridge to the boatyard where the car had been parked. Jill slipped ashore as soon as they were out of the reflected lights from the high street.

When she reached the car, Cass switched off the motor and nudged into the bank. Tying off the painter to a mooring post, she stepped ashore. The man stepped out from behind the car, his hand holding a small automatic. The second man appeared behind him.

"Where is your little friend?" She asked calmly.

"He is waiting in the car," the taller man said. "We need it to take your friend from the boat to our friends."

"And who might that be, I wonder?" Cass asked, more in hope than expectation.

"You don't really expect me to tell you. Anyway you'll meet them soon enough."

"Just lay the gun down on the car wing," Jill said in a soft voice.

The tall man hesitated. "Mine is bigger than yours, and it is quiet too." Jill insisted. Cass took the gun from the car wing and pointing to the ground watched as the two men got down on their hands and knees. Then lay down hands crossed behind them.

Jill appeared and slipped the plastic loops over their crossed hands. She then frisked them both, retrieving an extra gun from an ankle holster and a knife from a sheath between the shoulder blades of the big man. Jill produced a bag from the car and slipped it over the head of the tall man. The other man looked anxious, so she found a bag for him too.

Between them the women loaded the inert body of Andrew into the back of the car, the tall man just managed to cramp into the trunk. His friend was left on the grass beside the canal.

"What about their car?" Cass asked.

"It has a puncture and a sleeping driver." Jill said succinctly.

***

They were back in the retreat in an hour and thirty-five minutes. The traffic on the M4 was slow due to an accident at the junction with the M25. Quin was there to help them unload the still sleeping Andrew. As he turned to shut the door to the garage, Jill said, "We should really bring the other one in."

Quin looked at them sharply. "The other one?"

Cass said, "The one in the trunk!" She popped the lid revealing the tall man crammed up against the spare tire.

"Ah, that other one," Quin grinned. "We have been busy, haven't we?"

"We decided you might wish to talk to someone." Jill volunteered.

"Quite right too," Quin said. "Let's get him out of there."

***

Later, in the retreat, their guest was seated on a chair in the center of a stark bare room which they had cleared especially for their purpose. Used normally as a storage room, it was kept without heat deliberately. Consequently, it was ideal as an interrogation chamber.

Jill suggested getting the right gear for the actual questioning. She had in mind something after the design of the Nazi SS uniforms. Quin said no, since there were no such uniforms in the retreat anyway.

Eventually, Quin spoke to the man. "What were you doing waving guns at my staff?"

The man looked at Quin then talked.

"I was ordered to take the guy, Andrew, from the boat and make a prisoner of one of the girls talking to him. Nobody mentioned that I was up against trained agents. Nor was it made clear why we were supposed to do it.

The man was quite comfortable now, thinking that he had talked himself out of trouble. These people were obviously amateurs. Calling them trained agents was flannel to make them think they had fooled him.

Cass looked at the man calculatingly. "Let's get rid of this one now. Strip him and put him in with the crocodiles."

Jill said, "No, you know that their diet has to be carefully regulated in this climate. We can drop him in the snake pit. They would have no diet problems."

The man was looking a little more uncomfortable now. "Look, I haven't done anything to you two and I wouldn't have harmed you. I was only there to collect the man in the boat."

Quin came in and, reading from the contents of the man's wallet, said, "Are you Allan Wharton?"

"No, I'm Michael Smith. Wharton was my partner, the guy you left on the ground at Newbury."

Quin looked at the second wallet. "Well, Mr Smith. you appear to answer to several different names according to your papers here."

"That is just part of my cover as a private detective."

"Since when did private detectives carry guns in this country? I was under the impression that not only was it discouraged but it was actually illegal."

Smith made no reply, being on dangerous ground here. After some thought he decided that the people who had taken him were possibly working on the same side as he was. He changed the subject. "In fact I have been working undercover to trace and protect certain people. The man on the boat was I believe, one of the people in question. I carried a gun because several of the people we sought had been killed. It had been suspected for some time that there was a cabal at work finding and killing the group we were seeking. I hooked up with one of the opposition search groups and that is where I encountered your formidable ladies."

"Why should we believe you?" Quin said guardedly.

"If you pass me my wallet I'll prove it." Smith said holding his hand out.

Quin passed the wallet over.

Smith took the identity card from the wallet and split the plastic. Inside was a warrant card with photograph stating that Michael Smith was a Detective Sgt in Special Branch.

Chapter ten

Horses for courses

As Mike Smith pointed out, since they were all singing from the same hymn sheet, there was a real case for sharing information.

Both search teams had come to the same target at the same time. The next target was probably the only other one surviving. According to Smith the last man was in Brussels, and there were two other groups searching already. The searchers were looking in the wrong place as far as he was aware since the target had been a member of the EU Civil Service for the past 30 years. He had not been listed at the meeting attended by all the others, as he was a member of the staff at that time rather than an invited guest.

The SB had the list of staff attendant at the function and they had narrowed it down to four possibles; though of the possibles one had never even been in the room with the others.

Quin said, "Well, that probably settles it, 'the man who never was.' My bet is that he is the one."

Cass looked at him with eyebrow raised. "Why?"

Quin smiled. "As the meeting had been vetted every way from Sunday, by using a staff member they introduce a firebreak into the program, a wild card if you will. It is the invisible men and women who are always ignored. In this case we have a man who is on duty, but not present. Where is he? Is he a guard on security? No. We already know all the guard detail. Is he a chef? No. He is a clerical officer about to be promoted, just 'Joe Soap' doing his job and hanging around the meeting room as ordered. Halfway through he gets called in and is given a Mickey Finn. He wakes with a sore head in the arms of a floozy that his wife might not approve of. He doesn't question. He panics and fades into the woodwork perhaps with the unneeded threat that he should never speak of it.

"Now thirty years on, he has forgotten the incident. There is just the undiscovered mark on the back of his neck, and the vague memory that is now a dream of the forgotten dalliance with a young girl, whom he cannot recall consorting with prior to waking up naked at her side."

"If I am correct we should really get to this man before someone else decides to take a look at the staff." Quin turned to Smith. "Do you have a team on this man?"

"In this instance, no!" Smith looked embarrassed. "I am the SB effort to assist M15. My boss said that the spooks were so busy demonstrating how busy and efficient they are, they do not have the manpower. We got lumbered on the understanding that when we are ready to move they will step in to make the arrest. Thus they will garner the glory, and we will get back to the servile spot where we belong. Foot soldiers, in the eternal battle for good." He sounded bitter at this point."

Quin looked at him sharply.

Smith raised his hands. "Don't get the wrong idea. I am sick of the Branch being made a convenience of for the benefit of extra funding for the spooks. But my loyalties still lie with my department. I have not crossed to the dark side, honest!"

Quin left him with Charlie and spoke quietly to Cass in their room. "I believe that he is what he says he is. So we can let him loose when we have found the last piece of the puzzle. Under no circumstances must he be allowed to find out about this place. We can leave with the closed van for the airport and, if necessary, drop him off to fetch passports etc., once we are down the road."

Cass nodded her agreement, "No use showing all our cards this early in the game. He's maybe a little too plausible perhaps?"

For Andrew Card the relocation to the retreat was a new experience. He heard the explanation given by Quin and appreciated the fact that he had been in serious danger because his cover had been exposed. His place at the retreat was comfortable and, while he missed the life on the canal, he did realize that the situation would return to normal and he would be able to return in good time.

***

The Brussels streets were busy with hurrying people trying to get out of the soft rain that was falling on the city; blurring the glass of the window where the watcher waited. He looked at his watch and turned away, drawing the long curtains to shut out the damp scene below in the street.

The other occupants consisted of one seated in front of the fire blazing in the big reproduction marble fireplace, the other making a drink from the decanters on the sideboard. The room was furnished with a collection of faux antiques, giving an impression of fussiness. The Englishness was at odds with the roll of canvas lying on the floor beside the window bay. On it lay a long-barrelled rifle with a tripod. There were two other weapons on the canvas, an H&K sub-machine gun with two magazines and an automatic pistol.

In the corner of the room behind the settee, an inert figure lay, a trickle of blood had formed a small puddle below his half-open mouth. The man was breathing, albeit shallowly. As he lay there, his eyes opened slightly. He continued breathing in the same manner while he looked at the three other people in the room. He tried to move his hands and found that he was not tied. His head hurt the bullet had cut a groove and there was a cut inside his mouth which had created the blood on the floor beside his face.

He though briefly about the comments his landlady would make, if she saw the canvas roll with the guns on her polished wooden floor. Seeing the guns, he realized that there was nothing personal in this intrusion. It was just that this house was in the right position for the job in hand.

He guessed that there was a target of some sort expected and this was the ambush point of choice.

He gave his situation some thought. Either they thought he was dead, or they didn't care as long as he was out of it. Though he was not what he could call fully fit, he could bear the injuries. All he needed was the chance to either escape or take them on. All three men were now seated discussing something in Serbo-Croat. The language was not important. The fact was, they were talking and no one was taking any notice of the man behind the settee.

He tried moving, and found that there was life in his legs. That was a re-assurance, since it meant that, despite the injury, he was still alive and probably mobile.

He rose to his feet while the men had their backs to him. His image appeared in the mirror, and the shock of seeing his bloody head nearly threw him. None of the men had realized that he had regained his feet. He shrugged, stepped over to the canvas on the floor and picked up the automatic. Turning to the astonished men. he cocked the automatic, a 9mm Walther. "Up!" He said to the three men.

They shot to their feet looking unhappy at this Lazarus's resurrection before them.

"We found you where you lay," the man in charge, who had been seated, said. "We arranged with the Patron to use this room and here you were."

He smiled. "Ah. so I suppose I have someone else to thank for this new parting I have acquired."

"Certainly. We would have given assistance but we thought you were dead. I was surprised, as I had been informed that you were a resourceful man, unlikely to be in the position we found you in. I suppose you are Ian Bennet?"

The man at the settee seemed quite sure that man before him would understand and believe him.

Bennet told the other two men to lie down on their faces with their hands behind their backs, and gestured for the leader to sit once more.

Then, "So there is just the explanation. Why the guns are here? and why are you here?" He asked the questions lightly and watched the seated man closely.

For the first time the man was not at ease. "We brought the guns, of course. I came to see you about a security matter, a little problem that turned up at my company HQ last week."

"Why me? I am not even in the book as a security consultant?"

"You were recommended to me by a friend in the business."

"Name?"

"I cannot recall at this moment. I was told of you some time ago at meeting of the Institute of Directors. I cannot remember who told me but I do remember that I valued his opinion."

"Up on your feet. Take your friends with you. Oh, before you leave, what have you done with my landlady?"

"She is below, unharmed I assure you," the spokesman said. "We did not injure her in any way."

"Who was the target you were after?" Bennet asked quietly.

"Gio.......oops, you nearly caused me to misinform you." The man was all urbane charm once more.

"What is your name?" Bennet asked, not anticipating an answer.

"I am called Smith, Peter Smith." Came the reply

"Are there lots of Smiths in Croatia?" Bennet suggested.

"It's a common enough name, anywhere in the world." Smith replied. My name translates as Smith. So I use that name in the West. It simplifies matters."

They left the canvas roll and guns on the floor, and descended to the front door.

Bennet's head was throbbing, so he waved them through the door and saw them drive off in a grey BMW.

The door to the ground floor apartment was open. The voice of his landlady talking to someone on the phone was advising them that the situation was in hand and no harm had come to her. Ian called out that he was going to bed. He had a headache. He did not hear her reply. so just continued up the stair to his apartment.

Reaction was setting in and, as he stumbled through his door, he collapsed.

***

The voice was persistent it sounded foggy and strange. There was something wrong with his eyes and his head was pounding. A cool softness descended onto his aching brow. Gentle hands caressed the painful area on the side of his head. As consciousness returned he realized that there really was a voice, only it was clear now. The anxious county accents verifying that his aristocratic landlady was attending him. Memory returned in a rush. His wound!

The startled move advised Naomie that he was awake. "Just lie still while I get this mess cleared up. Then we'll get you through to bed."

He tried a wry grin. "I never thought I would hear you make that sort of proposal."

"You never asked." Her reply was prompt and she did not stop cleaning his wound. He felt her apply a pad, and then bandage it in place. He tried to open his eyes.

"Give me a moment, while I clear the blood away. You must have started the bleeding again when you fell." The soft wet cloth bathed his eyes. When he was able to open them he looked into the clear blue, rather anxious looking eyes of the Hon. Naomie Price-Hamilton, his landlady.

"Take it easy and see if you can sit up." The voice was soft but the determination was in the firm help of the arm behind his back helping him sit up.

"I do apologize for messing up the floor like this." He indicated the blood that had leaked from his wound, and the gun laden canvas roll that still lay on the floor. "I had nothing to do with all this," he said still a little vague about things.

"Bed first. We can discuss the in's and out's later when you are feeling a little better."

With the help of her surprisingly strong, slender body he managed to get to his feet and stumble through to the bedroom, his arm round the shoulders and leaning heavily on her.

He stood swaying beside the bed, waiting for her to leave.

"Well, come on. Get your clothes off. You cannot go to bed fully dressed." She started undoing his shirt. When he took over, she pushed his jacket off his shoulders removing his arms in turn. Having draped the jacket on the chair beside the bed, she undid his belt and zip and dragged his trousers down. He sat on the bed in his shorts while she hauled his shoes off allowing his trousers to slip over his feet. She folded them and put them beside his jacket. His shirt was half off revealing the fact that he wore no vest, so with that and his socks removed she left it at that. Hauling back the duvet, she pushed his legs under arranging him lengthways in the bed. She placed a towel from the bathroom across the pillow in case the bleeding started again and stood back checking over her efforts.

"You shouldn't….." He started to say, but she interrupted him.

"I let those people in, so this is my fault. It's the least I can do." She fetched water from the sink and put a jug and glass on the bedside table. "Now, is there anything else you need—for now, that is?"

"An aspirin would help." Bennet said faintly.

"Oh, I knew there was something," she said and dashed down to her apartment, returning with a bottle of painkillers.

She fed him two with some water, then settled him back on the pillows.

"Thank you. I am very grateful for all you have done for me. There was the hint of a grin on his face as he added, "When I feel better, I'll take you up on that com….." The rest of his comment slurred and he lapsed into unconsciousness again.

The lady looked at the recumbent figure, and whispered, "You just get your head together again, and I might just make that offer again." With a smile she turned the light off and left him sleeping.

***

The doctor appeared the following morning, apparently summoned by Naomie. At least she escorted him into the apartment.

Bennet was awake by then and accepted the ministrations from the pair with good grace. His head felt better after the doctor had reduced the size of the dressing, and declared himself satisfied that Naomie could be left in charge of any nursing needed. "I'll call in two days' time. The dressing can come off then and you should be back on your feet." With a cheerful wave he departed.

Bennet heard the front door close after him and was contemplating getting up to make breakfast, when the room door opened. Naomie appeared laden with a tray of poached egg on toast, coffee and yoghurt.

"You can get up later. But I want you to get some food inside you. After losing so much blood you need to make it up as quickly as possible. I'll return and help you with your bath later, so just take it easy meanwhile. The doctor agreed to let you stay here as long as I took care of you. He also agreed not to report your injury to the police. He is an old friend. He understands. He knew what my husband was involved in."

Surprised, Bennet looked up at the mention of her husband. "I did not realize you were married?"

"I was. My husband, Alec, died two years ago in Pakistan. In his business this sort of thing happened occasionally."

"This sort of thing? What did your husband do?"

Naomie looked at him directly her clear blue eyes weighing him up, then she spoke. "My husband was a spook, Mr Bennet, a spy for the British Government. He was captured by Afghan terrorists, and they sent him home in a box.

"I learned a lot of odd things during our time together. That was why I knew what to do when this happened." She turned and left the room leaving Bennet to his breakfast.

She returned after he had eaten wearing a wrap-around apron and helped him out of bed, he was still wearing his shorts and nothing else. She steadied him on his feet and walked him through to the bathroom. She leaned him against the wall while she started the shower, checking the temperature of the water. Satisfied she turned to Bennet and looked at him steadily. He was still upright but not as steady as she liked. Making her mind up she said, "Right, shorts off and in we go." He started to protest but she said, "Oh, don't be so silly," and yanked the shorts down. She slipped out of the wrap-around revealing her own nakedness. "Like you, I've seen it all before. But you need a shower and you cannot do it yourself."

Bennet stood under the warm water, luxuriating in the feel of the sweat and blood running off into the drain by his feet. The sponge was applied by gentle hands. He wondered how he had shared the house with this woman for so long, without knowing her.

Naomie turned the water off and reached round Bennet to get the towel, her breast brushing against his arm. The intimacy of the moment occurred to them both, but both ignored it. Once he was wrapped in the bath towel, she manoeuvred him out of the stall onto the bathmat, where she rubbed him down efficiently and impersonally. He was able to help himself into the dressing gown she provided. After drying herself, she helped him back to the bedroom. Having parked him in a chair, she stripped the bed and remade it with fresh sheets. Once he was back in bed she left him, taking the discarded breakfast tray with her.

***

The doctor called early the following day, his brisk examination resulted in a smaller dressing that he could replace himself, a small box of pills in case the pain required them and the advice not to stand too near to a pistol next time.

By that morning he was well enough to get out of bed and, when she appeared with breakfast, he was shaving carefully.

"Thank you, Naomie. I could really get accustomed to this." For some reason, he felt suddenly embarrassed when he made the remark.

He did not notice the tinge of color that had appeared on her cheek at his remark.

He sat down at the table to have the breakfast she had provided, "Please keep me company. Have some coffee while I eat."

She collected a cup of coffee and sat opposite him at the small table. The symbolism of their encounter was not lost on them. There was an aura of unfinished business over their situation but neither was willing to raise the subject. Both had been there before with others, and both were apprehensive, not sure if they were ready to venture into the uncharted waters between them.

Having eaten and now with coffee in front of him Bennet took the plunge. "You miss your husband?"

"Not really. After the first flush of enthusiasm he was always wrapped up in his work. He was away more often than here at home. I quickly learned that if I did not have a life of my own I would become a cabbage. So I bought this house and ran the apartments, first of all on short term lets. Then when Roger was killed, I sold our house and moved in downstairs. My tenant left last year when you took up the lease." She spoke in a matter-of-fact voice. "I confess I did not anticipate the events of two nights ago."

"Nor did I," Bennet said. "The whole business left me mystified until I realized that there was nothing personal in the attack. It was to gain access to my apartment to assassinate someone apparently, so at least what happened to me saved someone else's life."

Naomie looked at him unblinkingly. "Are you saying that you have had no training in this sort of thing?"

Thinking fast Bennet decided that the truth would be his best bet. "No, I was not. It was just that I heard them talking about their target when they thought I was dead."

"So what branch of the service are you, or were you, involved with?" The question was inevitable so Bennet after little thought answered truthfully.

"I was M16. I resigned two months ago. I was steered to this apartment because the service has it listed. I had just returned from Moscow. I had not been back in England for several years. My fiancé had sold my apartment the first year I was away. Then she married her boss so I had nowhere to return to. I took the Brussels post when I came here first.

"Over the past year plus, I have been at a desk in the Euro/HQ. I resigned out of sheer boredom and since then I have been helping out an old friend in his private detective agency."

Naomie smiled. "You're a Private Eye?" she said incredulously.

"I suppose so!" Bennet smiled in return, fascinated by the way her face lit up when she smiled. Now tell me why a beautiful woman like you, what 30/32 years old, is sitting here talking to me when you should be the target of every eligible man in the immediate area?"

She blushed. "Perhaps I am not as beautiful as you think. Or even that there are no available so-called eligible bachelors to target me. Maybe even a combination of the two." She paused for a moment. "Then again it is possible that I have not been interested in looking around after all this time alone."

Bennet smiled again. She noticed that his eyes crinkled at the corners when he did that. Why was she so aware of him?

"In the circumstances," he said seriously, "I would consider it a favor if you would allow me to take you out somewhere special for dinner, and perhaps a show? If there are no others to consider then I won't feel I am stepping on anyone's toes."

Naomie took a few moments to answer, and Bennet found himself anxiously awaiting her answer.

"I think I would enjoy a West End night out," she said eventually. "Tomorrow night perhaps?"

With tongue in cheek Bennet suggested, "If I book us in at the Grosvenor House, we can leave tomorrow morning and be in town by lunchtime. You could, if you wish, go shopping. Then we return the following day, if that will suit. It will save any rushing about and give us a little time to get to know each other?"

Chapter eleven

Back in the groove

Quin and Cass were strolling down Park Lane when Bennet and Naomie arrived in a taxi at the Grosvenor House. Cass, holding Quin's arm felt the immediate tension that was instantly relaxed at the sighting of the arriving pair.

"What?" She asked.

"An old friend!" He said tersely.

They came up to the pair. Quin caught Bennet's eye and wheeled Cass through the glass doors of the hotel entrance.

Inside he seated her in the lounge, while Bennet and his companion checked in.

Quin ordered tea for them both and sat down. "We may have just got lucky." he commented. That is Ian Bennet, a past colleague, and now an independent contractor based in Brussels. He will join us shortly to say 'hullo' either with or without his companion, who also looks familiar."

Bennet and Naomie appeared from the elevator about ten minutes later. Locating them, Bennet steered Naomie over to join them. The ladies were introduced and Quin realized he had known Naomi's husband, and in fact had, on one occasion, met Naomi at a reception. Both the ladies noticed that the two men greeted each other like old friends and the ensuing conversation verified this observation. Introduced as Quin's wife, Cass was amused at the surprised reaction this got from both the others.

"Why the surprise? Did you think it would never happen? Or is that I don't fit the image?"

Both Bennet and Naomie burst out laughing at this. When they had calmed down Naomie explained that she was the widow of a spook and Bennet a retired spook, whom she was currently keeping at arm's-length until she worked out if he was worth keeping or throwing back into the water.

At this the entire group collapsed with laughter once more. After tea they decided that they would join forces and, after dinner at L'Escargot in Leicester Square, take in the show together. The two men left the ladies to arrange for reservations with the Concierge. While they were away Cass turned to Naomie. "Why do I feel you were not joking about Ian?"

"I had not discussed it with him certainly. Nor have we been together, though we have been acquainted for over a year. You may have noticed the wound on his head?" At Cass's nod she continued and told the story as she knew it. "So you see this was never scheduled. I think it came out of gratitude for my help. Perhaps because of my husband I had some sympathy for an ex-spook." She paused once more. "I was wary at first. Having survived being married to a spook, I was not inclined to repeat the experience. I was certainly on the prospect list for a while. Dinner invitations and Embassy functions, it took time but they finally got the message. I confess this incident opened my eyes to the fact that my tenant was an attractive man and I was interested to say the least. I had the impression that he thought the same of me. Do you think I overplayed my hand?" She looked at Cass just a touch anxiously.

Cass smiled. "I think that was just the right thing to say. It put the matter on the table in case there was real interest, and allowed for a light dalliance if there was no commitment. Left the doors open to you both, so to speak!"

"Well, that sounds reasonable. I can live with that." Naomie sounded relieved.

"By the way, for what it is worth in my opinion, Ian is definitely interested." Cass commented. "His body language shouts it."

When the two men rejoined them, by common consent they adjourned to the suite Ian had booked where they could talk more freely.

Not surprisingly the conversation came round to what they were all doing at present. Hearing that Bennet was freelancing currently, Quin looked thoughtful.

Eventually, during a lull in conversation Quin spoke directly to Ian. "We have something going on at the moment with a Brussels connection. Would you be interested in working with us? He turned to Naomi hurriedly. "I am no longer working for HMG, though in some ways this is a hangover from those days."

Naomi smiled. "I'm intrigued by the idea that finally, I may get to know a little about my former husband's work. It's something he would never talk about."

"We operate under slightly different rules," Cass said.

Naomi spun round to face her. "Are you involved?"

"I certainly am. We met when we were involved with a mutual problem." She nodded at Quin. I have been involved ever since."

"So what are we talking about?" Ian jumped in before the conversation got completely out of hand.

Quin started. "This stays here. It can go no further than the four of us." He looked at each in turn. Satisfied he told the story. "It's now down to the last one. He is apparently in Brussels and we have an idea who he is."

Naomi interjected. "You are talking about the Partiman group, which means the man you want is Robert Anderson."

The other three looked at her in astonishment. Eventually Quin said, "How...."

She stopped him raising her hand. "On one occasion my husband got drunk and I put him to bed. He insisted on telling me something. I told him not to be so silly. He never ever told me anything. That is why he said, 'I am telling you something now. You will never be able to say that I never told you anything again!'"

She paused. "He poured out the story that you have just told us with some minor differences. He gave me names. He would not stop until he told all. I remember most of them, several that you mentioned, Shepherd, Rogerson, and Myers. He said that Anderson was important because he was not one of the group. He was a wild card. That was the way he put it. If they get that far they will think it's Haddon."

Quin looked at Cass and then turned to Naomi. "You are sure of this?"

"Absolutely. Anderson is in a nursing home here in Britain."

"Do you remember where?" Quin insisted.

"Just a minute. It was near his home, the place where he was born. I know it was a village near Oban..... Ben something," She shut her eyes and concentrated. Then "Benderloch! That was it."

"Where is Haddon?" Quin asked her.

"Oh, he's still in Brussels. He and his wife have a tea room in Nossegem on the road to Lueven, not far to the east of Brussels. Haddon was younger than the others and has only just retired. I know the Haddons, you see. When Alec was in Brussels I used to meet him at the office. It was separate from the Embassy of course and Haddon was the face of the office for several years. I got to know his wife socially so she kept in touch when Alec died. What do we do next?"

The other three looked at each other. Then Ian said, "All for one!"

Quin shrugged and took out his cell phone and called Charlie. "I need you to go to Brussels, actually Nossegem—on the road to Lueven—at the tea room there, a man and his wife named Haddon. They are not our target but they may be identified as the one by others. That can mean terminal trouble, going by what has happened in the past. Explain and get them into a safe place. This is serious, Charlie. Can you manage?"

"Will do, Quin. I'll get on the road now. I'll be in touch when we've sorted things."

***

The office was small though not exactly pokey. The furniture was good quality, not new but in good shape. The person sitting at the desk was angry, her face a little flushed, reflecting her feelings toward the man in front of her. Cass would have recognized the small man even without his dog.

As for him he was terrified. The incredibly beautiful woman in front of him, normally icily calm, was anything but at this moment. And, though he had not been told that her temper was something to be avoided, he had never really thought about having to face it.

"You let them make fools of you. Three grown men, so-called agents, experts at your jobs. Now we have lost our man through your stupidity.

"But surely we can find him, or just get that last on the list?"

"We are not even sure that we know who that could be. All we have is the vague word of a dying man that the last person was not a guest. "

"But we do have a name. I'm sure we had a name."

"We have part of a name and up to now we are guessing. We really do not need any more slip-ups like the one you lot made earlier. Killing that wrong man was unnecessary. It put others on the track. Up until then we were legal, free and clear. Now we have one suspect we know of. My research says it's a man called Haddon. He is retired and runs a tearoom with his wife in a place near Brussels. Do not let him see you, and do not kill him or his wife if they are the wrong people. Do you understand?"

The small man nodded anxious not to arouse that anger again.

"So go! Get this one right and I'll keep your last escapade between us. But, if this goes wrong, your boss will get to know."

Harper scuttled from the office, seriously frightened.

***

In the small town the tearoom was a well-used popular haunt for the local people. The Englishness of the establishment made it a must for the ex-patriots living in the town. There were many of them, as the bloated civil service of the EU swelled with the ever-increasing demands of the machine driving the European Union.

James Haddon looked fondly at his wife, Molly. She was placing clotted cream on the individual plates already set with scones and strawberry jam. He set the teapot and milk jug down on the tray beside the stacked cups and saucers, and backed through the swing door into the tearoom itself.

The room was crowded as usual, the waitresses bustling to and fro between tables and kitchen. James took his tray to the table he was serving and placed the contents for them to serve themselves, then returned to the kitchen where his wife had prepared the four plates with their scone, cream and jam.

He caught up the waiting tray and delivered them before returning to sit for a moment's break.

Charlie poked his head into the kitchen door from the delivery area behind the premises. "Jim Haddon, I presume. " His voice was friendly and re-assuring.

"Who wants to know?" Jim said smiling.

"I'm from the Service." Charlie produced an identity card that proclaimed his membership of M16 cloned from Quin's card.

"What can I do for you?" James said, handing back the card.

"Remember when you served with Robert Anderson?"

"Yes. I remember Robert well. What about it?"

"There has been a glitch in the system somewhere. I need to ask if you recall some odd happenings at that time?"

"Oddly enough I do. I was reading in the paper the other day about one of the people from that time being killed and it brought it all back to mind. Of course Robert was involved in some way. He was very close-mouthed about the whole business I recall, most unlike him. I suppose the old bugger is long retired by now. So what is up? What do you want me for?"

Charlie felt this was going his way and he stuck his neck out. "Is there anyone you can leave in charge of the business, if I snatch you and your wife for a break in UK for a week or so. Just until we get the wrinkles out of this situation. I promise you there are no ongoing disasters coming your way. You may get to have a reunion with your old friends. It would be most helpful and convenient for us all."

James scratched his chin. "There is a way as a matter of fact. Two weeks, you say?"

"Yes. No more than that." Charlie smiled.

James turned to his wife and spoke very closely to her ear. She smiled and took her apron off.

James then picked up the phone and pressed a speed dial. He spoke in Dutch. He received an answer, replied and placed the phone back on the hook.

"Right. We're ready." He looked at Charlie, eyebrow raised.

Charlie, startled. Jumped up from the chair he had taken and said, "Now?"

James smiled. "We always have bags packed ready. At our age time can be important. We leave them in the hall cupboard of the apartment. It's on the way to the airport, so we can go as soon as you like."

At the apartment the bags were produced as promised and, after a short toilet delay to allow packing their toilet bags, they were back on the way to England.

Charlie called Jill from Heathrow Airport. "I'll be with you shortly. Put the kettle on. Two guests for tea. Call Quin and let him know, will you?"

***

Sheila LeBec was not happy. Back in her apartment in Shepperton she tore off her clothes and switched on her shower. Gradually she cooled off. Her anger at the stupidity of the people given her to perform the most basic of tasks dissipated. There were things about this current deal which were causing her to question her whole association with the Board. The accidental death of the man mistakenly identified was one accident too many, as far as she was concerned. Her mention of the subject at the last Board meeting had had little effect on any of the other members, apart from Sir Anthony Merrick and Marcus Warren. All the others just shrugged it off as collateral damage, in the face of the expected rewards they were gambling on. After drying off she selected clean underwear and a black cocktail dress. Her appointment with the others on the Board was for dinner at the Hilton, in Park Lane. She took her overnight case with a change of clothes for the morning. She was booked into the hotel so there would be no lengthy midnight journeys.

The Rolls was at the door when she was ready. To her surprise Marcus Warren was already seated in the car when she entered it at the door to her apartment building.

As they made their way to the M4, Marcus closed the screen behind the driver and turned to Sheila. "Drink?" He suggested.

"Love one. It's been a shitty day so far."

He opened the cabinet and made a performance of opening a small bottle of Champagne and pouring two glasses.

"Tell me. Where are we on the recovery program?"

"Probably just two to go. Though we know one of them has been lifted by somebody else."

"That is not good news. You can bet Anton will make you well aware of it."

"There is nothing I can do right as far as that Russian pig is concerned. Ever since I refused the invitation to join his harem he has done everything to balk any move I make."

"He is a very rich man and we need his wealth on the Board. So please try not to provoke him tonight, I fear he travels with his own execution squad."

"I will not provoke him. But, if he provokes me, then he will discover that I too have an execution squad."

Marcus sat back in surprise. "You?"

Sheila drew up her skirt revealing her creamy thigh, a flash of black lingerie and a flat black holster with a .22 Walther automatic snuggled into it. Having allowed Marcus to glimpse her preparations, she smoothed her skirt back down.

Marcus was exhibiting signs of agitation which amused Sheila. She was well used to the effect she had on men. Marcus was married, happily as far as she knew, but he was like most men susceptible to a little flirtation if the chance arose.

They arrived at the Hilton in good time for Sheila to check in and freshen-up in her room before descending to the private dining room for the dinner and Board meeting to follow.

As she walked into the private room to join the others, she was aware immediately of the presence of Anton Grovich, the Russian billionaire. She crossed the room to greet the Chairman of the group, Sir Anthony Merrick, feeling the Russian's eyes following her.

Sir Anthony was charming as always, complementing her on her dress and enquiring after her health.

"Tony, as you well know I am revoltingly fit, and I wore this same dress to our last meeting."

"But, Sheila darling, you cannot expect me to remember that far back. By the way, our Russian friend is currently devouring you from the ground up. I do suggest you avoid sitting next to him at dinner, or on any other occasion. I fear he will be investigating your knickers at the first opportunity."

"Always the bon-mot and such a charming turn of phrase Tony, I can always depend on you to make everything so abundantly clear."

"As you know, love, I have always had your welfare in mind, especially at these little get-togethers. The rapacious nature of our colleagues is such a feature of the company business. Now, come and sit with me. Then you can be sure that, though I may accidently touch your thigh, my hand will stop at that point in deference to the fact that my wife will grill me on your appearance and conduct. As you know she scares me to death and I am likely to give away any details of our encounter before I have had time to think."

"As ever, the perfect gentleman. Why did you marry her, Tony?"

"Why does anyone in our circle marry? She was rich, and the estate needed an influx of cash to keep the writs at bay. Come now. Let's sit and get on with this ghastly meeting. The sooner we can get to the serious business of the night, the better."

Sheila smiled to herself. For Tony the serious business meant a visit to a flat in Soho where he had his little friend ensconced. It was strange that Lady Marion Merrick had no problems with any other woman, apart from Sheila. It seemed as if there was something special about Sheila that was, in her mind, different and a threat that other women did not pose.

When Sheila asked Sir Anthony about it he had passed it off as nothing, just a foible. Then, when he had had a little too much on one occasion, he announced that his wife, in an unguarded moment, admitted to being attracted to Sheila herself.

At the meeting, Sheila was queried about progress in the collection of the secret microchips. Her lack of success in obtaining the final two was met with silent disapproval. Sir Anthony dissembled the hostile atmosphere.

"As you know this exercise was always going to be a chancy matter. It's been a long time and people have moved, died and disappeared. We do not even know who the last person is. The clues we have point in a certain direction, but they are by no means conclusive. The mistake made by the eager efforts of our Russian colleague earlier in the search created publicity we could well have done without. It now seems that it started rival seekers into action. They appear to have got hold of one of our subjects ahead of us which implies, whoever they are, they are aware of the significance of the group we are chasing. Since we are still not aware of the nature of this so-called treasure in the form of information to be found in these micro-chips. I propose we end this apparently hopeless search which has cost the life of an innocent man already."

On the face of it, the proposal by Sir Anthony was passed.

This was Sir Anthony at his best, Sheila thought, the reason he was chairman of WOAD, (World Organization for Aid Distribution) the Board of which controlled such a huge proportion of the world's wealth. She looked around the table at the other eight members of the Board: The Arab, Jer Shahib, oil: Marcus Warren, Tea and Coffee: Peter Noble, the American shipping magnate: Marianne Philippe, Martinique-French, probably drugs: the Russian, Anton Grovich, oligarch, oil, gas, and transport::Avo Ranala, the Estonian mob boss! Sitting beside him, a Jesuit priest, Father Aldo, Banking: And finally Sir Anthony himself, newspapers internet communications and who knows what.

Her own wealth had been garnered from the inheritance of her mother's string of prostitutes. Under the hand of her mother, tasked with information gathering, they had supported Sheila's journey through University. From there she had gone from degree course to broking. Using the information gathered through the network of prostitutes, she had swiftly accumulated her first million.

Her association with the inherited prostitution ring had long been officially severed, though there was still a residual escort agency. The million turned into a billion with the skilled manipulation of her portfolio. It had been her meeting with Sir Anthony which had led to her association with WOAD.

The fact that the company actually distributed aid throughout the third world made a cover for the distribution of drugs and weapons. With a reputation for charity, the day to day running of the organization was conducted by the right people, selected for their antecedents and experience.

The Board conducted their deliberations in secret. The management Board met under the chair of Sir Anthony on a month to month basis. The Charity management had no knowledge of the alternative operations of the Board of the charity. Nor had Sheila until recently. The rough and tumble of international trade had never bothered her too much. Always there were things that brushed the edges of criminality. These were mostly tax and local regulation infringements. Had she been aware of the drug and gun running she would never have been involved. When she had brought the matter up with Sir Anthony, he confessed that he had known eventually about it, but found it easier to turn a blind eye. They now agreed that if it became possible to get out of the operation they would take the opportunity.

Sheila was not convinced that this situation would remain for much longer. The violence, that had been becoming more and more a feature of the Board's activities, was now getting more obvious, as matters were getting out of hand. Too many of the members seemed to consider that their wealth excused all.

Chapter twelve

Northern Lights

Benderloch was a small village, approached from the south through Oban. The nursing home was a modern building on the right of the main road to Fort William.

Robert Anderson was white-haired and with-it. Naomie had suggested that it was possible that he was in the home because of family pressure. In fact, he was there from choice. Since the death of his wife he was really not interested in the family politics and consequently preferred to have control of his own destiny as long as he was able. From that time forward, his lawyer and he had conspired to ensure that whatever his will declared would be carried out, regardless of family dispute.

When Cass and Quin arrived, following a telephone call to arrange an appointment, Robert was prepared to receive them in his own room.

He insisted on having tea served before anything else. Then, when the staff member disappeared and all had tea in front of them, he said, "Right. Now tell me what this is all about."

Quin studied him, assessing his condition—apparently health and a relaxed manner. "Remember the occasion, many years ago when you were on staff at a Brussels conference, an incident occurred."

Robert looked at him and slowly smiled. "Ah, I wondered when this would come up. Now Molly is gone, it doesn't really matter what comes out about that little incident. I was never convinced, you know. It would have been so out of character for me to do anything like that. What have you really come about?"

"If it is any comfort to you, the only thing that happened to you that night was that you were rendered unconscious along with many of the people at that meeting you were servicing. While you were unconscious they inserted a small microchip in the back of your neck. It was part of a set of instructions for a particularly nasty invention which, later research revealed, would have resulted in destroying entire nations; supposedly controllable but actually uncontrollable once it was released into the atmosphere. It seems the doomsday weapon has been invented. The formula has been carried around by the people from that meeting ever since."

Robert looked at Quin searchingly. "You are joking, surely?"

"I'm afraid not. Remember, at the time, this was not regarded as anything more than a nasty tactical weapon among many other nasty tactical weapons more easily acceptable to the public. The entire record of the development was reduced to microchips installed into thirty men and women. Over the years people have died and others disappeared for various reasons. However, though it was believed that all thirty would be needed to reproduce this—for want of a better name 'Dark Material'—it has now been realized that the last five chips alone would be sufficient with modern techniques, to reproduce it. The one chip vital for this process, and containing the so-called antidote, is the one we believe you are carrying."

"Me? Why me? I was not even aware that this stuff existed unto you just mentioned it."

"You, because you are the wild card; not present at the meeting but in the building nevertheless. This broke the chain, if you see what I mean."

Robert sat there nodding silently. Then, "I see the logic. So what has changed?"

Cass spoke, "There is a group in existence that has been trying to get all the chips. They have not been gentle about it. An innocent man, mistakenly identified as one of the people who attended that meeting, was killed despite the fact that he was not involved. He was killed out of hand anyway. You may recall your old colleague, James Haddon?"

"Of course, a good friend for many years. Is he dead?"

"No, but we have him in a safe place, because all the evidence pointed to him being the final chip recipient." Cass continued, "He and his wife are in a safe place for now and we would like to get you in a safe place, too. It would be all too easy for the opposition to kidnap you from here. You look as if you are enjoying life too much to just throw it away!

"We can arrange for the chip to be removed and destroyed, and also for your own safety, a safe place to stay until the danger is past."

Robert said, "You mean I will disappear completely for a week or so?"

"Yes!" Cass nodded. "Just until it is safe for you to return."

"I was getting bored here anyway. When can we leave?"

Quin and Cass looked at each other. "Now," they said in unison.

As they cruised down the A82 toward Glasgow, Robert revealed that he was delighted to get away from the confines of the rest home. As he explained, "They look after me extremely well. The members of staff are great, and nothing is too much trouble. The problem is that I am still quite active and I would really like to get out more often. They are protective and, since I don't drive, I feel hemmed-in at times. Where are we going?"

"Currently, to a house beside Loch Lomond. Then we head south to our place near London.

They checked in at Cameron House, taking connected rooms. Robert maintained his high good humour throughout the evening. By ten o'clock he was tired out and pleased to go to bed, leaving Quin and Cass to round out their evening enjoying the late summer evening beside the waters of the loch.

Cass looked at Quin searchingly. "Well, husband. Speak to me. I would like the answer to a couple of questions?"

It was still light, though by now it was after 10 pm. Quin looked enquiringly at Cass. Smiling he asked, "What questions would you like me to answer, wife?"

"We got married in a rush and, as you stated at the time, there was an element of mutual safety involved. Tell me. Do you regret marrying me?"

Quin smiled, "I wonder about you, too. As far as I am concerned, I never believed in love at first sight. When we met there were things going on and there was no time to think, let alone worry about the future. When I suggested we marry, I hoped against hope that you would say 'yes', because by that time I realized that I had at last met the woman I wanted to marry."

Cass looked at him with tears in her eyes. "I hoped you would say something like that." She reached up and wrapped her arms round his neck. "I was uncertain at first, but then I realized that, like you, I had actually stumbled into the person I had been looking for."

They made their way back to the room. Quin poked his head into Robert's room. Robert was sitting up in bed reading from an e-reader. "Mind if I just check the door, Robert?"

Robert looked up and smiled, "By all means, Quin. Please check. I have been known to forget things like that." Quin walked through and tested the room door. He confirmed it was locked.

"Goodnight, Robert. We are right next door if you need anything."

Robert waved, "Night to you both. See you in the morning." He returned to his book as Quin closed the door.

***

They reached the retreat after dark on purpose. Robert was asleep across the back seat as they drove in through the tunnel. He awoke as they stopped in the garage, where they were met by Jill.

Quin, Cass, and Robert followed Jill through the doors to the living quarters. Looking around as they walked through the retreat, Robert commented, "This is one of those 'cold war' bunkers, I suspect? You certainly seem to have made it habitable."

Quin did not comment immediately, deciding to wait until they were all seated in the lounge with the others present. It would be easier doing the job once rather than going through it twice.

Later in the lounge with everyone present, Cass started the explanation for the benefit of the Haddon's and Robert Anderson. Between Quin and Cass the story took some believing by the newcomers, but the examination of the small scar on the back of Robert's neck was all it needed to finally convince them that there was something in the story they were being told.

Robert, after some consideration, spoke, "From what you say, and I can find no real reason to doubt that you believe it to be true, this scar covers a microchip that has very sensitive information on it. Information that could lead to a nasty outcome for mankind. Despite the fact that I will not probably be around to witness any results, I still feel that the chip should be removed and destroyed, rather than it be removed from my cold, dead carcass to be exploited in the future.

"Can you arrange the removal and destruction forthwith, so that we may all sleep more securely in our beds?"

Quin looked at the others, the nods all round seemed to be a pretty good indication of their feelings in the matter. "I'll get the doctor here tomorrow and we will take things from there."

***

In fact it took two days to find a doctor. They ended up with a retired gentleman who was an old family friend of Cass. He had been a surgeon for most of his adult life and he cheerfully undertook the minor surgery needed. His acceptance of Cass's reassurance that all was in order, though discreet, was touching, though Quin thought the surgeon was actually a little touched in the head.

The fact that the actual operation was carried out with high good humour and deft hands was re-assuring. It was just a question of the surgeon, known as Doctor Sam by Cass, could, or would, keep his mouth shut.

Cass was adamant. "I have known Dr Sam all my life and I can tell you he will not talk about any specific operation. He is ultra-serious about disclosure and he has never mentioned any of his work except is general terms, and even then only to colleagues."

The friendly surgeon was duly returned to the bosom of his family by Cass, the others of the group set about the task of letting it be known that the final chip had been destroyed. The Haddons were transferred to the Hilton Hotel in Park Lane where they were permitted to finish their holiday in less spartan conditions.

At the request of Robert Anderson they allowed him to stay in the retreat, though only as long as the carer decided to stay with him. On their way to the Sussex house Quin asked Cass where the carer had come from.

"The lady had been employed in the Sussex house for many years. Her problems came with sunshine. It seemed she was perfectly fit whilst she remained out of direct sunlight. The effect of the sun's rays was not pretty on her sensitive skin." The suggestion that she would be an ideal caretaker for the retreat was something that had occurred to Cass. Since up until then, there had not really been a need for a caretaker, she had shelved the idea.

Robert suggested that he would rather not return to the home. "If it's possible I would be happy stay in the retreat, just to potter about making sure the systems are kept in order and keep the place clean for when you return."

Neither had a problem with Robert's suggestion, except for the fact that Robert really needed a companion to keep an eye on things.

It was then that Cass came up with the possibility of Mary from the Sussex house. "That is, if she agrees," she had finished hopefully.

Mary had been delighted after seeing the place. The prospect of keeping an eye on Robert did not seem to bother her. She pointed out that, having looked after her own father, it was a role she was accustomed to. The company would be welcome in the otherwise quiet location.

As for Robert, he liked the smiling lady and was happy with the arrangement.

***

While these arrangements were going on, in Brussels, Sheila LeBec was having problems. The men sent to collect the Haddons had discovered that they had disappeared off to London for a holiday. The other event had been the news that the James Haddon was not now perceived to be the person involved. The real target was a man who had been retired for many years but it seemed the chip had been removed and de-stroyed. That would have to be verified but, if it were true, the entire exercise by WOAD had been a waste of time and money. She called Sir Tony and let him know the latest news. "I know the search has been officially finished. But the infor-mation was not passed to the men in the field. I am trying to get this stopped but I need to get round the Russian

"Grovich is not going to like this news," Sir Tony said

"What do you think he will do?"

"My guess would be that he will find this Haddon man and torture him to death. Then, having learned who the real carrier is, he will seek him out and confirm whether it is true or not. It means another will die nastily and that will not be the end of it. The message is clear. We will not be in a position to stop him."

Sheila was thoughtful after the conversation with Sir Tony. She did not want more blood on her hands because of the savagery of the Russian. During the evening she consid-ered the matter, on and off, finally coming to a decision.

***

Ian Bennet picked up the telephone on the second ring. The voice at the other end was female. "I cannot stay long, so please don't interrupt. The people with the tearooms are in danger of extinction by a nasty Russian group. If you contact them please warn and, if necessary, protect them. The Russian is a vicious bastard." The call clicked off.

Ian switched off the recorder and removed the old-fashioned tape-cassette. He then tried to get the ring-back number. He was not surprised that the caller had not left her number.

He spoke to Quin immediately, catching him at the re-treat. "I think this has to be genuine." The tape played out. It's message clear.

Quin said, "They are staying at the Hilton. I'll get them out straight away." He rang off and called Cass. "We need to get hold of the James and Molly Haddon, fast! Call the Hilton and tell them to lock themselves in and open to no one but us."

As they drove out of the retreat Cass said "No answer from their suite. I've left a message with the reception to call me, But who knows?"

***

As they arrived at the Hilton they saw Mary Haddon being bundled into a black-windowed VW people carrier. Quin swung the car in an attempt to block off the other vehicle, but there was not enough time to do other than cause it to swerve.

The vehicle shot off down Park Lane with Quin following. The chase took them through the park up to Bayswater Road where it turned right and drove to Marble Arch. There it turned back into Park Lane and stopped at the third house down. Quin continued past to the Grosvenor House Hotel. There he stopped and spoke to the doorman, and passed over the keys.

They grabbed the ready bag from the trunk and set out up Park Lane to the house where the VW was parked.

The lights went on in the house as they approached. There was a man standing beside the steps down to the area in front of the house. Like most of the houses in the area there was a sunken area, with an entrance to the basement/kitchen of the house beside the steps leading up to the front door.

The man was obviously not happy. Cass heard him speak to someone below beside the basement door. The tone was surly!

Cass tugged Quin's sleeve and indicated that she would deal with the man.

She unzipped her jacket and opened the top two buttons of her white blouse, revealing a generous area of frontage. Pulling off her headband she released her hair to allow it to tumble around her face.

Quin looked at her and grinned. He felt briefly sorry for the man and stood aside as she adopted a loose casual walk and sauntered up to the surly watcher.

"Hey!" She breathed, "You look a little uptight. How about a little light relief?"

The man looked at the goods on display and showed immediate interest.

The person below was apparently female. "What are you doing up there?" The voice was suspicious.

"Just assessing the local talent. Mind your own business!"

"The boss said no distractions!" The voice persisted.

"If you feel like looking after me yourself, speak up by all means. Otherwise shut up and mind your own business!" The man sounded defiant and impatient.

"Does that mean we are in business?" Cass murmured softly.

The man grinned, "After you." He opened the gate and indicated the steps down to the area below. As he did he called to the other watcher, "Get up here and take over from me. This could take a little while."

The woman below swore and ran up the steps pushing past Cass on the way. Cass was aware that the woman was carrying a weapon in her hand as metal brushed against her hand when the woman passed.

The man was still on the steps when Cass reached the bottom . She turned to meet him as he descended, undoing his coat as he came.

The woman walked straight into Quin at the gate. She said, "Oh shit!" and collapsed into his arms as her jaw clicked shut from the impact of his fist. As she slumped forward, Quin jabbed the needle into her neck and depressed the plunger. Though not knocked out from the blow, her eyes glazed over. She lost consciousness from the effects of the drug injected from the syringe.

For Cass it was simpler. As her target reached the lower step he looked up and presented her with a clear view of his throat. Almost without thinking her fingers stabbed out and smashed his Adam's apple. He gagged and sagged to his knees desperately trying to breathe. Her other hand swung the cosh slamming it into the side of his head. He collapsed, still breathing harshly through his damaged throat, much to her relief. Cass had not set out to kill anyone.

Quin joined her at the bottom of the steps carrying his victim. Depositing her beside her colleague on the ground, he turned to the door standing ajar in front of them and said, "Shall we?"

The small scullery was empty. There was no sound from the kitchen next door, though the light was on. The door swung open at Quin's touch, revealing a large kitchen with an Aga cooker range. There was a kettle on the stove steaming quietly, but no other sign of life. As they stood and listened they heard approaching footsteps from the stairs within the house. Quin gestured to Cass to step behind the open door. He turned his back to the door and started clattering cups and saucers. The man who came into the kitchen was carrying an smg on a strap over his shoulder, but he did not seem surprised to find another man in the kitchen. He said something in Russian. Quin said, "Da! Da! Da!" Nodding his head in a universal gesture of frustration. Cass stepped out from behind the door. As Quin turned around to face him, Cass lifted the strap of the smg from the Russian's shoulder. The man looked at Quin in puzzlement.

Quin had his Glock in his hand. "Where is the boss?" He asked in English. The man started to say, "Up…." but did not finish the word.

Quin watched the man make up his mind to shout a warning. Cass hit him with her cosh, and the words didn't make it. He collapsed in an untidy heap on the floor. Between them the invading pair collected all the weapons they had accumulated so far: two smg's, three automatics, two 9mm, and one 7.25mm. Added to their own weapons, they considered that they probably had sufficient firepower to see them through.

They each took an smg to supplement their own automatics. Quin led the way upstairs to the room above showing a line of light beneath the door.

They could hear voices within and a cry of protest from what sounded like a woman. Checking their weapons, Quin looked at Cass. She nodded. Quin knocked and opened the door, stepping through with gun up and ready.

"Stand still everyone," he said quietly.

The room was occupied by four people. Two people standing, a man and a dramatic- looking woman. The two seated figures were James and Molly Haddon. Both were strapped to the chairs they were occupying.

The woman was standing beside James Haddon, hand raised. On James's cheek was the imprint of an earlier blow. Quin motioned the pair to move over to one side of the room away from the two captives. As the woman moved, she raised her leg, her hand lifted her skirt on one side catching the small automatic holstered on her thigh.

The plop of the silenced automatic was almost lost in the rustle of movement. The gun fell from the woman's hand and she looked at her sculpted bosom incredulously. The small hole rimmed crimson as the blood welled out. She collapsed forward onto the floor. A small trickle of blood ran out of the corner of her mouth, staining the carpet beneath her.

The man looked nervous and stood still where he was told. Cass entered, putting the small automatic into her pocket. She frisked the man, relieving him of the automatic and the knife strapped to his forearm. She found another small automatic in his ankle holster.

Cass then went and released the two from their straps and made sure that they were unhurt. "What now?" She asked, "A quick search?"

Quin nodded. Turning to James Haddon, he said, "Can you use this?" He held out one of the 9mm automatics.

James grinned. "I haven't handled one for about forty years. But I'm told it's like riding a bicycle. You never forget." He took the gun. Popped the magazine, cocked the gun ejecting the round in the breech, he slid it back into place in the magazine and replaced the magazine in the butt of the gun. He cocked it and set the safety. "Yes. They're right. You don't forget."

"Just in case, while we check the other rooms in the house."

"Leave it with me." James said, "They owe me."

Quin took the stairs, followed by Cass. While Quin went right up to the attic apartment, Cass dealt with the third floor rooms. She found the office on the second floor. All the rooms on the third were either bed or bathrooms. A swift search had produced clothing of several types but nothing of interest as far as illegal activities were concerned.

In the office she was joined by Quin Together they went through the desk drawers and file cabinets, finding little of real interest apart from some intriguing material on intercontinental movements of goods from strange origins to even stranger destinations. Using the photo-copier they copied all the relative documents they found. There was a safe but they had no way of opening it. Just in case Quin tried the handle. He had already started to turn away when he realized that the door was not locked. Unfortunately, though there was a stack of plastic envelopes containing money of various origins, there was nothing else apart from a key. Quin passed it by in his search. It was an ordinary cabinet key, or perhaps a drawer key. He picked it up almost as an afterthought, wondering why such a key would be left in the safe. He put it on the desk top. "Why would you put a key like this in the safe?"

Cass looked at it puzzled. "Maybe it belongs to a special lock? Does it fit the drawers?"

Quin tried it. It was stiff but it turned the lock.

"Are all the drawers and cupboards open?" Cass ventured.

"As far as I know we've tried them all," Quin said uncertainly.

Cass came around the desk, "Let's check again." She went down on her knees and studied all the drawers facing her on the pedestal on the left side of the desk. Quin dropped to his knees and studied the other.

"Why would there be a keyhole where there is no door or drawer?" Cass asked. She indicated a keyhole directly centred in the facing under the rim of the desk top. It was completely hidden from above by the overhang of the desk top.

"Let's try it and see." Quin inserted the key and turned it. Nothing appeared to happen until Quin leaned forward putting his hand against the desk top to steady himself.

The whole top of the desk slid forward revealing a shallow tray containing several documents. Once again the photocopier came into use. They copied the documents and replaced them before they returned the desk top to its proper position, locking it once more and returning the key to the safe. Cass folded the papers and thrust them into the inside pocket of her zip up jacket. They returned to the basement and James and Molly Haddon, who were waiting patiently for their return.

At the Grosvenor House Quin collected the car. They drove down to the Hilton where they settled the bill and collected the Haddon's luggage.

***

Back in the retreat Quin spoke to Ian about the warning message he had received. "Any idea of the identity of the lady?"

Ian took his time answering. Then he spoke slowly almost hesitantly. "I believe I might have. The Russian is a member of a very exclusive club, rich as Croesus, and a reputation for being a hard man to deal with. He is on the Board of an organization called World Organization for Aid Distribution, WOAD for short. All the other directors are billionaires and there are two women on the Board, Sheila LeBec and Marianne Philippe. The message I got was from a woman who sounded British, and as if she knew the Russian. But my impression was, as an equal, rather than an employee or menial. Do you know what I mean?"

"I think I do. Why don't you ring her up and thank her, saying her warning was in time and that James and Molly Haddon are quite safe, though it was a close run thing. That might confirm, or deny your suspicions."

"It's worth a try I suppose. I'll let you know how it goes. Is everything OK at your end?"

"So far so good. I'll be in touch anyway. I have a feeling that this business with the Russian is far from over. Take care." Quin rang off and returned to join the others in the rest room.

Chapter thirteen

for you the war is over

Sheila LeBec put the telephone down thoughtfully. Ian Bennet had been quite explicit, and obviously he had worked out who she was. The best of it was that James Haddon and Molly were safe and the needless murder avoided. She opened the drawer in front of her and retrieved a small electronic device. She switched it on and, horrified, watched the tell-tale light start blinking. The needle in the instrument was pointing at her telephone. Hardly daring to breathe she lifted the handset. The needle did not follow the movement of her hand. Laying the handset down she lifted the base station for the telephone, the needle followed the movement. As she lifted the base the bug was quite obvious, and that worried her more than anything. She replaced the base set onto the desk without touching the bug.

What she now had to worry about was survival. She opened the concealed door in her escritoire and retrieved the cell phone lying there. She left the apartment, carrying the bug detector, and checked out her car. There was no detectable bug there. Looking at her watch and confirming that he should be available, she pressed the speed-dial number and waited. There was a series of clicks as the line she had selected jumped through several relays. Finally a familiar voice said, "Hello, Sheila. what news has driven you to use the spy-phone?" Sir Tony sounded relaxed and in good humour.

"Can you talk?" Sheila asked.

"Never had a problem that way. But to answer your question, I am alone and unbuggable at present."

"I have interfered with our Russian friend's plans. I believed I was in the clear, but it seems I am not. You know the way the bastard's mind works, so I expect I will need to disappear for a while at least."

"Do I need to know what it is that has brought this on?" Tony's voice was no longer frivolous. He was all attention and concern."

"I warned that man, Ian Bennet, that Anton was contemplating collecting James Haddon and examining him, grilling him, then killing him. I am happy to say that somehow Bennet managed to retrieve Mr and Mrs Haddon from the Russian's clutches, unhurt, though not without damage to the Russian hit squad."

Sir Tony sighed. "I am delighted to hear it. The man is a menace. But why should that concern you?"

"I found a bug on my telephone this morning after I heard from Bennet."

"Where are you now?"

"I am in my car on my way to Keiheuval-Balen. I keep an aircraft there under another name. Do you think I could land at your place, without madam having a fit?"

"Madam is currently in Antigua, resting her bones. You are welcome here. I will arrange for the ground crew to expect you."

"I will be with you in about two hours in that case. If I call, will you meet me at the field?"

"Nothing could keep me away. I will have the guest bedroom prepared, in case you need to use it."

Sheila smiled. "Ever hopeful, Tony. Ever hopeful."

At the airfield she had her private twin Otter pulled out of its hanger and the starter plugged in. The field mechanic started the engines and ran them up, while Sheila walked round the aircraft. She climbed into the cabin and made her way to the cockpit. The interior of the aircraft was elegantly fitted out, with easy chairs and a writing desk, the colors taupe and dark brown.

Her pilot, John Langford, arrived in a rush and joined her in the cockpit. He took the right hand seat as she checked the controls and studied the instruments. Satisfied, she waved the chocks away and got permission to taxi. The airfield was not busy. Within minutes they were airborne and en-route to the English Channel.

***

They approached the airfield on the estate, performing a wide circuit to ensure there were no obstacles and no ambushes. Sheila brought the twin engine aircraft down in a smooth sideslip, lining the Otter up with the longest stretch of the field and allowing it to drop gently to the ground to roll smoothly, turning eventually to line up with the opening doors on the side wall of the barn. As they reached the threshold the doors were opened wide enough for the aircraft to taxi in without actually stopping. When the aircraft came to a halt the doors were already closing behind them.

Sheila rose from her seat and turned to John. "I'll leave it with you, John. Refuel and have things ready to go if needed. We will probably stay for a while, but who knows?" She said with a shrug and a wry grin. "Did you bring a gun?"

John grinned back at her. "As always, Madam." The colt .45 automatic appeared in his hand like magic.

"Good, keep it handy, Wyatt Earp. But no shooting until we know who we are shooting at."

As she stepped down from the air stair, Sir Anthony Merrick appeared through the side door of the barn, a broad smile of welcome on his face. "Darling Sheila, what a lovely surprise this has been. Come and relax in the Hall.

The Range-Rover standing outside the Barn was green and muddy. Inside it was reasonably clean, and Sheila, who had travelled in jeans and battered calf-high boots, clambered in without comment.

Sir Tony started the engine and began talking as soon as they were moving off down the dirt track. "Much though I would love to entertain you personally, as you know my wife is not only suspicious, but also seems react to any contact I have with you. She is not at home yet, but I now know she intends to surprise me tonight by returning unexpectedly."

Sheila turned and looked at him quizzically?

"Oh, surely you are aware that anyone travelling by air is logged in or out of wherever they board an aircraft, ferry or other transport. I was informed by the company that Lady Marion Merrick was travelling by private aircraft from West Indies to London City Airport. Her ETA will be 19.30 this evening." He glanced at her puzzled. "You did not know? All of us are followed someway or other. Your departure and flight plan will have been broadcast to the others, which is why I have made alternative arrangements for your accommodation with friends who have no connection with our business, nor even on an apparent social level."

"You have been busy. Where is our Russian friend now then?"

"He is still in Paris, but his Citation jet is warming up for a flight to London. I decided to take no chances and arranged with Cass Gilmore to put you up for a few days, or as long as you need to be. I hope I did the right thing?"

Sheila smiled. The Rover bumped over the track and turned off through woods following a faint trace through the mixed trees, winding in low gear between the trunks of what was an ancient forest.

They eventually stopped at a chained gate. Sir Tony blipped the horn twice.

A tall man appeared, a rifle slung over his shoulder. The peaked cap shaded his eyes. In Barber jacket and ankle boots, he looked every inch the gamekeeper.

Unlocking the gate he ushered Sheila through and accepted her case from Sir Tony.

"Good bye for now." Tony smiled. "I'll see you tonight at the party." To the man he said, "Look after her, Ian."

The man nodded and replaced the chain locking the padlock once more. He then turned and nodded to Sheila to follow him she was led through the surrounding trees to the small pick-up sitting waiting. He tossed the bag in the open back and slotted the rifle into the carrier behind the driver's seat. Then started the engine and drove off.

"Who are you?" Sheila asked.

"I am a friend of the Gilmore's, Ian Bennet at your service." He nodded to her with a small smile.

"You're the one...."

"Yes, I am. I am the one you spoke to, and who spoke to you this morning."

Sheila was puzzled. "What is going on? Why are you here? You told me that the Haddons were safe. So why all this cloak and dagger stuff?"

"Wait until we get to the house and all will be revealed." He thought, *at least all you need to know will be.*

The woods thinned out and the area became more disciplined as they came to a grassed area forming part of the rolling parkland. The grey stone house stood behind a tailored garden framed by the low hills of the South Downs.

Sheila breathed a silent "Wow!" at the scene.

Bennet noticed. "It sort of grabs you by the throat, doesn't it."

"It's stunning." Sheila admitted.

"Canonby Hall is the residence of Cassandra Gilmore, who is the Lady of the Manor at Canonby." Bennet sounded amused.

"What do you find so funny?" Sheila asked.

Bennet looked at her thoughtfully. He came to a decision. "I served with her husband for several years in various parts of the world. I never would have believed that he would become part of the landed gentry. I always knew he came from money, good education etc., but what once seemed entirely out of character, now fits him like a glove. In addition I have never seen him so happy. Quin and Cass fit together. You'll see."

"Quin?"

"Tarquin Gilmore, Quin to his friends."

Sheila nodded slowly.

The pick-up bumped over a curb and joined a tarmac road which approached the large house. Avoiding the front entrance Ian Bennet drove around to the rear of the house to the courtyard created by the two wings of the building standing at right angles to the main façade of the house. He drew to a halt beside an open door and the small group of people standing waiting to greet them.

"Everything go all right, Ian?" The tall man opened the door for Sheila.

Ian grinned, "Of course. Quin Gilmore, meet Sheila Le-Bec."

The tall man smiled and shook her extended hand. "The gorgeous lady behind me is my wife, Cass. This is Charlie. He waved at the other man present, and Jill is the bashful one standing beside the door."

Sheila was swept into the house which turned out to be as beautiful inside as it was outside. Cass's step-father had ensured that there had been no expense spared in the refurbishment of the house when he took it over. The furnishing and artwork reflected his good taste and his attention to historic detail. Cass had been the beneficiary of his taste and expenditure. When younger, she had not appreciated the effort he had made to get things exactly right. Now aware, her appreciation of the home he had created was the reason she enjoyed living here now. For Sheila the place was a revelation, the room she was given had a traditional four poster bed and the modern touches for comfort were concealed, but present.

That evening Sir Anthony appeared with his sister and three other couples, local people from neighbouring estates. They dined in the elegant dining room with silver, and crystal, and candelabra for lighting. The servants were swift and efficient, the food excellent. The conversation during the meal was the general chit chat of the local scene.

After the meal they adjourned to the drawing room where there were tables set out for bridge, and the evening was passed in a pleasant social atmosphere which Sheila found reassuring.

The guests departed. Sir Tony's sister left, driven by his chauffeur, by prior arrangement. The group re-assembled in the drawing room. The drinks tray was refreshed and the staff retired for the night.

The butler reported that he had made the rounds, ensuring that the doors and windows were secure before leaving them to themselves.

Sir Anthony said, "I am grateful for your cooperation in allowing my friend and colleague to stay here. As you know my wife has a particular foible about guests in her absence." He smiled quietly when he finished, well aware that the entire area knew of his wife's attitudes.

Quin waved a hand. "Absolutely no problem at all. We would have been happy to entertain Sheila without your input in any case. She was responsible for saving the lives of two friends, and for that alone she would have been welcomed."

Sheila looked at Ian Bennet searchingly, wondering who these people were. How do they fit into this business?'

Cass saw the questioning look and interjected, "Sheila, the business of the micro-chips, outstanding for so long, has finally been resolved. The final chip has been located and removed and, I'm happy to say, destroyed. That means that with the last two out of reach, there is no chance of the original designs being reproduced."

Sheila looked at her surprised. "I did not realize that you were aware of what WOAD was up to. I myself did not realize, that the information we were gathering was for a weapon of mass destruction until last week." She turned to Sir Anthony.

"Did you know?"

He looked uncomfortable. "Well, I had to know. After all I am the Chairman of the Board. What I did think was that we were recovering the information for the company, not Grovich and his associates in Russia. That was when I decided that the whole business was unacceptable."

Ian joined the discussion at that point. "What about this Russian? He is obviously going to be a real fly in the ointment. Are we going to go into hiding?"

Quin said, "I think we wait and see, but keep our guard up. There may be no reaction at all or we may get a real backlash. Whichever way it goes, I think we need to make sure that no one in this room travels anywhere without a companion, preferably another person from among the people in this room." He looked around at the gathering. "I called Naomie as soon as I heard about Sheila. We need her here before the Russian puts two and two together, and gathers her in as a bargaining point. There was the sound of an approaching vehicle outside. That should be her arriving now."

When the vehicle drew up outside the front door Ian was already there to open it. In the room they heard the murmur of voices followed by footsteps. The door opened to reveal

Naomie Price-Hamilton, closely followed by Ian Bennet. Cass stepped forward and ushered her into the room, saying. "This is Naomie, a member of the team."

Charlie and Jill had not met Naomie, although they were aware of her existence. There were introductions all round, and when they were all seated once more, Naomie told them of the events of her day.

Speaking slowly and clearly she said, "My day started fairly normally. After I had breakfast I was clearing up when I noticed that I had acquired a watcher. I didn't believe it at first. I really thought I was imagining things. Apart from anything else the watcher was so crass and obvious, I could not believe he posed a threat to me or anyone else. He sat in his car and watched my house through his binoculars. He was swarthy with lank, white hair. He also had broken teeth and acne."

Sir Tony said, "You saw all this through your window?"

Naomie looked at him coldly. "I have binoculars too, you understand."

She resumed her story. "I got the call from Quin. So I started to collect my things for the trip to UK. The car was in the garage. I have access through my kitchen, so I managed to load the car without being spotted. Having been married to a spook, I still have some of the equipment he used. My trust level now being at a pretty low ebb, I ran a scanner over the car before leaving. I found the tracker behind the rear fender. I removed it, but rather than dispose of it, I decided to keep it until I found a suitable place to put it.

"I locked the house up and started the car in the garage. I popped the remote. As the door rose, I saw my watcher on the phone. I drove out in a hurry and passed him going in the opposite direction. The last I saw of him he was trying to turn the car in the street with little success. I tossed the bug onto a truck from Paris, hoping that he was returning home.

"I met a black Galaxy. You know one of those models with dark windows, like those used by the FBI in the movies. It started to try crowding me off the road. I opened the side window of my car and put two bullets through his windscreen. He backed off. I noticed he crashed into another car coming out of a driveway, so I lost him at that point.

"I drove around the coast road to Dunkerque, decided not to bother and finished up at Dieppe. I left my car in a parking garage there, and took the ferry to Newhaven, where I rang Quin from a public telephone. He sent the car for me."

Sheila said, "You shot the driver of the Galaxy?"

"Well, I shot the windscreen of the car. I cannot claim to have shot the driver, though I would be quite pleased if I did. After all he was trying to crash my car, so he asked for all he got."

***

In Brussels, the driver of the Galaxy was swearing as she parked the car in the company garage. The damage was extensive, and would have been quite acceptable if the target woman had crashed and been injured or killed. As it was it was her own car and she was the one injured. The bandage around her arm showed blood from the bullet wound inflicted by the bitch who had made her crash.

Rachel Vishinski was 25 years old, a SVR agent and a veteran of an Afghanistan tour and one private excursion to Helmand Province. Her successful removal of the M16 agent, Alec Price-Hamilton, had been attributed to the Taliban. But it was her job and she did it. Now the removal of his widow was called for and she was a natural for the task. So far the bitch had been lucky. Next time things would be different. She made her way up to her apartment where she proceeded to shower and dress her wound properly. Recovered and refreshed with a gin and tonic in hand, she reported to Anton Grovich by phone.

The Russian was not pleased and, as he usually did, he raised his voice to tell her of his annoyance.

Rachel listened for a moment then slammed the phone down.

Her phone rang. She picked up. "Yes!"

At the other end a smooth voice said, "I am calling on behalf of Mr Grovich."

"What is up with the man then? Has he lost his voice?" Rachel was taking no prisoners.

The phone at the other end was snatched by the sound of it. "How dare you speak to me like that. I will not allow it."

"If you cannot keep a civil tongue in your head, then you can find someone else to do your dirty work." She slammed the phone down again. She knew she had slipped up but she was dammed if she would be shouted at by some peasant whose sole participation was to supply money to pay for others to risk their lives for his illegal enterprises.

Rachel was not worried by the Russian's fit of anger. She knew she was the best at what she did. There were no other alternatives. Also her loyalty was to a much higher authority than Grovich. Vladimir Putin did not suffer fools gladly, but he supported his staff fiercely. She prepared a light supper and went to bed early. She knew there would be information on the subject tomorrow, despite all the tantrums tonight.

***

Naomie's attitude impressed Ian. He had not realized that the same sang-froid which had carried her through the trauma and treatment situation when he had been wounded was part of her standard make up. He was pleased to see her here and assumed that she would partner him in any future action.

When the group broke up he accompanied her upstairs and invited her into his room for a nightcap. She accepted and joined him to split a bottle of wine to wind down.

"I invited you to relax with a glass because I am aware of the sort of reaction an escape like yours creates."

He popped the cork from a wine bottle and poured two glasses.

"I confess I had a private motive as well. As Quin mentioned he felt that we should team up and watch each other's back. I wondered if I could team up with you."

He handed her the glass he had just poured, looking directly at her as he did.

She accepted the wine and took a sip, then lifted her gaze to meet his eyes and said with a small smile, "I had the impression that you issued this invitation with something else in mind." She dropped her eyes modestly as she spoke.

Without hesitation Ian replied, "There was another reason for the invitation. I wanted to get your reaction to spending a lot of your time with me from now on, before I came to my next proposition."

"So you need my answer to teaming up with you first?"

"Exactly!"

"I have to tell you that I was invited by Sir Anthony downstairs." She noted the disappointment in his face that he did not quite hide.

"I actually turned him down, because I presumed you would be my partner. Does that answer your question?"

Ian stood up and took the glass from her hand, and drew her to her feet. The other thing was would you care to....."

She kissed him and stopped whatever he was saying, moving close to him and finding, in his willing acceptance of her, the reaction she had hoped for.

Chapter fourteen

War

The two following days were passed in discussion and planning for the future survival of the eight people involved.

As Sheila explained, the Russian commanded enormous wealth and consequent influence. He was very discreet in his public persona, making little impact publicly. In private however, his treatment of others was a reflection of his arrogant, cavalier attitude to the rest of humanity. Life was cheap. As far as his interests were concerned the path of his increasing wealth was splattered with the bodies of the people who interfered, or those he believed had interfered, with his interest.

"Anton Grovich, 36 years old, son of one of the first of the Mafioso to claim respectability after Gorbachov.

"Anton never actually played a part in the Russian Mafia, but his conduct as he grew in age and wealth proved he would have been comfortable in that company." She paused briefly, took a sip from her drink, and then continued.

"The fact is, he has a huge pool of labor at his disposal, and access to others on a mercenary basis. Based on his wealth that means he has, in effect, unlimited resources." Sheila having delivered this nugget of information followed it up with another snippet based on her membership of the Board of WOAD. "Jer Shahib, and Avo Ranala, both also Board members, are tight with Anton. They command a huge intelligence network. Any move we make from here will be difficult to conceal from their networks. It means that our efforts must be either well covered or completely unseen."

There was a period of silence following this statement as the others digested this information. Finally Cass broke the silence. "That went down well. The hopeless odds we face will be an advantage for us. The problem with having huge resources is the tendency to use them on a large scale. That, in our experience, is far less dangerous than a small dedicated team. I think we do have to consider the neutralisation of Anton Grovich, Avo Ranala and their Arab friend, Jer Shahib."

She sat back and let her eyes roam over the other players around the table. Despite the bad news no one seemed particularly bothered at the dissertation.

There was silence following her summing up.

"Do you mean we have to ki…. delete these people?" The hesitant words came from Sir Anthony Merrick.

Sheila answered him. "Tony, as I have just explained, these people are intending to kill us all. What would you suggest we do?"

Sir Anthony looked around the group. There were no other apparent dissenters there and, despite his own misgivings, he was beginning to understand what was really happening. Up until now he had been on the fringes of events which others had been involved in. It was easy to ignore the hints and suggestions that some of the actions of the Board of WOAD were skirting the edge of the law. The fact of the combined wealth of the directors certainly conferred the impression that they were above the level where the minor infringements they were aware of could touch them. He felt panic rising, and for once he could think of nothing to say. This was not people playing games at long range. This was real life, today, tomorrow. People might appear and shoot him without warning or even justification, simply because he annoyed someone. *No financial gain involved, just pique!*

The more he thought about it the angrier he got. For the first time in his life he felt he could kill another person. The panic dissolved in the wake of emotion as he faced the fact that there were people to whom life meant little, as long as it was someone else's.

The others had started discussing matters, based on the axiom that attack was their best form of defense. No one seemed too concerned about the thought that they were likely to be the main targets in any confrontation. The general attitude seemed to be that shooting accurately and first was the important thing.

Sheila turned and looked at him. She smiled. "How's your pistol shooting these days?"

With a wry smile he said, "I have not been doing too much recently. But when I last shot I was managing inners, four out of six. I understand they have a range here, so I'll get in some practice before I have to leave."

Sheila was surprised at the answer. She had not anticipated his being prepared to take up a gun seriously. Suddenly she felt a little better about being paired with him.

Over the next day the pairs practiced their marksmanship on the short range. Activity on the long range was confined to practice and instruction for them all on the sniper rifle and the GP assault rifle. To the surprise of himself, among others, Sir Tony was a natural on the sniper rifle. His military training from his course at Sandhurst had not obviously been forgotten, despite the fact that the death of his father had caused his military career to terminate before he could be posted to Iraq.

It was agreed between them all that Sheila and Sir Anthony would attend the next Board meeting, though it was clear that there would be back up from the entire group for the occasion.

Since the meeting was scheduled for three days hence, it required a certain amount of arranging for the others to be in the right place to be of use in emergency.

***

The Otter landed at Zaventem smoothly, the tires kissing the tarmac gently and turning into the taxiway indicated by the tower. They came to a stop on the apron in front of the private arrival area. The service team boarded as soon as Sheila and Sir Anthony disembarked. The limousine was awaiting their arrival. After they had checked through the reception area, they were carried swiftly off to the Intercontinental Hotel. When Sheila was escorted to her suite she found Jill already there waiting to greet her. Dressed in smart clerical grey skirt and jacket, with a white blouse, Sheila had to look twice before she realized that Jill's normally blond hair was under a brunette wig. With her eyebrows darkened and she looked the part of an efficient PA. As she welcomed Sheila she gave no sign of the personal relationship between them.

When the porter delivered the luggage, he left the two women together.

Jill said, "Good trip?"

Sheila grinned. "Apart from avoiding Tony's hands. Yes, fine!"

Jill did a twirl. "What do you think? Will I do as your PA?"

Sheila laughed. "Perfect. But where do you hide your gun?"

Jill lifted her skirt and disclosed hold-up stockings and a slim holster strapped to the inside of her thigh. "OK?"

"Just like mine." Sheila grinned lifting her own skirt to reveal her .22. "Right. Well, we will have to order in tonight. I am not keen on the idea of making myself available to Anton's goons in circumstances that we cannot control. Will that be alright with you?"

Jill shrugged. "Sounds great. I can get out of this strait-jacket for a while at least."

***

In his suite, Sir Tony was suggesting to Charlie that they hit one of the nightclubs to find some company.

Charlie was not cooperating. "For Pete's sake, Tony. This is Brussels. It isn't even our home ground. But it is the Russian's. We would be a sitting target for his goons on a night like this. There is not much fun in a night out when you need to spend your time watching your back! We could invite the girls in from next door, of course. What do you think?"

Sir Tony thought for a moment about Sheila then shook his head. "I think not. What's on television, anything interesting?"

***

The following day the two directors arrived at the location of the Board meeting, in good time for the social get-together beforehand. When they entered the office block on the Adolphe Lacomblelaan, they were met by their PA's who had preceded them to ensure that all was ready. Sheila was wearing clerical grey, her skirt two inches above the knee with an open mandarin collar to show off her white lace jabot to advantage. A stunning combination that was still lingering in the mind of her escort, Sir Anthony Merrick, who was dressed a little more soberly in navy blue pinstripe.

Their PA's, both dressed suitably in charcoal suits, Jill's skirt three inches above the knee, and both carrying black briefcases on behalf of their bosses.

The four people rose in the elevator to the 5th floor where the rented boardroom had been prepared for the WOAD Board meeting.

The reception on the landing was already tenanted by two of the other directors, Father Aldo in his regular black Armani suit, and Peter Noble the shipping magnate, a man she found unpleasantly familiar whenever the two were alone. A situation Sheila took trouble to avoid after their first encounter.

Father Aldo was standing with a glass of cognac in his hand listening to something that Peter Noble was saying. The conversation stopped as Sheila and Sir Anthony stepped out of the elevator. The PA's (minders) present were both looking alert until they recognized the two Board members. But both Charlie and Jill were subjected to speculative looks.

Jill commented to Charlie, "I've never seen a Catholic Priest wearing a shoulder holster before?"

Charlie's cynical reply was, "This one is special. His name is Ricardo. The last time he was in church he was stealing the silver."

Jill looked at Charlie. "What were you doing there?"

Charlie grinned ruefully. "I was lying on the floor trying to shoot him, and so wound–up I could not keep the bloody rifle steady. So the bastard got away."

"Does he know you?"

"Shouldn't think so. It was pretty hectic and there were bullets everywhere. I was just another soldier at the time, and in Bosnia they were pretty common. Make no mistake. Despite the dog collar, that man is very nasty. So don't get into a corner with him. It could be upsetting."

Charlie left her to talk to the other PA, while Jill nibbled a canapé and sipped coffee. The others arrived, Avo Ranala with a PA who looked as if she was just out of bed, and probably, Jill though, was. Anton Grovich arrived with Hannah Curtain in her guise of PA, complete with smart grey suit, white blouse, document case and black court shoes to match.

This time it was Jill who recognized her. Hannah had been Mossad trained and her defection from the Israeli forces to private practice had been a shock which had resounded through the Israeli services.

Jill encountered Charlie, "Do you know the woman with Grovich?"

Charlie said thoughtfully, "A fit looking lady. Not the Russians squeeze, I think."

Jill chuckled quietly. "The lady is Hannah Curtain, nearly as lethal as me, I would say. We came from the same stable, though our ways diverged in Gaza. She buggered off with our target, the price was, I believe, half a million dollars. She does not come cheap, and is reputed to always finish what she starts."

Hannah approached Jill while the others were still milling about. Marianne Philippe arrived with Jer Habib, and in the flurry Jill heard Hannah speak. "We attended the same school I remember, though you were in the class below mine."

"You have a good memory. I never circulated in your circle as I remember."

"I seem to recall you were with my snatch group in Gaza when I broke contact with the group"

"Ah, you refer to your desertion with our target. Yes. I was there indeed. I actually missed you that day. I have been practicing since then."

"I'm so pleased to hear that. I do hate sitting ducks."

"You must be working with the Russian. The Estonian would have had your knickers off before you could draw your first paycheque."

"I think not, but he would certainly try. I look forward to our next meeting."

As she turned to go Jill said, "Missed out last time. Perhaps you should retire?"

Hannah spun round, then stopped and she relaxed. Smiling. "I won't miss out next time, once is too many as far as I am concerned. See you then, perhaps."

Rachel Vishinski watched the assembly, ensuring she knew all present for future reference. As company security for the Russian oligarch, her place was in the room at the meeting. She turned and joined her current employer going into the Board room. Jill, Charlie and Hannah Curtain took their places with the others while the Board entered the private meeting room.

***

Sheila told the Board the situation regarding the collection of the microchips, stressing the fact that the final chips had been ruined and the hoped-for information lost. Anton said, "How do we know that you did not acquire the information before the chips were destroyed?" His manner was abrupt and his suspicions obviously shared by many of the others around the table.

Sheila got to her feet, leaned across the table and started into the Russian's face from just over a foot away. "You all gave me the job. No-one offered to help in any way. All you were interested in was results. You personally poked your nose in once, and demonstrated what a stupid bastard you are, finishing up by murdering the wrong man because you mistakenly identified him. You killed him because you were annoyed at your own mistake. In this situation I recommend you shut your big mouth and keep well out of my way. I have wasted enough time on this Board, playing stupid games in an attempt to make a difference in this life. Between us we control a recognisable proportion of the wealth of this world. It is clear to me that, despite the charitable title this committee operated under, there is no charity involved in your input.

"I resign from this Board as of now. I will be happy to never set eyes on you unscrupulous bunch of crooks again."

The Board members sat stunned by this outburst. Outside Charlie and Jill were on their feet watching the rest of the group. Hands on the briefcases they both carried, Hannah spoke to the room in general. "There will be a limited exodus from the meeting room in a few moments. I suggest the rest of you do not make any rash moves whatever may be whispered or shouted to you. I have personal experience with our two colleagues here. Take my advice. Do not interfere."

At Hannah's words two of the other PA's went pale. Their earpieces had obviously passed on instructions. The trouble was that Hannah Curtain's was a most feared voice to argue with. A lethal lady whose advice it would be fatal to ignore.

Within the meeting room, Sir Anthony rose to his feet and hit the table with the file in front of him. When he had the Board's attention he said quietly, "I also resign. I want no part of any group that uses blackmail and murder to achieve its goals."

Marianne Philippe rose gracefully to her feet. "May I join you, Sir Anthony? The smell of corruption is becoming overpowering." The three people left the meeting room and were joined by their PA's in the outer room. None of the others made any move to prevent their leaving.

Outside Marianne turned to the other two. "You realize we have, in effect, painted targets on our backs. In the circumstances I am sure you will understand that I will be going my own way. I do have a place in mind that I am not prepared to share."

Her minder pressed a remote button for her limousine. Jill shouted to Charlie. They grabbed Sheila, Sir Anthony and Marianne between them and tumbled to the ground. The exploding vehicle shredded the minder with a shower of metal, splattering the immediate area with bloody fragments.

Charlie and Jill were back on their feet in moments, hurrying the trio down the street and around the first corner, out of sight of any watchers. The glass from the windows of the building they had just left was still falling when they reached the Roodebeeklaan, still running. There they stopped and looked at themselves. There were some indications of their ordeal but remarkably few. Marianne has a small tear in her jacket where the automatic she had started to draw when Charlie threw her down had caught on the seam. Sheila had laddered her stockings and scraped her knee. Sir Anthony showed no outward sign. But he was pale with shock. As he straightened his tie, the anger was beginning to get through. Jill and Charlie were apparently untouched by the whole affair. Jill was calling a cab as they gathered themselves together. The taxi stopped and they piled in.

"Airport!" Jill said. The driver set his meter and drove off. As they all started to speak, Charlie put up his hand and put his finger to his lips. Frustrated they all sat back while the cab threaded through the traffic, already being blocked by the screaming emergency vehicles racing to the scene of the explosion.

Jill spoke to the hotel, instructing them to collect the luggage in the two suites, to await collection, and to cancel the bookings.

At the airport the Otter was ready to fly. The pilot had remained with it the entire time they were in Brussels. It was there that Marianne left them, boarding a private jet to Paris, or elsewhere it seemed. Her comment was vague on the subject.

Sheila flew them to the private airfield and watched the aircraft being concealed in the converted barn. She turned to the pilot, John Langford, who had been with her for five years. "John! You always said you would like to try your hand as a bush pilot in Canada or New Zealand. Well, your opportunity has just occurred. She reached into the cockpit bag she had brought from the Otter. "There are the papers, all signed and notarized. The Otter is yours. I suggest you start out today, because it's possible the plane may be targeted. Mind you, the weather in Greenland is pretty good at present, if you considered breaking your journey there.

John Langford looked at his boss. "You don't have to do this, Madam. You have always been fair to me and I am quite willing to continue looking after the Otter for you."

Sheila smiled. "John I, never doubted you for one moment. But I have to go undercover for a while until I have some current problems ironed out. When I come out again, I'll think about another aircraft. But it is pointless keeping you hanging about while all this goes on, as well as the problems you may get from my enemies. In the circumstances I had always intended handing the Otter over to you anyway. It's a little sooner than I thought. But what is a month or so among friends?" She leaned forward and gave him a hug. "Bye, John. Smooth landings."

As he watched her climb in to the Range Rover, John Langford's thoughts swung between regret at what might have been and excitement at what the future held. Finally, when the Rover was out of sight, he walked over to the hanger and rolled the doors back. He had no wife or family to worry about after all. He had been saving for years in anticipation of the day he could go to Canada and buy himself a Beaver at least to fly in the wilderness of Northern Canada. Now he had an aircraft, he could use his savings to set up operations. There was nothing in his flat in Newbury he could not live without. His laptop was in his bag with his passport and licences.

He fuelled the Otter and he contemplated his future. Starting up, he rolled out of the hanger. The engines were still warm from the flight in. As he lined up to take off he saw the two cars racing toward the field gate. Without hesitation, he pushed both throttles forward and raced down the field lifting the wheels from the ground as the first car reached the field gate. His last glimpse was of the shattered wood from the gate flying in the air as the car smashed through. As he rose over the trees at the top of the rise at the far end of the field he disappeared from sight of the men in the car. As a precaution he banked to port, at right angles to his take-off path. In his mirror he saw the missile fly roughly where he would have been, had he not changed course. He continued climbing on his present course until he reached 3000 feet, then he made a long turn to starboard, still climbing on a course that would take him to Stornoway from where he could file a plan to Iceland, and points West.

Chapter fifteen

Skirmishing

The Range Rover bumped across the grass through the woodland to the adjoining estate. Charlie stopped when he reached the boundary. They could hear the report of the missile exploding, but were unaware of its significance. The drone of the departing Otter was audible, and Sheila concluded that James must have got away quickly. She realized that the engines would still have been hot. There would have been no need to sit and warm them.

Her cell phone rang. John Langford said over the background noise of the Otter. "Two cars, loaded for bear from the looks of it. Get out as fast as you can. They are on your tail. Good luck!"

"Thanks, John. Clear skies to Canada." Sheila said.

Charlie said, "I think they will follow us through the woods. So I suggest we go back and make them welcome."

Sir Anthony nodded. "I think you are right. It would be better if they disappeared; completely, if possible."

Charlie turned the Rover and drove back into the deeper woods before turning off and concealing it behind a copse of trees. Opening the boot he began passing out weapons to the others.

He gave the shoulder-fired missile to Jill, passed a rifle to Anthony and selected the bipod-mounted machine gun for himself. Jill got down behind a dead tree trunk and lined up the missile launcher on the next bend in the road. She placed the H&K smg next to her on the ground with a bandolier of magazines. Charlie placed himself on the other side of the track. He positioned the bipod to give himself the maximum cover and view of the track. His second weapon was an Uzi. Sir Anthony took position behind Jill to her left to cover her if needed. He checked his Glock automatic, a habit he was cultivating in the present circumstances. Sheila settled down beside Charlie with a NATO issue M16A4-45mm semi-automatic rifle. As she settled into place the sound of the two vehicles became louder as they neared the ambush position. The sudden appearance of the first, a Nissan all-terrain-vehicle with smoked windows, nearly startled her into action. Charlie's voice came, "Steady! Wait for the other one." Calm, she even relaxed under the influence of his own relaxed attitude. The second vehicle appeared. The missile launched from Jill's weapon hissed out and touched the careering Toyota land cruiser, converting it into a mobile tangled ruin. The machine gun beside Sheila opened up on the Nissan, striking sparks from the metal and shattering the windscreen and side windows.

Sheila heard the measured shots of Sir Anthony's rifle as she fired her first shots at the Nissan already riddled with bullet holes. The charging vehicle came to a halt. As a grenade rolled under the collapsing chassis, the whole thing blew up with a bang, the combination of fuel and explosive eliminating any chance of survival from the occupants of the vehicle.

Charlie said to Sheila, "Stay here!" He dashed off, cocking the Uzi as he joined Jill who was already running to the bend in the track.

Charlie cut the corner. Sheila saw him drop to one knee and lift the Uzi to fire at something she could not see. Then she heard the H&K join in, firing three bursts. Then silence descended on the woodland once more. Sheila stayed where she was until Charlie and Jill eventually returned. The two ambushed vehicles burned themselves out, the smouldering wreckage hissing as rain started to fall on the site.

***

In the house the other four were waiting to hear what had happened at the Board meeting. Charlie first of all detailed the facts about the ambush in the woods. "I have no way of knowing if there was anyone left behind at the airfield. We do know that there was an attempt to shoot the Otter down. That was what first warned us. That, plus a call from the pilot telling us we were being followed. We set up the ambush and I'm pretty confident that all the people in the two cars were dealt with. There are the two wrecks to be removed, by the way."

Cass said, "The tractor is there with the big trailer, as we speak."

Sheila said, "Whoever it was knew of the private airfield on Tony's place."

"It was no secret really, I'm afraid. There are plenty of people who knew about it. It is listed as an emergency alternate for smaller aircraft." Sir Anthony said slowly. "The bit I do not understand is how anyone knew your Otter was using the place, unless someone was watching the airfield, or somebody passed the information on for some other reason." He looked thoughtful, running a list of various people through his mind. The problem was that there were few people who would bother to mention the movements of Sheila on the estate as worth commenting on. He came to the conclusion that really there was only one who might be vindictive enough to want to harm Sheila.

He was astonished at the anger he felt at his wife. Sheila had been a friend for years and despite the easy relationship between them there had never been any real suggestion of impropriety between them. He had never really understood

- 164 -

the antagonism that his wife felt for Sheila. She was away at the moment, apparently visiting her sister in Gloucester.

He opened his cell phone and rang Charlotte, his sister-in-law's, number. "Put Marion on, Lotte, please."

"Oh, hullo, Tony. Marion isn't here I'm afraid."

"Ask her to call me when she gets back will you?"

"But she isn't...." Charlotte hesitated for a moment, then, "Marion never came here. She rang up and arranged to be here. Only then I got a call saying she was going to Paris instead. Sorry, Tony. I don't know where she is."

Sir Anthony put his cell phone away thoughtfully, wondering why she wished him to think she was in Gloucester. If it was an affair, why would she bother? There was no suggestion that their marriage was anything but a convenience. His flat in Soho was an open secret, and he suspected that his wife Marion was more interested in women than men. They had never had a normal relationship after the rather drunken first night of their marriage, when both made an effort to consummate their relationship. The resultant debacle had made it clear that whatever else happened, their marriage would always be one of convenience only.

Tony had found his friend in Soho, and he never did know what arrangement Marion made. He had not really cared.

He called his sister back and established that all was well at her home. He did not mention where he was speaking from, just in case.

Quin announced at dinner that night that he was of the opinion that the attempt at the removal of Sheila and Sir Anthony was an unplanned reaction to the resignation of the pair from the so-secret cabal which was the charity Board of WOAD. Of the other directors only Marcus Warren and Marianne Philippe could be regarded as non-partisan. Thus the remaining group seemed all to approve the actions of the Russian.

"I have the impression that if the Russian was not there the others would be quite amenable to let sleeping dogs lie, and forget who you are on a quid-pro-quo basis. In that case I think it best that we concentrate on the removal of the Russian before all others, with the possible exception of Avo Ranala, the Estonian. How do you all feel about that?"

With little further discussion of the matter, it was agreed that the Russian, being the main threat, should be the initial target.

Charlie raised the most important question. "How do we get to him?"

Jill suggested that a surveillance team be set up to try and establish a pattern of behavior.

"We are all known, to one or the other of them. It could be difficult without using some outside help," Ian commented.

Quin said, "I think this house is going to be difficult to operate from. The track through the woods implies communication between the estates . I'm sure we will be under surveillance ourselves before too long. So I propose we change our base to the refuge. Even if it becomes known it can be defended. What do you think?"

Naomie asked, "The refuge. What is that?"

Cass explained. "So you see, there is a place that only we know. It is on land that we own and it is built to withstand a nuclear attack. It is supplied with all things to keep us going, including weapons. And it is handy for London."

The decision was made. The party scheduled the move for the following morning.

***

The group met after settling into the retreat. They gathered in the lounge area nursing coffee cups, all in the casual dress they had travelled up in. They had come by different routes, and different methods. Cass was first to enter, Quin last. He had established a security watch on the arrivals to make sure there were no unwanted visitors.

Now, at the meeting he made a speech. He wasn't accustomed to doing it, but it was needed, and because of that he made the situation clear to them all. "This place is called the retreat because it is our sanctuary if we need to drop out of sight. No-one beyond the walls of this room is aware of the existence of the retreat. It must remain our secret. From here, we can attend to the threat to our lives posed by the existence of people like Anton Grovich and his friends."

He stopped and looked around at the group, eyes searching to see if there was any surprise or opposition to this idea. Finding none, he went on. "I think we should let the opposition know that they have more on their plate than they expect. They are undoubtedly wondering what happened to the team they sent out to take out the Otter as well as Sheila and Tony."

Charlie said, "I take it we are discussing the elimination of the Russian, Ranala, the Arab, and who else?"

Sheila said, "I think we can discount Marcus Warren, and Marianne Philippe. But I do wonder about the American Peter Noble. Father Aldo bothers me too. His PA is, according to Charlie, a gunman for hire, so I do not trust him."

She looked around the group. "I cannot believe that things have gone this far so soon. I realized that things were getting bad when Anton killed the man who was mistaken for one of the carriers. I confess I was looking for a way out from that time onwards. I seem to have pulled Tony in, and I suspect Marcus, though he went to ground in a hurry after the last meeting."

Quin said, "Before we go any further, we are not talking about a hit here. What I am suggesting is that, if there is any sign that we are being hunted, we retaliate. Otherwise we let things chill." He held his hand up to stop the comments which were obviously about to interrupt his remarks. "I expect everyone to be armed and ready all the time from now on. We travel in pairs and watch each other's back. What we don't do is look for trouble! If there is any sign of trouble, run and call. For the present, when you go out log in your destination and, if you change things when you are out, call in. We are talking life and death here. No games, please.

"If you think I am being overdramatic, I have something to show you all."

Cass handed over a file with a set of photographs in it.

Sheila took the file and opened it. Her gasp of horror shocked them all.

When the pictures had been circulated among all present, Cass commented, "That was Sheila's apartment in Brussels. The cat was her next door neighbor's. The neighbor was out at the time, luckily. The destruction occurred within thirty minutes of Sheila's departure, after her resignation. The chances of the opposition doing a forgive and forget are…" She hesitated, and then said, "Nil!"

***

Sheila sat in her room alone. It was after the meeting and tears were running unchecked down her cheeks. She was not making any noise, just quietly crying for the life she once had in the apartment where everything she had treasured from her parent, was now gone. Only her mother's wedding ring remained. She rotated it on her little finger as she sat saying a private farewell to her past. She knew it was her own fault. Greed had driven her reason to join the Board of WOAD. Now she admitted it, and accepted that her current situation arose from that fact.

After a few more minutes she rose to her feet, stripped off and stepped into the en-suite shower. After five minutes of high pressure battering, her skin tingled and her mood was upbeat. She stepped out and towelled herself dry. Her hair, blown dry, fell around her face like a blond halo. She dressed in black chinos and a loose sweatshirt, covering the presence of the Walther PPK tucked into the back of her waistband. The little thigh gun and holster was packed into her carry-bag.

When she went out to join the others she was her normal cool self.

***

Ian and Naomie were going to London to do some shopping. They were in England with a weekend bag, only having not anticipated the need for more.

After the planned negotiation of the tunnel, they had been able to gather sufficient extra clothing to cover their needs for the next week or so at least. They checked into the Hilton in Kensington rather than rush straight back to the retreat. Ian thought the chances were good that their presence would not be noticed unless by accident. If that occurred then they would take action at that time.

They were still learning to be together and their anonymity was especially precious to them at this time.

***

In Brussels, Anton Grovich was furious. "How can eight professional killers just disappear?" He smashed the telephone down on the desk. It shattered into a collection of components in his hands, broken plastic cutting his palm. "Fuck, fuck, fuck!" He spluttered.

"Get rid of this." He shouted, waving his hand at the mess, and shedding drops of blood on the papers on his desk at the same time.

"Get hold of that fucking bitch who was supposed to clean the slate for me."

From the corner of the office, out of immediate range, his assistant hesitated. Then shrugging he said, "Hannah Curtain will not answer our calls. You put out a contract on her."

- 169 -

Anton Grovich put his head in his hands, the blood from the wounds in his palm staining his hair. Through gritted teeth he muttered, "Then find someone else. I want this matter cleared up before the next Board meeting!"

His assistant, Eric Hanson, slipped out of the office. He was reaching for his cell phone as he passed through the door. To the woman seated at the desk in the neighbouring office he nodded at the door and said. "Plaster and antiseptic swabs. The boss has smashed his phone and cut his hand."

The woman picked up a spare handset from the drawer of her desk. From the cabinet behind her she took a small bottle and a first-aid kit. Rising to her feet she sighed, and walked into the other office closing the door behind her.

Hanson put his phone to his ear and spoke to someone. "Take out Hannah Curtain!" He listened for a moment. Then, "I don't remembering asking you anything. I'm giving orders. Get on with it!"

He cut off the contact and stabbed another button on the keyboard of the cell. After a pause he spoke. Sheila LeBec, Sir Anthony Merrick, Marcus Warren. Delete all three!"

He listened for a moment. "How the fuck should I know. You're the experts. You find them and do the business. That's what your being paid for!" He switched off and stood thinking for a minute. Then, hearing movement from the office next door, he left.

Chapter sixteen

Battle Lines

Hannah Curtain was enjoying her coffee outside Pret-a-Manger, on Tottenham Court Road in London. The sun was a welcome enhancement to her enjoyment of the moment. She had leaned forward to pick up the discarded newspaper laying on the next table when she spotted the shooter. It was with a sigh of exasperation that she rolled forward behind the cover of the tables, rising behind the corner of the entrance to the shop next to the café. She entered the shop which sold perfume. Through the front window she verified the shooter's position. She put her gun away into a brief case and started to walk away towards Oxford Street. Hannah pulled off the jacket she had been wearing and pulled a Hermes scarf from the pocket. Wrapping it round her head and carrying her jacket, she set off down the street following the shooter.

The woman walked into a souvenir shop on Oxford Street. Hannah pulled out her cell phone and pressed a speed dial number. "Wally? Who operates from Hammond's, London. It's a... all right so you know it. Answer the question!" She listened for a few moments, then. "I owe you one, Wally. I'll be in touch." Closing the cell phone, she turned and walked away, checking shop windows to make sure she was not being followed. Finally, she took a cab to the Hilton Hotel in Park Lane. From there another taxi took her to the Churchill Hotel, where she was currently staying.

She guessed that the Russian had put out the contract he had threatened her with.

***

Quin Gilmore raised his eyes from the screen in front of him. "Take a look at this." He said. "Your friend, Hannah is named on a contract. It's worth half a million."

Jill looked up from the map she was studying. "Looking at their website, are you?" Her tone was derisive.

"As a matter of fact, I am." Quin said, not at all bothered by her tone.

"Why do I suspect that you are not joking?" Jill said warily.

"Probably, because I am not." Quin said with a smile.

Jill looked over his shoulder at the website he had brought up. It looked like many other of the sites available. Mystified, she turned to him. "What am I looking at?"

As Quin pointed things out on the screen she began to see what he meant, interpreting the coded information contained in the make-up of the web site.

"I see we are also invited to remove Sheila LeBec, Sir Anthony Merrick and Marcus Warren. That is not very friendly!"

"Well, I have made a few additions for the benefit of our friends in Brussels."

As Jill watched, more coded names appeared on the screen. She deciphered the coded names and suddenly laughed. "Cheeky bugger, they will not be happy with that."

She told the others what Quin had done and joined into the laughter at the idea that Anton and his associates had joined the list of targets on the website.

"While it is good to have a laugh at the expense of our enemies, we really must get some sort of positive action under way. Ian and Naomie are preparing to return to Brussels this week." Quin nodded to Ian. "They are determined to face the enemy in their own back yard. Now we are aware that they do not link you two directly with Sheila and Tony, so they should not be looking for problems from your direction. But keep the lines open. We may be completely wrong about this. We would not like to lose either of you through underestimating the opposition!"

Cass mentioned the other thing to take into account. "Hannah Curtain! From what we know she is likely to hunt them down rather than the other way round. With a little luck, she will save us a lot of bother. Whatever, she is not a factor to be ignored.

Now are there any questions?"

"Should we try for a link-up with Hannah?" Jill made the suggestion.

Quin looked around the group, the question open for comment.

Charlie spoke up. "She is a pro, and I understand a very successful one at that. It could work for both of us."

Sheila and Tony both nodded slowly. Sheila said, "Worth a try perhaps. It's a yes or no question. From then on of course it would be a matter of trust."

Jill said, "I think, if she commits, she'll keep the agreement. After all, her entire reputation is based on carrying through a contract. If you agree I'll make the approach. At least she knows who I am."

Quin shrugged. "We can try, at least. But there can be no disclosure of the location of the retreat until we are convinced that she is genuine. Agreed?"

There was a chorus of agreement from the rest of the assembly and the matter was left there.

Since both Sheila and Sir Tony had business to attend to in London, both expressed the wish to get on with things. "I know we are hoping to go on the offensive against the Russian's thugs. It occurred to me—and I did discuss this with Sir Tony—that if we emerged in public they might be drawn out into the open. With us as bait, I mean. After all, we pulled you all into this mess. It is really up to us to get us out of it if we can." She looked at Sir Tony. He nodded his head in agreement.

"Please make no mistake, ladies and gentlemen/ I am scared at the prospect. But I am, like Sheila, determined to get on with life. We cannot hide forever. What Sheila is suggesting, using us for bait, does give us a chance to identify and eliminate at least some of the scum threatening us." Sir Anthony stopped abruptly, embarrassed at showing emotion quite so openly.

Quin looked at him with respect. Both of the former Board members surprised him with the strength they were displaying in their current situation.

"Two conditions," he said. "You both wear vests full time in public. We cover you at all times until either they spring or another reason makes it clear that the risk is over."

Sheila looked relieved. "I have no problem with that. Do you, Tony?"

Tony grinned. "I was hoping you would say something like that. Yes. I—we both agree and thank you for all you have done so far. I do realize that our own acceptance of the situation on the Board was responsible for the problems we are all facing. So we both appreciate the help you have all given and the fact that, without you, we would probably be either dead, or wish that we were."

Sheila was nodding her agreement as he finished his statement.

"Okay. Let's get down to the planning." Cass rose to her feet and the meeting broke up.

Charlie turned to Jill. "How are you going to contact Hannah?"

***

The conversation was brief.

"Hannah? It's Jill Mather. We met again a few days ago."

"So?" The answer was clipped and uninterested.

"We have a common enemy. I wonder if we could discuss the matter?"

"What's to discuss? I will be removing the problem in my own time."

"I just thought we might cooperate on the task. I have the impression that the problem comprises more than one particular target. Because of that I would suggest that having someone to watch your back could be to your advantage as well as ours." Jill waited, fingers crossed.

"What do you suggest?" Hannah said warily.

"Meet at a place you choose. I'll bring a friend, who leads our team."

"Who?"

"Quin Gilmore!"

"I'll call you on your cell number."

The phone cut off.

Jill turned to Charlie, thumbs up, grinning. "She's hooked," she said. "She will play for sure."

"Certain. Are you?" Charlie said with a straight face.

Jill hesitated for a moment, not quite sure if Charlie really doubted her. Then she realized that he was pulling her leg. Her dive on him was not elegant but it was effective, driving the wind from his lungs with a whoosh. Laughing and gasping at the same time is difficult, as he swiftly found out.

***

Hannah Curtain put the phone down carefully. She was not concerned with the fact that Jill knew her number. She was aware that they were both professionals. It was part of the job description to learn things like that. What Jill had said was interesting, and it did link with her own thoughts on the threats made by Anton Grovich. Whatever the level of expertise the Russian commanded, one on one, or even two on one she could cope with. The trouble could be that, with unlimited numbers and some basic training, there was no way that one person could escape and evade forever. Sheer numbers would prevail in the end. Hannah was not a fool. Aware that she could not get things right every time, she did need someone she could trust to guard her back when things did go wrong. She had no illusions about being immortal at 35years old, she had the scars to prove it. What Jill had said made sense. All she needed now was to make some calls and see just what sort of outfit Jill was hooked up with. If it was all Jill said, or at least implied it was, then it could be worth hooking up with them, albeit temporarily.

***

The WOAD Board met at the Park Lane Hilton. Attending was Anton Grovich, Jer Sahib, Peter Noble, and Avo Ranala. Unsurprisingly, Marianne Philippe was not there nor indeed was the Chairman Sir Anthony Merrick or Sheila LeBec. Father Aldo slipped in at the last minute.

The priest was enjoying the current inactivity, but he was quick to approve the actions. It did not require his personal intervention. Thus he felt he could distance himself from any fallout the action would generate.

He touched his collar. Even, after all these years, he was able to marvel at the immunity it had given him. When in the Congo, engaged in the battle for survival, he had personally slaughtered many of the local populace to ensure his own survival. His association with the rebel faction required him to bend several rules imposed by his cloth.

The rapes, torture, and murder would never earn him forgiveness and in truth he did not expect it. He was genuinely appalled at his own acceptance of these excesses. Even now the urges were present. Life back in civilized society was a continuous battle with his urges and desires. It was a battle he did not always win.

There were at least two countries who would have been surprised and pleased to receive samples of his DNA, to compare with DNA taken at, up to now, unsolved murders of a particularly brutal nature.

He left the meeting having heard the deliberations of the remainder of the Board who, in deference to his cloth, walked all around the agreement to hunt down and eliminate the absent Chairman and Sheila LeBec. It amused him to realize that they were unaware of his past and therefore treated him with the respect they felt his collar deserved. He had already decided that, if Hannah Curtain and/or the other targets, did not remove Grovich, Sahib and Ranala, then he would.

Pleased that he had made the decision, he made his way to the Airport and shuttled to Paris for the weekend.

***

Anton Grovich was unhappy. It was a regular occurrence these days for some reason. His condition was exacerbated by the syphilis which he had developed after the shipment of so-called virgin teenagers he had been sent from a source in Uzbekistan. Unwilling to wait for the medical inspection which would have weeded out the infected girl, he had chosen the most virginal-looking to share her first experience with him, not realizing that the look which had attracted him had been the reason she had arrived in the infected condition.

The discovery that the poor girl was in fact no longer a virgin had resulted in a rage vented on her person. Now the body was divided into several segments distributed through the sewage system of the city. Her legacy was causing his ill health and irritation from this as yet undiagnosed source.

All his aides were being extra cautious in their dealings with him at present. They were under the mistaken impression that his present mood would pass, and things would simmer down to their normal level.

The first sign of real trouble came from Avo Ranala. There were several lines of enquiry out seeking Sir Anthony and Sheila. All leads appeared to end at the time when they had disappeared until Ranala, who had been waiting for Grovich in the Russian's office, happened to see a note scribbled and screwed up under the edge of the desk where it had missed the waste bin standing next to it.

He picked it up and opened it idly scanning the message written there.

He read, *'The plane traced to Sir Anthony's estate. A party sent to intercept. The entire party and vehicles have all been lost without trace. No trace of aircraft. Bullets found in the nearby woodland suggest that a successful ambush was effective in wiping out the entire team and concealing the vehicles. A subsequent detailed search of the area revealed nothing except the aforementioned expended bullets.'*

The message was signed by, C. Bertram, (Security Plus. London)

It was dated the date of the last meeting attended by Sir Anthony and Sheila LeBec.

Avo Ranala tapped the note against his teeth. He sat wondering why he had not been told of this at the time. He wondered if anyone else had been told. It seemed that Anton Grovich was working to his own agenda. The agenda obviously excluded him.

He rose to his feet and walked out of the office. Anton was just coming back. "Where do you think you are going?" Anton said aggressively.

"It's none of your business, obviously." Ranala replied, and made to push past the Russian.

Grovich grabbed his arm. "Just what does that mean?" The Russian's voice rose menacingly.

Ranala shook off the restraining hand. He raised the note and shook it at the Russian, "This is you, working together with us. Is it?"

Grovich read the note, he smiled. "I arranged this contact before we came to our agreement. That is why I did not bother to mention it. I would have told you all at our meeting today." He put his arm round Avo's shoulder. "Come!" He said. "We will have a drink before the meeting." He wheeled the Estonian back through the door into his office, screwing up the note once more.

Chapter seventeen

Hannah Curtain

She stood in front of the mirror examining her body critically. She had to admit there were one or two scars visible but apart from them it was a pretty good picture she was looking at.

Not too bad for 35, she thought. *Nothing sagging yet, anyway.* She laughed mocking herself, but secretly pleased that she was maintaining the trim figure she had honed since her service with the Israeli Special Forces.

Seated in the lounge, now fully clothed, she contemplated the suggestion that Jill Mather had made about combining forces against Anton Grovich. The idea was attractive in some ways. It would make a change to have someone watching her back for once. Over the past few years there were occasions where a backup would have saved her at least one of the scars she had noticed earlier. That was for sure! It would not hurt to talk to Jill and find out what they had to offer. Which she did not already have.

She reached out and took hold of her phone. It was a rechargeable cordless type standing upright in its docking base. She felt resistance from the usually easily removable handset. She was rolling off the chair and behind the settee immediately. There was a two second pause. She could hear the dial tone inviting her to punch in the number. She had shut her eyes and started to open them when the bomb blew. It was not a huge bang, no big fireworks. Contained, it wrecked the chair she had been using, the table on which it was sited, and the collection of bric-a-brac which had accumulated there over the past two weeks.

Hannah rose to her feet reached behind the sofa and re-trieved her carry bag. She checked her passports, money and reserve gun, and the key to the locker in the Railway Station. By the time she reached the front door, the bomb in the bed-room had detonated.

Despite all, she nodded her appreciation at whoever had set things up. The bedroom would be where she might have gone having survived the first bomb, to pack a bag to move out in a hurry. So a delayed second bomb would fit nicely into the set-up.

She stopped without touching the front door. Putting her bag down she started examining the door and its surrounds. She almost missed it. A narrow pressure switch inside the door jamb, hidden within the carpet. It was the small drop plate attached to the bottom of the actual door. In the up position, perfectly safe. In the dropped position, when the door was opened, it would impact the pressure switch, and bingo!

Back into the kitchen, Hannah found the reel of duct-tape and a ball of string. At the front door she taped the flap up in the safe position. Tying the string to the lock, she opened the Yale movement and locked it open without moving the door, reeling out the string she picked up her bag and, standing sheltered behind the corner where the kitchen entrance was, pulled the front door open with the string.

***

Avo Ranala was not happy. Despite the assurances, he did not trust the Russian. As he left the building he turned left, then right, then left again. He stopped in a doorway and waited. Nothing. No one appeared. He pressed his cell phone speed dial. "Where are you?"

At the other end the voice started to answer. Then a gurgle. Then noise. Just noise. Then nothing. He smashed the phone against the wall and set off on foot.

The footsteps that coming behind him made just enough noise for his hyper-tuned hearing to register. As the assassin reached for him, he swung round with a sideways kick that took the legs from under the man. Avo was merciless. His assailant hit the ground on his face and Avon smashed his foot to the back of the man's neck. There was a crunch and a clatter of the knife the man had been carrying as it hit the pavement. Death followed almost immediately. Avo dropped to the ground beside the dead man and rolled him over. The head flopped awkwardly. Running his hand through the pockets of the man was the work of seconds. Wallet, watch, ring, money clip, and Browning automatic.

At the railway station Avo Boarded the Paris train. He bought a cell phone at the first stop. Phoning ahead, he was able to reach his PA. The word and the warning went out.

By evening Avo was in Tallin. For the first time that day he felt safe.

***

Hannah collected her bags from the locker at the Gare du Nord in Paris. Neither of them realized that they had shared the train for their escape from the clutches of the man they now both regarded as the mad Russian.

***

In London Father Aldo was seated, eyeing the passing array of people in the foyer of the Cumberland hotel. He could identify the prostitutes even though the elegance of their dress would give a different impression.

It was while he sat playing this game that he spotted Hannah Curtain. He knew who she was. She had been pointed out when she was in attendance at a meeting as the Russian's PA.

Father Aldo smiled at that. The bunch of PA's at that meeting could have armed an uprising with the weapons they carried. Even after they had lodged their weapons, they had been well armed. He had no doubts. Now here was Hannah Curtain in London. He watched and observed her meet with a pretty blonde. It looked as if they knew each other. Having met, they left. Aldo considered following them, then shrugged as another pretty woman passed him. 'Pretty Woman' that made him smile once more, and he hummed the music as he decided there was more than a passing resemblance to the movie star of the name and the profession of the lady.

Piqued, he rose to his feet and engaged the services of the lady in question.

She raised her eyebrow looking pointedly at his dog collar. He shrugged and led the way to his room.

***

Hannah and Jill were seated in the apartment in the Grosvenor House, reserved by Hannah under her travel name. Between them on a tray were biscuits and tea. Neither woman had touched them.

Jill eventually opened the conversation. "Tea?"

Hannah smiled a crooked smile and nodded. "Yes. Why not."

When the tea had been poured and the biscuits passed, Hannah said, "Okay. Now we know who we are and have got our tea. What is this all about, really?"

Jill took her time answering. "I understand that there is a little current activity involving you and Sir Anthony Merrick, and Sheila LeBec? Oops, I forgot to mention Anton Grovich."

At the mention of the Russian Jill noticed the momentary start, though Hannah's face was immediately blank once more. She waited but Hannah made no comment. Jill continued. "There has been a contract issued on Merrick and LeBec, and, I now observe, on you. In other circumstances I would have imagined that you would possibly have been involved in a rather different role. But in fact it seems we have a common enemy. I am still contracted to protect my client, Madam Le-Bec!"

"Are you seriously suggesting that we join forces to remove this objectionable Russian? If you are, I should point out that he is surrounded at all times with an efficient group of former Russian Special Services personnel. They, themselves, are daunting, Grovich himself. apart from being quite loathsome, is also adept at martial arts, and no slouch with a weapon."

Jill smiled slowly though Hannah noticed it did not reach her eyes. "We are aware of Grovich's achievements and have had a brush with the bodyguards already. There are a bunch of Estonians, belonging to Avo Ranala, I presume, who tried to intercept my clients. They now have a lonely grave in Sussex. I'm not playing with amateurs."

"What do you want me for? You obviously have an efficient team already." There was the hint of a sneer in the voice which Jill noticed but ignored.

"We decided to ask you in for one reason only. Knowing you would not leave things as they are, we would rather cooperate with you than cross paths and possibly bugger-up your operation and ours also. If we team up, at least we will all be playing from the same game-plan."

She sat back and let Hannah take that in, pouring more tea while she waited .

"You realize that Father Aldo is in the Cumberland hotel?"

"Of course. He is there, picking up a prostitute. It is one of his particular idiosyncrasies." Jill said calmly.

"Are you aware of his other unpleasant characteristics?" Hannah said quietly.

"I am not, though I am not his biggest fan. He would not be my choice companion for a dark and foggy night." Jill looked at Hannah curiously.

"When younger, the Father discovered that the collar gave him anonymity and protection from suspicion. It gave him the opportunity to explore his baser instincts with choirgirls and schoolgirls who came within his sphere of influence. He used the wrath of God to seal their lips. Then he slipped up and went too far. A girl he abused became desperate. He silenced her. In making the decision he used the occasion to indulge his personal fantasies. He got away with it, at the expense of an idiot boy who did not know which way was up, who took the blame. He enjoyed the process obviously because he performed three more gruesome murders in that district of Italy.

"He was relocated to Rome where there were several other unsolved murders. By this time he had discovered there were ways he could turn his fetish into cash. He set up an anonymous personal removal business, specializing in unwanted wives, and embarrassing ex-mistresses. It seemed there was a danger of his being unmasked. That is when he moved to France, where he now is ensconced.

"With his financial future more or less secure, he has kept his nose clean in France, as you've seen, even coming to London for his relief."

Hannah sat back and drank the cooling tea.

"Why do I get the impression that you know an awful lot about this creep?"

"He has been on my personal list for redemption for the past year. This is the first opportune moment, if you know what I mean."

"I see." Jill nodded her head. "So this meeting was fortuitous?"

"Exactly. But having heard what you have to say, I will make sure that it does not create a problem. I will seriously consider what you have suggested. It makes sense. I will contact you in two days with my reply. There will be no hangover, I promise. Is that okay?"

Jill shrugged. "Until then." She said, "He does know you are here."

"He doesn't know why!" Hannah said, "It could be he will draw the Russian here."

The two girls parted. By the time Hannah returned, Father Aldo had not re-appeared, though his selected lady had resumed her patrol through the public areas of the Cumberland hotel.

Hannah Curtain had decided that the opportunity had now arrived to rid the world of a particularly nasty individual.

It is true that Hannah was in effect, a gun for hire, but she had always insisted on vetting selected targets. She did not just dispose of anyone who was subject to a contract. There was always research involved, and, as in the case of Sheila and Sir Anthony, it was a marginal call, since they worked as partners to a vicious criminal. She shrugged. It hadn't happened anyway.

Here though, in the case of Father Aldo, she had come to know a person who had suffered from his attentions. The victim had not died, but she had been scarred for life. Other discreet enquiries had assured her that Father Aldo was not what he seemed to the respectable world.

Hannah found it hard to believe this was not known to the Mother Church. Frustratingly, having established the facts, by that time Aldo disappeared.

Hannah had been only recently separated from the Israeli forces. The opportunity to deal with Father Aldo had been lost because he had left Italy to live in France before she could act.

The sighting of Father Aldo in London was fortuitous. She knew that the priest was aware of her identity, but he should not know that he was on her target list.

She changed her clothes in her room and donned a wig. When she left the room, with her wig and tinted glasses, she was a different person. She seated herself in the reception area and waited. Eventually Father Aldo appeared, smartly dressed, complete with dog collar.

She slipped out ahead of Aldo, passing through the glass doors as he started across the room. She was with him as he entered Marble Arch underground station.

Aldo was contemplating his next destination. He had, in the past, been close to a family who had emigrated from Italy to England. Knowing that they had links to the Mafia, he expected that they would be part of the crime scene in London. He had called and been welcomed. Having decided to settle in England, he would need accommodation and contacts to carry on his particular lifestyle.

The platform at Marble Arch was as always, crowded. The train which departed as he came through from the escalators had left the platform empty, but it was swiftly filled with people pushing and shoving in anticipation of the arrival of the next train.

As the platform became crowded he thought of changing his mind and taking a cab. but with the flood of people entering the station that would be difficult.

Wary of the warning line on the edge of the platform, he found himself jostled back and forth. Despite being a big man, force majeure actually drove him and many others over the line toward the platform edge. The rumble of the approaching train and the gust of air driven in front of the train warned the crowd that relief was imminent.

For Father Aldo, unused to the habits of the travelling crowd, it was not easy to hold his position. He turned his back on the crowd and heaved. Feeling slight give behind him, he prepared to push again. The train entered the station now slowing as it travelled along the platform. Deciding he was well clear, Aldo had started to relax when he felt the sharp jab in the center of his back. A knife. It was a knife. In reaction he jerked forward away from the threat to his kidneys. The crowd surged as train neared. Aldo had no chance. Already off balance from the jab, his arms windmilled but did nothing to halt his meeting with the front of the train. He had a glimpse of the driver's horrified face as he fell, bouncing off the front of the carriage and onto the rails below. The flash of electricity, as he earthed the live rail, came just before he was divided into bloody pieces by the wheels on the steel rails.

Hannah was already leaving, working her way through the crowd as the cries of alarm and shock were echoing from the tiled walls.

In the ladies' room back at the hotel, she entered a booth and removed her wig and the tinted glasses, waiting for several minutes before emerging as several others entered. She was rummaging in her handbag as she passed them. head down until she was past and out in the lobby once more.

For Hannah, the death of the priest was a favor to mankind. In her head she thought of the victim who had identified her tormentor. Mentally she nodded in approval.

***

Jill called the retreat, using the cut-out number. Cass answered "Baxter's!" the code for all clear.

Jill said, "Just to let you know, the weather is good here, and Hannah's on the hook." The arranged message indicated all was clear. Quin had insisted that they become accustomed to coded call signals, as, once the action heated up, their security had to be instinctive.

Satisfied, Jill continued, "It looks as if Hannah will come in. She had a loose end to tie up before committing herself finally. I will stay here until tomorrow. Could one of the men meet me for lunch? There is a possibility that Grovich will be here and, since I will be at the restaurant he normally uses, I would appreciate some cover."

"I'll arrange it. But he knows what you look like. Won't that be a risk? Being there, I mean."

"He knows me as a blonde. I will be a grey-haired secretary in a business suit and spectacles, when I am in view. I would like to meet my escort before I go into the restaurant."

"I'll get back to you. I'm not quite sure who it will be, so don't take risks. Stay close until he arrives. I'll get back as soon as I can."

Cass spoke to Quin about Jill's suggestion and request for cover.

"It's short notice, I know. But is there anyone there in London we can call on?" Cass was serious about this. Although Jill was competent, quite capable of looking after herself, the Russian was dangerous and he travelled with several security staff at all times. Another pair of eyes was always important under the circumstances.

Quin thought a moment. "Gerald Butler!"

Cass looked at him. "The lawyer?"

Quin grinned. "What did you think of Gerald? Nice suit, trim, fit-looking, probably plays squash to keep fit?"

"Well, yes! I suppose I did."

"Gerald Butler was my immediate superior when I entered the Regiment at Hereford. We trained together. He was wounded in Iraq and invalided out. He returned to his law studies and joined his father's law firm. His fitness is nothing to do with squash. He is sensei of his local karate club in his spare time. I'll call him and see if he is available."

Cass shook her head. The image of the lawyer, smart slim, just under six foot tall, nice face, but not outstanding. The well-spoken image suddenly transformed into the man Quin described. Trim. toned figure, clear grey eyes that could look right through you. She shook her head. It was amazing how people appeared to be who you think they are, rather than who they really are.

***

On the other end of the phone Gerald Butler was smiling grimly. As far as he was concerned, meeting Jill for lunch was a much better prospect than a sandwich and coffee at the local Starbucks.

"Delighted to oblige. Your lady friend sounds much more appealing than the crush at the coffee shop."

Gerald rang Jill from reception. "Hullo, Jill. It's your escort service, supplied through the retreat."

"Name?" The voice sounded interesting.

"Gerald Butler. Say, five minutes in the foyer. Forgive the business suit. But I did bring a red rose as instructed."

"I'll find you." The phone went down and Gerald found a seat, where he inspected the plastic sheathed red rose curiously.

Jill rang Cass. "Gerald Butler! Who is he? Carrying a red rose?"

Cass giggled. "Cheeky sod. Sorry, Jill. Gerald is Quin's lawyer, ex SAS, current karate expert, though, most important to Quin and me, our lawyer. He's not married. I understand that is not because he isn't interested. Still waiting for the right one. So you could get lucky. He is a nice guy and no pushover, okay?"

Mollified, Jill said, "Okay, thanks, Cass." She put the phone down and arranged her grey wig. The short hair went well with the tinted rimmed glasses complementing her ensemble. In the mirror, a slender grey haired woman looked back at her. The charcoal skirt and jacket were combined with plain white blouse, natural tights and black court shoes.

Collecting her bag, Jill left the room, ensuring the lock secured the door behind her.

Chapter eighteen

Skirmish

In the reception area she spotted Gerald sitting across the room, briefcase beside him and the red rose encased in plastic on his knee. Despite her grey hair she drew male eyes as she crossed the room. Gerald saw her coming and rose to his feet. Jill approved. He looked ordinary, nice ordinary she decided.

Gerald decided that, if all Quin's friends were as attractive as Cass and Jill, he should get on to more social acquaintance as soon as possible.

"You are Jill. The rose is for you, by the way." His voice was cultured and nice,

Wow! Jill thought. *I'm going to lunch with Mr Nice.* Aloud she said, "Gerald, how kind! You really shouldn't. You know it's not a date." The flutter in her voice was for the benefit of the people sitting around some of whom were taking an interest in the proceedings.

"Jill, for me lunch with you always seems like a date. I look forward to it with the same anticipation." He took her hand and squeezed it gently. "Shall we go straight in?"

He steered her through the hotel reception area, and through to the restaurant.

***

The Russian arrived shortly afterwards with a flurry of activity as his several security men were found seats where they could keep him secure from interference. Gerald and Jill were sitting several tables away across the room. Both Gerald and Jill studied the man as he gave his orders and started on the champagne already awaiting his arrival.

"Not a nice person." Gerald said mildly. I have heard of him of course. His finger is in a multitude of pies." He noticed Jill's eyebrow raised at this comment. "Local vernacular, I'm afraid. It's just that the man seems to be involved in all sorts of things."

Jill grinned. She was beginning to understand what Quin and Cass saw in this quiet man. There was a contained quality about him, and a natural charm that she found appealing. She contemplated this while carrying on polite conversation with her escort.

As for Gerald he was intrigued. The attractive woman seated on the other side of the table was, as far as he was concerned, well able to look after herself. His impression was of a self-reliant fit lady, attractive rather than pretty in the accepted sense, but bright, apparently intelligent and definitely dangerous. *Why?* he thought to himself. *Whenever I meet somebody I would like to get to know better, do I always seem to choose somebody I cannot get near.* At that moment Jill asked a question.

Flustered for once, he said, "I beg your pardon. I missed that."

Jill repeated her question. "How does your wife like the idea of you entertaining a strange woman for lunch?"

Gerald thought about that. "Is that a trick question?"

Jill looked puzzled. Shaking her head, she said, "Not as far as I am concerned?"

"There is no wife to be answered to, I'm afraid. Whenever I meet someone I would consider marrying, she is either already married, engaged or lesbian." He grinned ruefully, sighed loudly, "And now it's happening again."

At this Jill looked up sharply, her clear eyes uncomfortably direct looking Gerald in the eye.

He returned the look unflinchingly.

Eventually, she smiled. "You are a most interesting man, Gerald Butler."

"I was just thinking the same thing about you, Jill. Our subject, by the way, has started to move."

The disturbing moment passed as life intruded once more. Gerald called the waiter for the bill.

The other side of the dining room erupted into a flurry of activity as Grovich and his entourage left. Gerald and Jill left quietly in the wake of the Russian party.

"What is the drill now?" Gerald asked.

"I will be keeping in touch with the Russian." Jill said. "Thank you for covering the dining room for me, and entertaining me throughout lunch." She kissed his cheek. "I'll return the favor one day."

"I'll hold you to that," he said with a smile.

As Jill departed Gerald touched his cheek where he had been kissed. He nodded to himself. There would be another time.

***

Jill wandered along Baker Street. She had altered her appearance. The long chestnut hair now rested on her shoulders. No longer wearing the jacket of her suit, it was now carried turned inside out, the red silk lining exposed. Her blouse now open at the neck showed her tanned skin and a hint of lace. The knee-length charcoal skirt displayed considerably more leg than earlier in the day. The waistband folded down to lift the hem. There was little to link her with the grey-haired secretary at the lunch table. On the other side of the road the limousine carrying Grovich and his party was sitting with engine running. Around the corner, Jill's taxi was sitting, awaiting her return.

Gerald spotted her as he left Selfridges by the Orchard Street exit. He had turned up toward Baker Street intending to take the rest of the day off. He now had a carrier bag with provisions from the food hall in Selfridges in addition to his brief case. As he crossed Wigmore Street he saw the flash of red from the silk lining of Jill's jacket. His eyes lingered on the legs displayed. He had the feeling that there was something familiar about the chestnut-haired girl who owned them, but he did not at the time make the connection. It was only when she looked around that he realized who it was.

At the same time the door of the limousine opened and two of the entourage emerged. They split and crossed the road, performing a pincer movement on Jill.

Without thinking, Gerald started running. He called out, "Jill!"

She looked round and spotted the two men approaching her. The nearest man threw himself forward and grabbed her arm. The other was drawing his automatic from an underarm holster, while he ran to support his partner. Gerald hit him on the run, and sent him flying head first into the wall of the building on the left. His cry was abruptly stopped by the impact of his face on the unforgiving bricks.

The man who had grabbed Jill found himself clutching her jacket as his face, encountered her lifted knee. Staggered, he straightened up and swung a fist, connecting with a glancing impact on Jill's cheek. She reeled back, stunned by the force of the blow, shoulders against the wall. As the thug recovered his own balance, Jill shook her head and came away from the wall. Her straight-armed fist to the throat missed his Adam's apple, but caused him to gasp and stagger back. The other thug stood with bloody face, weaving, but now lifting his gun to shoot Jill. Gerald, who had dropped his provisions though he still had his brief case, scooped up a tin of beans and slammed the unfortunate thug on the jaw with enough force to split the can. The man's eyes glazed over. The gun dropped as his knees buckled. He collapsed to the pavement. Jill followed up her punch with a demonstration of what to use a stiletto heel for apart from walking. Her foot swung and smashed into the cheek and jaw of her attacker, the heel tearing his skin, scribing a scarlet slash diagonally from ear to mouth. As he spun with the impact he grabbed at her leg. He released it as a second can of beans impacted the back of his head with a dull thud. Jill hopped off balance and would have fallen had it not been for the steadying grasp of Gerald's hand.

"Whee! That was fun." Jill laughed as she turned to look at Gerald. "Where did you come from?"

Gerald noticed the limousine was no longer waiting. He turned to look at the two thugs as he answered her. "I was going home early, having decided to take the rest of the day off. I called at Selfridges to get some food." He looked ruefully at his wrecked supplies. The two thugs were leaving the scene, supporting each other like two drunks. Gerald picked up the discarded automatic, and put it into his brief case. The people on the street were distancing themselves, ignoring the pair, unwilling to get involved. Jill laughed and collected her discarded jacket and handbag from the gutter where it had fallen.

"Takeaway again, I'm afraid." Gerald sighed.

Jill took his arm. "Come on. I'll cook you dinner. Oops. I forgot. I don't have a flat in London any more. Where do you live?"

"In Sherlock Mews, further up Baker Street." Gerald said warily.

Jill surveyed the pavement, where the remains of the provisions were being rapidly kicked into the gutter. "Back to

Selfridges first." She took his arm and they set off through the square. In the shadow of the trees Jill stopped and shrugged her skirt down to its original length. She slipped her coat on. Respectable once more, they made their way to the Food Hall in the department store, where Jill bought the requirements for her decided menu. Outside, she hailed a cab.

***

Cass put the phone down and turned to Quin. "It seems that the Russian recognized Jill despite all. He put two of his dogs onto her in Baker Street."

Guessing Jill survived, Quin said, "How did she get out of that one?"

Cass laughed. "Gerald was going home early after taking Jill to lunch. He had called at Selfridges for provisions on his way home. He spotted Jill in Baker Street, just as the two thugs got out of the limo to mug, or whatever, to Jill. Gerald ran to the rescue, shouting a warning to Jill. He took out the nearest thug. Bashed him into the wall from behind, then burst a can of baked beans over his head."

"Wow! Sounds painful. What then?"

"Jill punched the other one, then kicked him in the face with her stiletto heel. As he came back for more, Gerald intervened with another of his trusty cans and belted him round the ear. The car took off leaving them all about. the public dashed past as fast as possible seeing nothing of course. The thugs left Gerald with a Browning 9mm automatic."

"Where is Jill now?"

"She is cooking dinner for Gerald in his apartment." Cass looked at Quin and shrugged. "She felt guilty for ruining his shopping. And possibly grateful for the help, d'you think?"

Quin shrugged in turn. "I'll let Charlie know. She will probably spend the night in town."

Cass took Quin's arm and they walked through to the lounge where Sir Anthony sat glowering behind his newspaper. Side by side on the settee, Charlie and Sheila were playing Ludo. Both were laughing, heads close together, as they competed to complete their game.

Cass and Quin looked at each other. They turned to go and Charlie called out, "Don't tell me. Jill won't be coming back tonight. I suppose she will be staying, and going out with her dishy lawyer?" He didn't sound too upset. He turned to Sheila. "There! I knew it. We will be able to go to the 'Lamb' at Feltham after all. So, it's casual clothes and drinking boots at the pub buffet." He turned to the room. "Anyone else interested?" he called. Quin looked at Cass. She nodded. "We're in. Coming, Tony?"

Sir Tony put the paper down with a resigned sigh. "I think I'll have an early night if you don't mind. I'll stay and watch the shop."

Sir Tony was feeling miffed. His not-so-secret passion for Sheila LeBec seemed to have been frustrated even more by the unexpected charms of Charlie. He resented it briefly, but in fact, he had never really expected his suit to get anywhere.

He put the paper down, and for the first time in years he sat examining himself coldly and clinically. His laughable marriage to Marion, a woman he did not even like, and who did not like him. Her, increasingly, open preference for her own sex was a badly kept secret. It was time to cut the tie. Her refusal to consider divorce no longer meant anything, in view of her lesbian preferences. He could merely threaten to allow the fact to be known to ensure her agreement.

He collected a whisky from the tray on the sideboard, then sat and contemplated his future. James Haddon came in. He stopped when he saw Sir Tony.

Tony said, "James, isn't it? would you like a drink?"

"Th-thanks, a gin and tonic please, for my wife."

"What about yourself?" Tony asked as he poured the gin into a tall glass.

"Perhaps a small brandy." James said diffidently.

The door opened once more as Robert came in. "Hello all." He said cheerfully, "Am I in time for a snifter?"

Robert was sipping his whisky when Mary came through to tell them dinner would be ready in half an hour. "Just finish your drinks." She said, "Sir Tony picked the wine. So you'll not need to bring them through." She left, leaving the faint tantalising smell of the game pie which was the basis of the menu for the evening.

James went to fetch Molly. And when she joined them, to Tony's surprise the conversation was lively. The entire group was laughing together when dinner was called.

***

Three miles away in the 'Lamb' in Feltham the four people sat around a table in the crowded bar enjoying a relaxed meal together. The ladies departed to the restroom together, making their way through the good-natured crowd.

Quin turned to Charlie when the Cass and Sheila left. "So what's happening?"

Charlie looked at him surprised. "What?"

"Jill, Sheila, what is going on?"

Charlie smiled. "Sorry. You didn't realize about Jill and me. We had a thing on the boat but we never really expected or intended it as more than that. We both realized there was no romantic future for us. We are friends and a team. I think we always will be, but, no more than that. She knows that I have a thing for Sheila, and I reckon Sheila has a thing for me. We'll see how it develops." He sat back and looked at the crowd milling around the popular bar. "They have no idea what goes on under the surface. I sometimes think it's like living in a goldfish bowl. We are in our world and they are in theirs."

Quin grinned. "How many drinks have you had, Charlie?"

Embarrassed, Charlie smiled and shrugged. The ladies returned and saved him from having to reply.

***

Back in the retreat, Cass spoke to Quin. "Did Charlie tell you?"

"About Sheila, Jill, and himself? Yes, he did mention it."

"It never occurred to me, I suppose, because they have always been so in tune." Cass said thoughtfully.

"I think they still are, on a working level. Charlie said they are still friends and, as far as he knows, they always will be. Apparently they realized that friendship was the bond between them some time ago. It seems that Sheila's arrival confirmed what they already knew.

He turned to Cass. "If that is what you have in mind?" He hesitated and found himself enveloped in Cass's arms facing her eye to eye.

"No chance! We made a deal. No second thoughts, no diversions, us for life."

Quin smiled and hugged her. "You are sure? No doubts?"

"Beast! Don't you dare even think about it!" He stopped her talking with a kiss, and switched off the light.

Chapter nineteen

Time to kill.

Grovich was angry. It wasn't an unusual thing to happen. But nevertheless, the others in the house, being aware of the mood, walked quietly and avoided any unnecessary contact.

It was as if the beautiful house was holding its breath,

Sitting at his desk, simmering was probably the best way to describe it. Thinking to himself, *Why me? Why am I surrounded by incompetent idiots?*

The man who had interfered with the attack last night was just a bloody lawyer, on his way home with the shopping. He gave Pavel a concussion with a tin of garden peas, and broke Klaus's cheekbone with another tin of some unspecified food. "Why does my fate rest on a can-wielding lawyer? Why me?" He said aloud.

He picked up the telephone and punched in a number. "Avo! Where are you? I have tried all your local numbers and nobody is there."

"Hello, Anton. I just came home to sort out some local business. There has been some activity here while I was away. That Latvian bastard Horvach has been trying to take over the milk-run to Finland. Not any more, though," He chuckled, "An explosive encounter with his new Ferrari changed his image, and widened his coverage." Again, the laugh. "But he spread himself too thin this time." The laughter bellowed down the line.

Anton Grovich laughed dutifully, thinking, *crude bastard*, though he kept his thoughts to himself.

"We need you back here," Anton said. "I was going to punish Sir Anthony and that stuck-up bitch, LeBec. I have however decided to forget them and get on with business. My problem at the moment is that Hannah Curtain seems to have dropped out of sight. I need some specialists to take over the awkward subjects. Can I count on you?"

"Always, Anton. Are we not like brothers you and I? My men are at your disposal as always. I found a few more recruits to give us a little more muscle where we need it. They are all ex-guards from a Stasi prison camp in Prussia. All countrymen of mine I am happy to say. I will be with you by tonight. I bring the 737 today as I have too many for the Lear jet."

"Great, my friend. It will be good to see you since I am surrounded by idiots here. I will have a car to meet you, and a coach for your team to take them direct to the guest house. You come to London City, or Heathrow?"

"It will be City. I have a cargo for the plane to bring back which is in a warehouse in Aldgate. Just between us, I picked up the 1922 Bugatti last month and have not got round to shipping it home. The 737 can manage, so that is good for me."

Grovich was not interested in what he regarded as a juvenile hobby which his associate went ridiculous lengths to satisfy. But he made the right noises and closed off the conversation as soon as he could."

Still irritated, but in a slightly better mood, he called his secretary in. "Get the Board of WOAD together. We need to see where we stand at the moment."

"What about the Chairman and Ms LeBec?" She asked.

"What about them? They are on the Board. Are they not? If they come, they come. If they don't, that will be up to the rest of the Board to decide." With this gruff but non-violent answer, she had to be content. Neither he nor the rest of the Board had informed the charity committee that Sir Tony and Sheila had resigned. No letter of resignation had been received. The notices would go out as usual.

***

Hannah spoke to Jill, the call coming as she was still in the shower. She switched off the water and took her phone from the shelf above the sink.

"Yes, Hannah!"

"I'm in. When and where?"

"Where are you now?" Jill reached for the towel.

"Oxford Street." She glanced around. "Near the Circus."

"Get a taxi here. Have you had breakfast?"

"You're kidding. It's 10 am."

Jill gave the address of Gerald's apartment. "Keep an eye out for tails. I had a run in last night." She added.

She put the phone down and called to Gerald. "We have a visitor coming. Get decent before you give the old lady a shock."

"What old lady?"

Jill walked through to the bedroom still drying off. "Come on, lazybones, she'll be here in a minute."

Gerald reached out to grab her, catching the towel only as Jill let it go and reached for her clothes.

***

Hannah was at the street door while Gerald was still struggling into his pants. By the time she reached his second floor apartment he was respectable at least.

Jill answered the door, mentioning in passing, "Best call the office. We are going to need a trip to the retreat to sort out how we'll organize things. So you'll have to let them know you're not going to be there today!"

Gerald opened his mouth to protest. Then he closed it as he recalled the attack last evening. Jill was right. He would now be known and was probably vulnerable.

Hannah walked in, followed by Jill. She looked at Gerald, surprised to see him.

Jill said, "Hannah, meet Gerald. He joined me in the scuffle last night. Smashed a can of beans over one man's head, and knocked another out with a second can."

Gerald grinned, "I'm now the 'can do' man, or something like that. How do you do, Hannah? Coffee?"

She shook his extended hand. "Hello, Gerald. Yes, please. Black, no sugar."

Gerald went through to the kitchen for the coffee, leaving the two women alone.

Hannah looked at Jill. "I thought that you and Charlie? Have I got the name right?"

Jill grinned. "Yes. Charlie and I were partners but we both realized we were more friends than otherwise, though as working partners we are still good. Gerald just happened. Right place, right time, I suppose. Don't be fooled by the lawyer look. He is fast, and, I believe, lethal."

Hannah shrugged. "Whatever pushes your boat out. I've been too busy to bother much lately. So when do I get to meet the rest of the team?"

"Not all of them for some time. Two are in Brussels at the moment, But the boss man soon enough. I think he and Cass and maybe Charlie and the others will get together later today. We'll have a formal briefing then."

Gerald came in with the coffee for them all and a plate of shortbread. "Here we are. Relax and help yourselves. He picked up the pot and poured for them all, passed the sugar to the two women and took cream for himself. "What is the plan for today? More Russian bashing or chill-out at Madam Tussauds?"

Hannah looked puzzled, "Madam Tussauds?"

"It's the wax museum on Marylebone Road, a few minutes' walk from here. It seems Gerald goes there when he wishes to avoid people and have a little time to himself."

Gerald commented. "Hey. Remember I'm here while you are talking about me. Before you go any further, I do use the Planetarium. It has a parade of stars and galaxies, and is of course, kept fairly dark for obvious reasons. It allows me to think about matters in isolation.

So what is the program? I presume with Hannah here that her business has been concluded to her satisfaction."

"It has!"

The succinct reply closed the subject.

"Where does the Russian stay in London? Does he have a house here?" Gerald was just curious.

Hannah answered. "He has a house everywhere. A man like Grovich always likes to know he is secure. With his wealth he has no problem. There is a place set aside wherever he goes, staffed by his pet goons. When he comes to London he stays near Regent's Park, an apartment in one of those houses that overlook the park.

Gerald looked at the two women. "Does he know you are here? Or even where here is?"

Jill said, "Unless he knows who you are, probably no. But if he is aware of your identity, we should be moving on." Hannah looked out of the window carefully, peering from behind the curtains without exposing herself to view. "Black BMW, 60 reg." She said succinctly, parked on a yellow line.

"Sounds interesting. They looked at each other and Gerald went to pack a bag. "Are you armed?" He called.

Hannah smiled grimly. "Just a knife, "she said. "I left my gun at home."

Jill just shook her head.

Gerald tapped a part of the wall behind the bedroom door. A piece of the skirting popped out. He reached in and pulled out an oilskin bag. From it he produced a pair of Walther PPK's and the Browning .45 obtained the night before. He checked the magazine from the Browning, popping out the cartridges remaining in the magazine. "Only eight bullets here!" He said passing the gun to Hannah. There were full magazines for both Walthers, and a spare. "If it's not enough for now, we're in real trouble."

He finished packing his bag and slipped one of the Walthers into his waistband. He gave Jill the other. "Now we take the elevator to the garage. The Range Rover is not mine, but I have the keys. We use it. Jill, drive without the wig and we," he indicated Hannah and himself, "Lie low until we are clear." He looked at the two women. He spoke quietly. Both nodded without comment, allowing him to assume command without questions.

In the underground car park beneath the apartment block there were several cars scattered about the area. Gerald's own Jaguar was near the elevator doors, but he ignored it in favor of the big grey Range Rover standing on the far side of the area. He pressed the key to unlock it. The engine started throbbing quietly. They hurried across to the vehicle. Jill took the driving seat. Gerald pointed out the remote for the metal drop door at the exit. She locked in her seat belt, checked that both were hidden in the rear of the vehicle, and drove off.

***

There was an air of quiet confidence at the meeting in the retreat later that day. Appropriately, the group sat around the table in what had been intended to be the conference room. The chairs were leather covered and roomy enough to confirm that this bunker had been intended for higher echelon survivors. The lighting, by modern standards, was rather basic. The fluorescent tubes were shaded to reduce the glare they would otherwise have given off. The center of the long table was occupied by tea and coffee pots and the group was able to help themselves. James and his wife, with Robert and Mary, the housekeeper, were not present by their own choice. They were happy to leave the planning to the others.

Sir Anthony had taken the seat at the end of the table and, from there, was contemplating the group around him. "Before we start, I would just like to say that without you all, Sheila and I would probably not be here. I certainly had no problem in working things out. The Russian had us targeted and, if hadn't been for you people, we would have been dead the day we flew in from Brussels." He paused and then continued. "I guess that this meeting is all about what we are going to do about Anton Grovich. So, before we go any further, I would like to make a suggestion. Both Sheila and I are very wealthy. We are aware of the fact that we will be targets for Grovich's men. Neither of us can afford to be cut off for too long from our businesses. So I would like to offer myself as a 'Stalking Horse', hopefully to concentrate Grovich's men on me so that you can identify and neutralize them. I have things to do, arrangements to make. With the confidence that you're presence gives me, I can accomplish them, and at the same time help give Grovich a bloody nose!"

Sheila looked around the group. "I have an idea of the situation that Tony is facing. In my own case things are not quite so critical. This business has confirmed the decision I had already made. I have already made more money than I ever imagined. It means that whatever this group decides or wishes to accomplish, I can—and—will fund." There were tears in her eyes as she continued. "During the past few weeks I have been seeking the people who carried the various chips, like Andrew, and Robert, without the knowledge that Anton was prepared to kill for them. I was also unaware of the exact nature of the technology we sought. Only that it was virtually priceless. I started to get seriously uneasy when the Russian had the man we mistakenly identified, killed. At first I accepted that it was an accident, but realized when I got the full story that it was murder. Anton had him killed deliberately."

She turned and looked around the table. "You put your lives on the line for me, knowing nothing about me. I will also step forward into public view. I have bills to settle and business to wind-up. Tony and I have already decided to ensure the family of the murdered man is looked after." She looked at Gerald. "I believe Tony has already talked to you about that?"

Gerald looked up from the pad in front of him. "My office is working on the arrangements already." He added, "I have also commenced the procedure for setting up a company to permit us to operate, and finance, operations out of the public eye. Because it must be legitimate, it must be seen to be profitable. It needs also to be international. I have come up with a suggestion which I think will be the answer."

Quin raised his head and spoke for the first time. "If Tony is going to stick his head up, we need to make arrangements to cover him. So I suggest, if Hannah is willing," he nodded at Hannah, "I will ask her to become Tony's PA for the present, as the most skilled operative present. I know how difficult the job can be. Charlie, it seems you will be needed to become PA to Sheila, providing that is agreeable to you both. For the rest of us, Jill and Gerald, mutual protection, and Cass and I to cover any and all other situations. I stress that for the foreseeable future, it will be necessary for us all to be available at all times, to back each other up."

Cass added, "In the case of Tony and Sheila, I would like to suggest they work as closely together as possible. As targets it will concentrate the enemy resources and make it easier for us to identify and neutralize them."

The group around the table looked around at each other, adjusting their minds to the concept of the forthcoming offensive.

Quin looked at Cass and smiled. She smiled back, aware that he had been fretting at being forced to sit back and allow things to happen, reacting rather than initiating. It must have been as galling for him as it had been for her. She shifted in her chair, aware of the Walther in her waistband. Quin had insisted on all of them being armed at all times, until the present situation had been resolved. She squeezed Quin's hand. It seemed to her that the situation for them personally was never really going to change. Some people seem to attract trouble without trying. Her husband, Quin, was one of those people. She decided that she would not have things any other way.

Hannah was puzzled at her own reaction to the briefing and allocation of tasks which had just taken place. Accustomed to working alone, she had always in the past discouraged cooperation with others. Maybe she was getting old. Perhaps she was losing her edge? As she sat there quietly examining her feelings amid the chatter of friendly conversation, she realized that the entire group were of one mind, and more important, common purpose. They were a team which included Hannah Curtain, assassin-extraordinaire, and she felt part of it. It was something that she had never really felt in the Israeli army. Trained as a specialist even when she had led a squad, she had had no compunction at abandoning them. She looked at Sir Tony thoughtfully.

Sir Anthony Merrick was confused. Now he was wondering what he had let himself in for. His offer was a reaction to the way the group had, over the past three days, rearranged itself into pairs.

His idea had been to make a noble sacrifice, employ a team of bodyguards, and go back to work. This vision of self-sacrifice had dominated his thoughts and he hadn't thought beyond that point. He looked at Hannah Curtain. She was looking at him. They sat and looked at each other for some time. Then Hannah nodded slightly and turned her gaze elsewhere. Tony started, tensing as they broke eye contact. Then he relaxed reassured. It would be alright. She had accepted him, and her role in keeping him alive.

When the meeting broke up Hannah sought Sir Tony out. "Sir Tony! Can I have a word?" She smiled wryly. "We are now, I presume, partners."

Tony smiled back at her. "Since you put it that way, yes we are. Before we go any further I would like to make it clear that it is Tony or Anthony. The 'Sir' is for occasions and employees. Between friends, it does not exist."

"You hardly know me, Tony."

"Ah, superficially that is true. Though I should point out, in this company you are accepted, without query, on your own word. I feel therefore that I know you well, and I hope to know you even better over the next few days." He held his hand out to her. "I am pleased to meet you, Ms Curtain."

Disconcerted for a moment Hannah reacted quickly, taking the extended hand. "Please call me Hannah. I am pleased to meet you, Tony."

Tony felt the slim hand in his, the skin hardened in places, a practical working hand with a firm grip, a dependable hand. He was convinced that he had judged her correctly. "Tell me about yourself." He said as they walked through to the lounge to have a drink prior to dinner.

Gerald was wondering how he had got himself into this situation. Of course, he had not actually done anything. The situation had developed around him and he had merely reacted. Being honest with himself, if the same circumstances had arisen before he would have done the same thing, acted the same way and been in the same situation, without a team around him.

With a bunch like this, things seemed a lot less likely to go wrong. Provided he kept his cool and a firm grip on Jill, he should manage. At the thought of Jill he felt a warm glow that he was not accustomed to. It had been a long time since he had been this close to someone. He reminded himself not to get too carried away. Things did not always work out the way they do in Mills and Boone stories. He looked across the room where Jill was laughing at a comment made by Robert, who had joined the party in the lounge after the meeting. He had a feeling that this time it might.

***

The morning after was fine and dry, sky blue and just enough breeze to make it worthwhile wearing a light coat. Sir Tony and Sheila shared the Rolls, with Hannah and Charlie. All were dressed in business clothes. Gerald and Jill had departed by the underground for his office in Bentinck Street. They had discussed sharing the Rolls but decided that arriving thus at the office would draw attention to the connection with the others. Although the Russian was probably aware by now, they decided that there was no point in making it obvious. At the office there was no apparent sign of watchers. Gerald introduced Jill to his colleagues and staff. If they were surprised they were too well mannered to say so. The fact that Jill seemed completely at ease with the office computer and could touch type at speed made a difference during her first day at the office. They kept in touch with Tony and Sheila during the day.

Sheila found the advice of the Board meeting on her iPad at her office when she arrived. She contacted Sir Anthony to find that he also was advised of the same meeting. He suggested that the Russian had failed to tell the administrator that Sheila and he had resigned at the last meeting. Called for by head office of the Charity after lunch, she agreed with the Chairman that they would both attend.

It was Sheila who passed the news along to Cass at the retreat. Hearing this, Quin told Jill to remain with Gerald and sent Cass to join Charlie in keeping Sheila company. Quin came to town himself, joining Hannah and Sir Tony. He was concerned at the apparent change of attitude by Grovich.

***

At the meeting the Board members gathered warily. The only member absent was Father Aldo. The secretary reported that he had suffered a rather tragic accident, apparently he had fallen in the path of a Central line train as it entered the station at Marble Arch. In the terms of their agreement the investment made by Father Aldo was forfeit to the charity.

Sir Anthony Merrick and Sheila LeBec retired from the Board formally, both willing to forfeit their initial investment. Though Sheila mentioned afterwards, her biggest shock was at the attitude of Grovich who, while not friendly, was polite for the entire period of their presence at the meeting. Sir Anthony made a point of speaking to the charity administrator, whose office was in the building, but who did not sit on the Board. He informed her that he was still available for assistance, however not through the current Board.

With that cryptic statement he left the building with Hannah and followed by Quin they went to meet with Sheila at the Grosvenor House. Hannah informed him en-route that they had acquired a tail.

"I am relieved about that," Sir Tony observed. "To be blunt, I found it quite unnerving, dealing with Grovich when he is being so polite and reasonable." He considered for a few moments as the Rolls drifted to a stop outside the Hotel. "Tell me, Hannah. Would it be possible to send a message to the Russian through his minion, so to speak?"

Hannah looked at Sir Tony, surprised. "Why, sir. You do continue to surprise me. Of course it would be a straightforward task. I suggest, to simplify matters I will have a few words with Cassandra. She will also have a shadow. Between us I am sure we will come up with something inventive.

Chapter twenty

Games

The two followers did not know how it happened. One minute they were quietly obeying orders, observing the movement of their targets and waiting for the phone call to remove them. Grovich had made it clear to both of them. They were not to attempt to remove either target until he gave them specific instructions. Karpov had worked with Grovich for several years now, from the time when both had been operatives with KGB. He would carry out the order to the letter. It was the reason he had survived so long in Grovich's employ. That, and the fact that he knew things that no-one else knew. He had them in writing and lodged where no one else could get at them. If he died, Grovich died.

Baron, the other follower, had difficulty reading and writing, but he could strip an AK47 and re-assemble it inside a minute. Importantly, what he aimed at, he hit. It meant that if you wound him up you could set him off and forget him. When he returned the job would be done. At least that is what had happened so far. This, Karpov thought, was where reputation met hard cold fact.

The floor where the two men lay tied was cold and rough. It felt like concrete, a workshop perhaps or a garage floor?

The two lay on the floor of the store room in the underground car park below Gerald's old apartment. There was nothing to use there to assist an escape. The little room was lit through a high level window. Such light as there was filtered through the tufts of ground level grass obscuring the dirty narrow panes. On the other side of the window there was only an area of broken concrete with oil stains in a small yard which once had been the hard standing for the householder's car. Both car and house had been gone now for several years. The yard was now a small forgotten area, occupied by birds, litter, and the odd prowling cat. The room itself no longer held the bench once used as a work table by the janitor of the building. Now administered by the janitor of the next block, the room had been cleared for use as a store. But when the janitor was no longer required, it had been forgotten about. Gerald had been given the key to store some of his things when he moved in. When he left to come to his present address the key had come with him.

Hannah had suggested they eliminate the followers, but had compromised when the alternative plan was proposed and the key produced.

Hannah kept her own council on the subject, but she suspected they had not heard the last of Karpov and his companion.

***

Grovich, having dismissed the problem of the two directors from his immediate consideration, had already moved on with WOAD. He was now the Chairman and the de-facto voice of the organization; the other directors being more concerned with the money they were making than the ethics of the way they were making it.

The loss of Father Aldo had resulted in the need to reorganize the enforcement section, to make up for missing the close Mafia association they had enjoyed during the lifetime of the Reverend Father. There were still the business contacts revolving around the provision of drugs, and the protection of assets. But the personal touch linked to Father Aldo's interests was now missing.

Looking around the table, the Russian was thinking that, with the exception of Marcus Warren, he had just about the most criminal bunch of greedy individualists in the world under his thumb. Marcus Warren disturbed him. Up to now he had hidden in the shadow of the more antagonistic Sheila LeBec and her friend, Sir Anthony Bloody Merrick. Both had only entered his past operations with conditions that, in essence, diluted his efforts at major gains. It now remained to be seen if Marcus Warren tried the same tactics now they were no longer here.

***

Sheila LeBec was confused. Her new association with Charlie Smith was exhilarating and frightening. Always so controlled in the past, she felt as if somehow the brakes had been loosened and she was free to race where she formerly strolled. Previously when she had been with others she had dictated the pace, controlled the direction of her life. Now she was unsure, and it frightened her and excited her at the same time.

Sitting in her office, considering where her future lay just made things more confused. When the telephone rang and Sir Anthony was announced, she greeted him with relief as a diversion from her private thoughts, curious at his call. Up to now their only business connection had been WOAD.

"Well, Tony. What brings you here?" She smiled in welcome, to take the edge off her comment. "Can I offer you coffee or a drink?"

He was looking a little used, she thought.

"Both, please. Whisky followed by coffee." He sat down in a guest chair with a sigh.

Sheila called for the coffee and went to the bar in what she thought of as the social side of the office, and poured a generous measure of Black Label into a crystal tumbler. Passing it to him, she poured a gin and tonic for herself and joined him.

Noticing his mood she waited for him to speak.

"Sheila, I know we have only been acquainted for the months that we shared on the Board of WOAD, but over that time I like to think we became friends. I am here today on that basis. I have no business to discuss, but I do not have anyone close to confide in..."

Sheila sat back wondering what was coming.

"I, I've left Marion!"

Sheila smiled. "About time too."

Tony looked up, surprised at her reaction, immediate and positive. "She said she had been considering divorce herself. She had decided that she was not really into the man-woman bit. She had a lady friend who made her happier than she had ever been. Sheila, she thanked me for my forbearance, and said, for a man, I had always shown consideration for her moods. Now she knew why she had always been unhappy." He sat back and finished his drink.

A knock at the door and Charlie appeared., "Coffee coming up." He stood aside as the office girl brought in coffee pot, cups and a plate of biscuits.

Charlie and the girl disappeared. Sheila passed over coffee to Tony. "Another drink?" She asked.

"Please!" Tony smiled and sat back. "She is a different person," he said. "And I am now feeling as if I have woken to a new life. She said if I wanted a divorce I could have one. She would not contest it. But, if I was happy to leave things the way they are, she would play her part in public, provided her partner could move in with us. Of course the same rules would apply for me. What do you think?"

"Tony! Why me? I accept we are friends, but I ..."

He interrupted her, "Sheila, I respect your opinion above most others. You and I have survived a near death experience.

Just let me know what do you think? What is your immediate reaction?"

"Go for it. Give it time. If it gets tricky, reconsider at that time. What can you lose?"

"Thank you, Sheila. Now..."

She stopped him. "Stand up. Take off your coat." He stood up and removed his overcoat. Sheila took it and placed it on the coat-stand. "Now, finish your coffee. We will move over to the desk. If as I suspect you wish to talk business that is the place for it."

At the desk Tony leaned forward and spoke earnestly on the subject of Grovich. "I cannot see myself having a chance to take advantage of the new life I am offered, with that man looking over my shoulder. I would seriously like to do anything positive I can to get him out of my/our lives."

"Agreed! Any suggestion?"

Tony sat back in his chair. "WOAD!" He said. "It is an international charity. He is using it as a channel to move arms and drugs around the world. If we can link Grovich with that traffic, we can ruin him."

"True." Sheila said slowly, "But it will not remove him as a threat. He will likely find out that we have had something to do with the disclosure. Also, I suspect any threat to us is purely in abeyance at the moment. When he gets round to it, I think we will both become targets once more."

"We have nothing to lose. We are buzzard bait either way, if he lives. So let us destroy him."

Sir Tony's normal mild, good-humoured face was hard and unforgiving as he spoke. The recent events had had their effect. Tony Merrick was out for blood.

Sheila noted the look and the words. She was in agreement with his sentiments. Nodding slowly, she said, "Right. do we start?"

"We tell Quin and Cass what we have in mind, so that we don't cross lines between us. They also may have suggestions to make about where we start."

"I'm a businessman. Grovich has ploughed his way through so many people he has more enemies than Al Qaida. If we both get started on a list we can compare notes later, and see what we can come up with to destroy his business."

Sheila thought of an idea she had come up with. "What about rivals in the criminal world? It's my impression that he will have more enemies there than in law enforcement."

Sir Tony grinned wolfishly. "Yes, I believe that." He called through the intercom. "Hannah! Could you join us please?"

Hannah came in, eyes everywhere looking for possible threats. "You called?"

Tony nodded to Sheila who turned to Hannah. "Grovich must have stepped on a few toes in his upward progress through the criminal world. I'm sure his present position is not due to legitimate business practices. There must be plenty of rivals he has overcome in his history."

"You are asking if I know any of these people." She looked at Sheila enquiringly.

"I do not want to spend what life I have left looking over my shoulder." Sheila explained. "I want to find a way of removing that threat. Sir Tony is looking at the business end of things, I am looking at a possible permanent solution."

"Then we must go and speak with Quin and Cass, I think." Hannah said firmly. "I will call now." She took her cell phone and speed dialled Quin. "Quin, I am with Sir Tony and Sheila. We need to talk!"

Quin got the message. Hannah would not have phoned if it had not been serious. "Gerald and Jill are on the way to the retreat. Cass has been shadowing Charlie. I'll call her now and set things up there."

Hannah looked at the others and mimed 'now'. Both nodded. "We'll be there by lunchtime!" Quin let Cass know, and she called Mary. "We have a full house for lunch. Can you cope?"

"Of course!" The rather sharp reply made her smile. Mary could always cope. It was what she did.

***

Quin reached Cass, who was across the street from Sheila's office. She was still talking on the phone when he arrived. As his arm slid round her waist she murmured, "Are you ready?" Warm lips kissed her ear. "For you, I am always ready."

She laughed and removed his hand. "Right place, wrong time," She said. "Hannah was serious."

Quin sighed. "I'll make sure we have all the current information in place. I was just running through an idea I had for interference in the drug movements through Europe. I'll update with Ian and Naomie."

He turned and led her to the Jaguar which he had left ready to take them both back to the retreat.

***

Once there, he called Ian Bennet in Brussels. Naomie answered. "Ian is out at the moment. Can I help?"

Quin thought for a second then said, "What is going on at the moment? Can you update me?"

Naomie realized that Quin was serious so she said slowly. "There is a lot of activity in the border control sections here. The lobby for tighter regulation is being swamped with requests for the relaxation of rules. Ian is worried that this is the mob trying to ease the situation for the drug distributors. He thinks that, at present, Grovich has been benefiting from the tight regulation, the charity operation giving him an advantage over the more traditional methods of smuggling." She stopped and took a breath. "How am I doing?" She laughed a little nervously.

"Is that your assessment?" Quin asked slowly.

"I'm spending time putting things together. Ian says it helps him see things he might otherwise miss." Naomie stopped.

Quin realized that Naomie was a natural. She had encapsulated the situation he had been vaguely trying to get a fist on for the past few days.

"Naomie, can you bring Ian over here for a stay of at least a month? Is that possible?"

"Why? I suppose so. Is it important?"

"It's important!"

"How soon?"

"Today, if possible. We have a meeting at lunchtime today, but the group will probably stay overnight which give us a chance to get the complete group together. I would like your input from that meeting."

Not quite sure what that meant, Naomie rang off and called Ian on his cell phone.

By midday they were both on the shuttle. When they turned up at the retreat that afternoon, the others were all present to greet them.

***

The group assembled for official discussions the following morning.

Quin opened the meeting. "As we started to discuss yesterday, our efforts are now going to take the war to the enemy. Grovich is the target, and we intend to bring him down, remove him as a threat to our future lives. I've asked Naomie and Ian to join us because there will obviously be more than one target for our offensive. We have isolated two points we think will be vulnerable: smuggling and business. I am going to run through our findings quickly to give Ian and Naomie a chance to get completely up to date. I realize that during last evening you have all been chatting, but for the record…" He then did a run down on the discussions that had been going on the previous day.

There was a general murmur of conversation, then Cass interrupted. "Naomie, you have been elsewhere when a lot has been happening. What is your take on the current situation?"

The group stopped talking and Naomie became the center of attention. While she was aware that this might happen it was still embarrassing. She had to gather herself to take the floor in front of this assembly. Ian squeezed her hand. She began slowly at first, then out came her thoughts on the situation. As Quin had guessed, she had assessed and sorted all the factors under discussion. Without a note or aide-memoir she clearly and succinctly laid out her take on everything discussed, there was a silence as she finished.

She was disconcerted for a moment, until she realized that the people round the table were digesting what she had said.

Quin stood and said, "Thank you, Naomie. You have just demonstrated why I wanted you here for the duration of this operation."

Still a little overcome by the acceptance of what she regarded as an everyday function and they seemed to think was special, Naomie was happy to feel Ian's arm round her, reassuring her that things were fine. She decided that perhaps she might re-marry after all, despite it being to another man in a hazardous occupation.

With Hannah's help, Ian and Quin worked up a list of possible criminal allies in the battle to reduce Grovich's empire. At Hannah's suggestion they gave her the task of contacting the first, most likely subject.

The group had discussed the business aspect of Grovich's operations. Though Sheila and Sir Anthony were aware of some of the contacts Grovich had, it was obvious deeper penetration into his affairs would be needed before and real impact could be made.

Gerald had surprised everyone. "Please, I have an idea based on the location of his London office. I need time to research, but if I am correct it could put a real spanner in the works for his company."

Quin looked at the others. Sheila shrugged. Tony nodded. Gerald had already proved himself as far as the group was concerned. So the matter had been left with Gerald.

***

Italy 2009

In the north of Italy, Angelo Petrucci had been a hard working plumber until he had encountered Strotzi. He thought afterwards that it was fate which had thrown them together. He had a nice little business in Chivasso, north of Turin. The surrounding country was a delight for him to cover in his van. His wife and daughter, in a comfortable small house beside his workshop, had enough to keep them comfortable. They were his anchor in the ever more complex world he lived in.

Strotzi was Albanian/Macedonian, something like that. Angelo never found out, and never really wanted to. His clash with the man ended in disaster, costing him his wife, daughter and business. It turned Angelo into the man he was to be.

Angelo's workshop was coveted by Strotzi. As a small time villain, Strotzi was ambitious. He intended growing, becoming 'the man' in the region, in the whole of Italy perhaps. Strotzi had approached Angelo to sell him his workshop. That is to say he told Angelo that he would be needing it and to move out.

Not surprisingly, Angelo made a rude suggestion about Strotzi's parentage. These communications were all conducted over the telephone.

Whilst Angelo was on the other side of the valley the day following the conversation Strotzi moved in. When Maria Petrucci protested he, personally, slapped her round the head with the crowbar he had used to open the workshop. Her twelve year old daughter flung herself to assist her mother, Strotzi hit her on the backswing. Even Strotzi's right hand man was shocked. Strotzi commented, "Stupid peasants. Throw them in the house and torch it. I only need the workshop."

When Angelo returned to the village, his house was gone. His wife and daughter were gone also. His workshop was tenanted by a bunch of thugs who barred the way, and just shrugged when he asked about his house and the family.

A neighbor took Angelo in and told him about Strotzi, But they knew nothing of Maria, or Francesca, his daughter. The fire had been fierce and sudden. The fire service suggested there were solvents involved. They discovered the remains of two people in the ruins the following day.

Angelo caught Strotzi at the workshop. "What happened? Why are you here?"

Strotzi shrugged, and lied. "I gave the woman money to occupy this building. She was in the house when the fire happened. We could do nothing."

"You lie!" Angelo said through gritted teeth. My wife would not deal with you, I think you just moved in and burned my house. Did you kill them first?"

Two of Strotzi's men grabbed him as he raised his fist to hit Strotzi. Strotzi picked up a piece of timber and hit him again and again. The men threw the unconscious man into the ditch beside the road. Probably, they thought he was dead.

Angelo managed to crawl into the back of his parked van. There was water and food there. He had been going to stay in the van after losing his home.

It took three weeks for him to recover from the beating he had received. Strotzi heard that he was still alive. His comment was, "So what. If he comes back, I'll finish the job."

Angelo met Strotzi at the door of the workshop. He carried an automatic shotgun in his hands. He didn't argue or explain. He shot Strotzi, knocking him flat on his back. Strotzi got back on his feet, Angelo realized that Strotzi was wearing a bullet-proof vest. He was also pulling an automatic from his belt. So Angelo shot him in the groin. Strotzi screamed and doubled over clutching at his ruined body. He lay there, grovelling on the ground. None of his men came to help him. Angelo walked into the workshop, gun-up ready for trouble. The men and women who had been inside were all gone. The room was stacked with packets all down one wall. There was a safe behind the door, with the door unlocked. A row of weapons stood against the other wall, M16 Carbines, AK47 Semi-automatic rifles, and a box of automatic pistols. He stood there, bewildered.

When Sabine walked in he was still there, head in his hands, sobbing for his lost wife and daughter. Sabine was Maria's sister, a widow from Naples. She had only just arrived, and heard about the tragedy. "Who is the man outside?" Sabine asked.

Angelo looked up not realizing she was there. "Who are you?" He said, "If you are one of Strotzi's people you had better leave."

"You are Angelo Petrucci, my sister's man?"

"Sabine, is that you?" He peered up at her, only knowing her from photographs. Sabine had left the village to become an actress. The scandal had ensured that she would not return. Maria had kept in touch, despite the family disapproval.

"I'm just in time from the look of it. Come. Get that mess inside now before anyone else comes."

She dragged him to his feet. "Hurry!" She urged, pushing him to the open door. "Drag him in here. Strotzi was still alive at that time, sobbing and holding his body together.

Between them, they got him inside, out of sight. Ignoring the patch of blood outside Sabine dragged the door shut. She then started looking around in the building. "Find something that will burn, maybe explode!" She was all efficiency.

Angelo had recovered and, responding to her decisiveness, started searching the place. There was wrapping piled at one end of the building. At the weapon rack there were packets of C4 US army explosives. Sabine found fuses in a separate drawer. Pulling out one of the wrapping bags she stuffed it with the money from the safe without counting it. She filled the bag. The stack of packages were labelled 'H', 'C', and 'CC'.

What's this?" Angelo wondered.

"Where did you grow up? Sabine asked, then, "Never mind. Heroin, Cocaine, and possibly Crack Cocaine. Let's not bother about that. This is where we take the money and run."

He looked at her blankly?

Sabine took his hand and grabbed the bag in the other.

Poking her head out of the door she checked the coast was clear, and pulled him out.

"Where is your car?

Angelo pointed at the van, standing by the entrance to the workshop area.

"Go. Put this inside and start the engine. I will join you in a minute. Wait for me!"

Angelo nodded took the bag and walked to the van.

Sabine re-entered the workshop. Taking a fuse she inserted it into one of the C4 blocks. She snapped the fuse, turned and ran, slamming the door behind her. She ignored the man still groaning on the floor. The van was rolling down the street when the explosion came.

It was several months before Angelo discovered that Strotzi had been acting for a man called Grovich.

Chapter twenty-one

Reprisals

The French Riviera 2014

Angelo was actually, by now, a coming man in the criminal world of the Riviera, having crossed from Italy the same day the workshop blew up.

Hannah Curtain dropped in to the apartment in Beausoleil at 11am. She faced the camera and held up her Glock automatic before placing it on the mailbox at the door. "Good morning, Angelo. Ca va? I come in peace."

The speaker box squeaked, "Hannah, what a pleasant surprise. Please keep the weapon. We are friends here. The door for you is always open." The click and buzz as the door unlocked followed the comment. Hannah entered the small hallway of the rather ordinary flat. Nice but not opulent, comfort understated. Hannah liked it and wondered who had come into Angelo's life since she had last seen him. A door opened and she was engulfed in a warm embrace.

Angelo had kept himself trim, despite his unquestioned affluence garnered from the various enterprises he controlled.

"Sit, sit!" He indicated the chair opposite the seat he apparently occupied, a large chair which was set amid a semicircle of small tables, that each appeared to be overflowing with newspapers.

Hannah sat, commenting, "Still thirsting for news, I see."

Angelo shrugged, "I like to keep up to date with the world," he said casually.

A woman entered the room, small, trim, dark hair and a smile that seemed to light up the room. "Angelo, introduce me to your guest."

"Hannah, this is my friend, Sabine Rosetti. Cara, this is Hannah Curtain, an old friend.

Hannah rose to her feet to touch cheeks with Sabine.

"You will have coffee?" Sabine waited while Hannah nodded.

"I will fetch." Sabine left the room and Hannah sat down once more.

She looked at Angelo and with a mock sigh said, "So, Angelo. I am no longer the object of your affections."

Angelo laughed. "Hannah, you will always occupy a place in my heart. I do not forget friends, but a man must live."

Hannah smiled. "She is charming."

"Of course, would you expect less of me? She is my sister-in-law. When Maria died she saved my life and was responsible for setting up here in France. She was a widow and me…? Tell me, Hannah. How are you? The word is that you have stepped out of the market and are working with friends?"

Hannah thought for a moment, considering. Then she nodded, "News travels fast. I suppose that does rather sum it up. Friends!"

Angelo leaned forward and took her hands in his. "Hannah, Cara I am happy for you. Your life was looking a little crazy to me and your other friends. Working alone like that was, I think, a one way ticket. So what is it that has brought you to see Angelo? Do you need money, shelter? What I have is yours."

"What is this, Angelo? Are you giving away our beautiful home? Just as we have it the way we want it?" Sabine came through the door with a tray of coffee , cups, and pastries. The smile on her face took any sting out of her words.

Hannah laughed. "This man of yours is too generous by far. No. He is not giving me this beautiful home and I could not deprive you of it if he was. I will explain, after I have sampled those delicious looking pastries."

Sabine left them to it, calling on her way out, "If you are staying for lunch, it will be just one hour." The door closed over her last word.

"I came to discuss a man called Grovich!"

Angelo stiffened, the humour evaporated immediately from his handsome face. "You know Grovich?"

"I know him, and I will remove him. But before I do that, my friends and I wish him to pay, to suffer for what he and his men have done to friends of mine and, I believe, many others. He has many associates in the Russian Government. We understand that he was on the books of the FSB when they took over the role of the KGB. Grovich had been a former member of the KGB.

"He is currently running the WOAD charity. His operation is trading guns and drugs under the cover of the charity. We want to stop the trade and, if possible, cause him some of the pain he has caused others. His influence is felt throughout Europe. We are after cooperation from people like yourself in stopping this man. Killing him at present is difficult. His wealth means he can surround himself with several layers of security. If we can show him failing in his business, he will lose the current backing he gets from his Russian friends and his business partners."

Angelo sat thinking for a few minutes, then, leaning forward, he said quietly, "I do not know if you are aware of the way I started in this business. A local boss decided he wanted the building I used as a store for my plumbing business. I said no. The next day I was off on the other side of the valley on a job. He moved in, taking the store over for his drugs and other stuff. My house was beside the store. My wife came out and tried to stop them throwing my stuff out into the garden. Strotzi, that was his name, hit Maria. She went down, and he hit her again and again. My daughter rushed out to help her and he hit her also. His men were shocked but scared. Strotzi told them to burn the house. My wife and daughter were both dead. When I returned the house was gone, and my family. I was told she had run away with my daughter. But the fire service found their bones in the ashes of the house.

"I was able to destroy Strotzi and his store room, though I removed his collected money before I blew the place up. I thought that was it. Then I discovered that Grovich was the man behind him. I decided then that, one day, Grovich should pay. What would you like me to do?"

"We would like to rally the others in business here to block, hi-jack and otherwise expose and interfere with his operation where his goods are brought in.

"Marseilles is the major import point. He does have a warehouse there, one at least. Whatever is there is of no concern to us. Just make his life an absolute misery. We will do the rest."

"I will be happy to help with that, too." Angelo said, "I will certainly see if we can combine here to stop the trade. That will be for Grovich, of course. I could not guarantee the trade ceasing altogether."

Hannah smiled. "I would not believe you if you did." She put her hand up. "If it were you alone I would believe it. But between the bunch you are talking about, I would guess most would join in out of self-interest. As far as I am concerned this is one of those cases where the end justified the means. So, on that basis, let's do it." She held her hands out and took both of Angelo's. "I did not know about your wife, Angelo. I am truly sorry."

"I know you mean that, Hannah. I am touched by your sympathy. I will do my best for you in this matter."

**

The meeting in Beausoleil was tense. Three of the most feared figures in the Riviera crime scene sat at the table with Angelo. Hannah was there and Quin Gilmore, facing Lorenzo Grimaldi, Francois Carriere, and Albert Chung. Grimaldi had the floor and was detailing his conditions for joining the operation. His thin lips moved minimally as he spoke, his word sibilant, the scar on his face dragging the side of his mouth down with the movement of his lips.

"I will join, but I want the action from his dope imports exclusively." His final words were hardly uttered before the other two were protesting vociferously.

Quin stood up., All three immediately reached for concealed weapons.

Hannah spoke, "Shut up. Leave the guns alone!" The icy voice cut through tension like a razor slash. It was a tribute to the reputation Hannah had earned through the preceding years that it ensured immediate silence from them all.

Quin spoke quietly and directly. "You will be promised nothing! The only thing on the table will be the free market conditions the removal of this major player will create. How you carve that up between you is your business. The main object of this meeting is the removal of a very nasty man. If you cannot settle for that, plus of course the prospect of a hole in the market as a result, then I invite you to leave this meeting here and now." He sat down.

Albert Chung had a smooth oriental face with regular, handsome features. Until you looked at the eyes and saw the dead, expressionless gaze reflecting the cold nature of the man.

He was no fool. "I will take part in this scheme if I approve the planning. Francois Carriere looked sideways at Chung and nodded. "I also. What did you have in mind?"

Quin looked at Grimaldi. With an impatient gesture Grimaldi also nodded. "Count me in," he said. Let's take a look at the suggestions.

Angelo looked around the table and specifically at Hannah. She nodded, so he reached down to the case at his side and pulled out the roll of drawings there.

***

The night was warm and the light breeze carried the scent of the docks, a mixture of tar and rotting fish, with a hint of ozone.

Jill giggled at something Charlie said. Ian said, "Knock it off, you two. It looks as if there is some activity over there." He was looking through his glasses at the dock opposite their position. The doors to the warehouse on the other dock slid open, allowing a flood of light to spill over the quay area. Several men came from the warehouse. They scattered to various positions along the quay, making ready to accept the expected ship. On their side of the water, Quin called quietly to his group. Ian, with Cass and Jill, climbed into the open land rover and started the engine. He drove off the long way to approach the other quay from a different direction. Quin, Charlie, and Hannah dropped down into the boat moored alongside their quay. All the team were dressed in combat gear, Kevlar flak jackets, and helmets with adjustable night vision glasses. All carried H&K smgs, and, hooked to their webbing, smoke and flash-bang grenades.

The ship that came in was a dark shape looming out of the shadows. Obviously navigating by satnav and using the lights of the quay for orientation, the ship drifted into position and was secured alongside. Quin and his crew were, by then, alongside, hooked on to the bow rail of the coaster.

Above his head Quin read the name, *Campeche,* with the port of registration Monrovia, Liberia, in scabbed white paint. Checking that his people were prepared, Quin swarmed up the rope tethering the boat to the ship. One by one the others joined him on the after deck. Last of all he dragged up the bag of explosives. He released the rope tying the boat to the ship The other painter had been tied to the quay. The boat drifted down the length of the rope and ended up alongside the jetty.

All the activity was happening in the area amidships and forward where the hatches were being lifted off. The men involved were concentrated on what they were doing. In the background there were armed men, carrying AK47s. Quin counted six within sight. He called Ian and let him know what he could see.

Ian called back mentioning that there were three other armed men on the other side of the warehouse. Both parties waited while the ship was unloaded, the cargo being efficiently transferred direct to trailers pulled into place one by one, three of them taking the entire contents of the ship's hold.

The loaded trailers moved off the quay and through the open doors. The hatches were covered once more and the ship prepared to sail. The bulk of the men followed the cargo into the warehouse. Quin led the team across the deck and onto the quay. The ship parted from the shore, and went astern, swinging round to head back out to sea. Three power-boats provided by Lorenzo Grimaldi, Albert Chung, and Francois Carriere waited to intercept it offshore. Hannah fired her suppressed H&K three times and three men dropped from their position as guards. Hannah muttered in a disgusted voice,

"Smoking cigarettes on guard duty, where do they get these people?"

Quin said, "Quiet! It's time to go and spoil the party." He moved forward and ran to the spot where the three trailers were being hooked up to tractors for their onward journey to Grovich's distribution storage facility. It was suspected to be in the suburb of Marseilles, just past the airport at Vitrolles. With Ian and his party in the land-rover following, Quin and company intended boarding the third truck-trailer combination. Between them they intended taking out the distribution depot completely. There was activity where the trailer rigs were linking up. Hannah and Charlie from Ian's party, slipped over to the idling trucks one and two. They carried and inserted made-up bombs among the pallets of cargo. In the confusion of men moving about and hooking up the trailers nobody really noticed them.

When the stackers and packers finished they returned to the warehouse, smoking and laughing, leaving the three drivers to sort themselves out. It was then that Quin, Hannah and Cass boarded the number three truck. The three trucks took off and Quin contacted Ian by radio, allowing the following vehicle to shadow the trucks without becoming obvious.

As suspected the destination was the base in the industrial estate beyond the airport. One by one the trucks turned into the fenced and gated reservation around the warehouse building. The land-rover followed them in, taking out the gatemen on the way. The gates closed after them but were not actually locked.

As soon as the truck stopped, the stowaways dropped off and took cover beside the warehouse. The drivers all went inside and arranged the order of their unloading. From the size of the warehouse there was a huge amount of traffic stored there.

Quin did a reconnoiter, looking through gaps in the door and one of the windows. Then he called Ian, "I'm going in with the first truck. I will possibly manage to push it through to the far side. Charlie should go with truck two, aim for the center. Hannah will direct the third to this end and we will blow the lot once we are all out. Any problems?"

Ian considered. "Can we get right in like that?"

"There is a wide gap straight through to doors at the other end of the building. I spotted about fifteen men scattered through the place. Have the others ready to help us shoot our way out.

***

The drivers came out talking among themselves. They boarded their trucks and started their engines. Quin stood up and walked over to the first truck. He opened the passenger door and climbed in, waving the driver on. The driver saw the smg and the clothing and rolled the truck forward as ordered, the second followed, then the third. Quin hoped all was well. When the driver made to stop when he had the truck inside he said, "Keep going!" He lifted the smg to reinforce his orders. The truck drove on to the other end of the huge warehouse. The other trucks acted as he had ordered and the men inside the warehouse looked on in astonishment.

"Out!" Quin ordered his driver. As he left the truck he triggered the fuses. Once out of the vehicle he ran and dived behind a stack of loaded sacks then zigzagged his way back the way he had come, firing short bursts whenever he encountered anyone in his way. He and Ian were in time to support Hannah as she came under fire from some of the men who had woken up to the fact that this was a raid.

Truck one blew up shooting flaming packets everywhere across the expanse of the warehouse. Then number two followed. Ian pointed to two men flying across the area, one finishing smashed half way up one of the metal uprights supporting the warehouse roof. The body slid slowly down the pillar to the floor. Quin nudged Ian, "Your side!" Ian snapped out of his dream and opened fire on the three men who appeared, guns up looking for the intruders. Two went down the other got into cover. Ian pulled out a grenade, but the second load blew at that time and the hidden man was revealed stripped and screaming.

"Move!" Quin called, "Out now. While we can." The third truck was due to blow at any moment.

They made it to the wall beside the door before the third truck actually blew. They all huddled together battered by the force of the explosion. The entire interior of the warehouse was an inferno. They got through the small doorway. The big doors had been shut when the last truck went through.

Quin slammed the door after them. The noise was horrendous, the fire inside was absorbing the oxygen fast and the roof had been breached through the shattered skylights. There was no way the fire could be stopped now. People were running about coming from elsewhere on the estate. The landrover sat, engine running, waiting for the others to return. As they tumbled in, finally, Jill let out the clutch. They roared out of the main gates and drove back to the docks.

***

While they had been occupied, the teams from Angelo's group had captured the ship and destroyed the quayside warehouse. Jill drove onto the quay and the team boarded Angelo's power boat. They caught up to the *Campeche* within 40 minutes. The victorious flotilla made their way to a final rendezvous five miles offshore where they gathered and toasted the success of their raid before splitting up to go their separate ways.

Chapter twenty-two

Offensive

Due to the intervention of Quin Gilmore, the three men concerned with the seizure of the ship were even now contemplating a partnership. Having tested the water on this operation, it was now occurring to them that, though too small individually, as a combination they added up to a formidable force.

Back in England once more, loot from the raid was lodged in a safe place for redistribution to charity. Quin was musing over plans to take the fight to Europe and Grovich's own doorstep.

He was working-out in the gym, currently punching the heavy bag. Thud...Thud. His fists connected with the slowly swinging target. Sweat ran down his back as felt the stretch with his body loosened up after the tensions of the past few days. He danced over to the small ball mounted against the wall of the gym and set himself a fast flutter of blows before relaxing into a rhythm of speedy left and right punches, increasing and decreasing speed as he attacked the ball.

The voice behind him startled him. He had been completely in his own zone and had not heard Cass come in.

"Hi, Cass. Come to join me?"

"Dream on, husband. My workout is Tai Chi. It is more in tune with my body."

Quin turned to face her, accepting the towel she handed him. Then, stripping off his gloves, he wiped his face, leaned forward and kissed her.

He stood back and looked at her shapely slender figure. In a meek voice he said, "Okay, I surrender. You may use me as you will, mistress. I am but a slave to your beauty."

Cass giggled. "Shower! Idiot. We have work to do."

Quin spread his arms out, an appeal to the world at large. "What did I do to deserve this treatment? I must shower to prove my devotion."

He stepped forward taking Cass by surprise, caught her in his arms and sweeping her off her feet. "What is good for one, is good for all," he said, and carried her off protesting though still giggling to join him in the shower.

As they were drying off Cass said, "We are going straight in, I guess?"

Quin had debated about that. He was not surprised that Cass had reached the same conclusion. "I guess so. We would be foolish to allow him to regroup and re-establish his system, having interrupted things already."

***

Hannah put the phone down. "Angelo has been in touch with the others. They have decided that the partnership will continue for the immediate future. Currently, they are planning to intercept the suspected new route developed by Grovich through Toulon. One of Grovich's lawyers had been looking for a ship to purchase or hire. Albert Chung has one available. They are in negotiation as we speak. Needless to say, Grovich is not aware of the part Chung played in the Marseilles hit."

"Albert Chung has a ship?" Quin asked.

Hannah smiled. "I believe it is jointly owned by Petrucci, Grimaldi, and Chung. A new company in the shipping industry. It seems ideal for the task. Angelo said they will look after their end, and thank you." She stopped thinking for a moment, then, "Angelo would be most grateful if he could be invited in for the kill. It seems he regards Grovich as the man who was responsible for the deaths of his wife and daughter. He requests the chance to deal personally with Grovich when the time comes." Hannah looked Quin in the eye, her face like stone, and Quin realized that he would never want Hannah Curtain as his enemy.

"How do you feel about that?" He said quietly.

Hannah relaxed, and with a small smile said, "I can live with that. I understand his motivation. If he is lost I will undertake it for him."

***

Over the next two days the reports on the movements of the Board of WOAD came in. Ian reported that Grovich and Avo Ranala had gone to Tallin for some reason. Jer Shahib has returned to Yemen, apparently gathering an emergency shipment of heroin to replace Grovich's lost consignment. Marianne Philippe was negotiating an arms shipment, it seemed. Her meeting with Fedor Sikorsky, the arms supplier, was not only out of character, it seemed bizarre in the current circumstances. Peter Noble had dropped off the map. He was believed to have retreated to his Bermuda estate out of sight and out of reach. Marcus Warren was attending a ceremony in Venezuela.

"We have some breathing space to prepare for our next move."

"Why don't we stop Shahib?" Charlie asked. "Take out the drugs at source."

"It's not the source of the drugs, idiot." Jill said. "The source is where they all seem to come from, the far-east, Afghanistan and beyond. Yemen is just a safe clearing house."

"Ok, smart-ass. Why don't we close the clearing house?"

"We will make that suggestion number one." Quin said "Now, anyone else. Suggestions?"

Jill suggested closing the Brussels offices used by Grovich. "They are not part of the charity holdings. They actually are rented by Grovich."

Quin noted the suggestion. "Anything else?"

Hannah spoke, "I would normally offer to kill him. I had already decided to do this. But I am persuaded not to, for reasons. So I suggest we capture him, perhaps hand him over to the Taliban, or to Angelo. He did operate in Afghanistan. His dealings with the drug trade there are at arm's-length through a dummy corporation using a local agent, Martin Saville. I am sure the Taliban would enjoy a personal interview with Grovich. His name is not forgotten from the time of the Russian occupation, where his reputation and promotion was linked to his success at interrogation. Saville is an Australian grifter who stays there beyond the reach of Interpol. He is a nasty piece of garbage. It would be my pleasure to delete him."

Quin stood up and spoke of his own idea. "Grovich has an apartment here in London and another in Brussels. Both are rented. Both have interesting clauses." He picked up the phone. "Put Gerald on."

The screen on the wall of the conference room lit up and Gerald Butler's face appeared. He smiled, "Hullo, all. It's been a busy time for you I hear. I have been busy, too. It seems that our man, Grovich, tends to assume things he should really check before he goes too far. He has a lease on his apartment here in London and another on an apartment in Brussels. They were both prepared in London by the lawyers of the owner.

"It seems there is a clause in the London lease which precludes the use of his apartment for business purposes. In this area of London, the law states that any building which has a business within, must have a display plate on the street wall beside the door of all such premises, listing the name/s of the businesses within. Two things come out of this. One: The local law is being observed. The sign beside the front door of the apartment block displays the name of the business, Euroholdings Ltd. The address, and so on.

"Two: The lease expressly states that the lessee will be in default if the rule is not observed to the letter. Also he will be subject to immediate eviction without notice, as soon as the breach of contract is discovered. Which it demonstratedly has.

"Brussels is easier. The owner of the building is moving all his tenants out. There is a hazard warning. The building is unsafe. Since it is only six years old, the construction company is also under investigation. One of the biggest shareholders in the building is Anton Grovich, who represents several other Russians, one being a Mr Putin, a name you may be familiar with. The word is that all the shareholders will be held liable for not only the costs of demolition, and rebuilding, damages to all the other tenants, plus the legal fines and fees under civil proceedings and criminal charges under European Law.

"It seems Euroholdings ran the construction company. There is only one shareholder of Euroholdings, Anton Grovich." Gerald ended his speech with a grin and added, "The police authorities in Belgium and London are both conducting investigations and a warrant is out for the arrest of Grovich in both Brussels and London."

"What about the London apartment?" Quin asked.

"The bailiffs move in next week," Gerald said. Why don't we have a look around this week-end? I have a vacancy in my diary."

Quin smiled, "Funny you should say that. There are two people at least, free and ready to join you as we speak. Can you put Jill up?" He said innocently. "Hannah has her own studio apartment."

Gerald smiled at the group. "By all means, Quin. That would be perfectly fine." We could pop round to Anton's flat and make sure there is nothing embarrassing left there to cause problems when the bailiffs arrive."

Chapter twenty-three

Actions

Thud! The big man hit the floor without knowing what hit him. "Did I kill him?" Gerald asked. Hannah checked. "No. He'll live. Let's get on with it."

Hannah retrieved the gun from the man's inert figure and dropped it in her bag. Between them they dragged the man into the first room and left him with his hands bound to his ankles. Jill, Gerald and Hannah proceeded to search the apartment. Unaware of the silent alarm involved until too late, they found the concealed door to the hidden room was in the store room. It was there that the interesting stuff was to be found. The two women had left Gerald to keep an eye out while they went through the various things to be found within. Hannah found the silent alarm switch. She called to Gerald to come and help while they piled everything into bags, stripping the secret room and leaving the weapons for the police to find.

The three thugs arrived as they were leaving the apartment. All were armed and they opened fire on sight. Hannah dropped to the floor and shouted to Gerald and Jill. "Go! I've got this." She fired twice, her silenced Glock audible but not intrusive. Her opponent's weapons were also suppressed and the sibilant sounds of the traded shots caused no apparent alarm in the building. Hannah was an old hand at this sort of warfare. As the shooter at the corner of the corridor retreated, she rolled over to the opposite wall. Gerald and Jill, loaded with the bags they had brought, tottered down the stairway three floors to the ground floor. The separate door to the basement garage was locked. Gerald shot it, narrowly escaping the metal handle flying into the air as the lock was smashed apart. The handle buried itself in the plaster of the wall behind him. The shiver down his back reminded him of his instructor's forgotten words: *"Never casually shoot out the lock of a door. Always make sure you are in cover, or out or range, of flying shrapnel."* That handle could have been buried in his skull.

A chastened Gerald led the way to the car and tossed the bags in. Jill never said a word as she drove out of the garage and round to the main entrance of the building.

As they arrived Hannah strolled out peeling her rubber gloves off. The distant sound of police sirens approaching encouraged them to move off in a hurry.

***

At the retreat they unloaded the bags. The entire team went to work examining the haul.

"We seem to have hit the jackpot this time." Jill was smiling as she fanned a group of documents in front of the others. "This is a selection of properties which will be under the hammer during the next week. The only reason I can see for them being of interest is that they are all located in what we know as red light areas of the major cities in Southern England."

Charlie looked up from the money he was counting. "I have just reached my third hundred thousand, and I have another three bags to go, plus the other half of this one. I reckon over one million pounds.

Quin cut in at that point. "I have just found the address of the training house for prostitution. It is in Brussels-Sud." The silence after this announcement could have been carved into strips.

Eventually, Cass spoke. "How soon can we take it on?"

Quin looked at Naomi?

She said promptly, "36 hours."

Cass said, "We must do it sooner. They know we have these documents."

Quin said, "Gather your gear. We leave in thirty minutes." He stabbed a button on the phone system. It beeped and James Haddon's voice came through. Quin spoke, "James, book the limo and seven on the train to Brussels from Ashford. Make it three hours near as possible, but no less. Deliver the bookings to the car en-route."

"Got it!" James answered. "I'm on it now."

The party was under way within the half hour.

***

The Brussels target was alive with lights in the rain, the flickering neon distorted through the windscreen as the wipers did their business.

On the other side of the street, three people stood huddled in the doorway of number seventeen; a doorway crowded on both sides by a sex shop and a quickie brothel. At least that is how Cass interpreted it. The rather drunken sign read, '30 Euros, 39 minutes'. The others in the car all had a go at working it out, but they found no common answer.

As Cass watched, the three people huddled in the doorway disappeared into the house.

"Pull over to the other side of the street," Cass said to Jill, who was driving. "They may be out in a hurry."

"Or they may not," Naomi commented drily from her place in the rear.

Jill laughed, "Do not forget that Hannah is there."

Naomi growled in her best French, "So what. Zis ees ze 21st century., com ci, com ca. Now-a-days, does it matter?"

Both the others burst out laughing.

The street door opened. Ian came out and slipped into the back seat beside Naomi.

"Beat me to it, girls. I came out to call you over and here you are. The others will be out in a few minutes. It will be a crush. There are six girls being groomed."

"What happened to the keepers?"

Ian shrugged his shoulders. "Omelettes and eggs." He described, the picture of the four men and the woman they had found inside, the half-dressed man and the semi-stripped woman 'instructing', both with electric prods in hand, teaching the finer points of the sex trade to tearful girls. The man and woman both now dead. The other two minders, too slow, all now locked in a macabre group like some scene from a Zombie movie.

The girls stated to run out through the front door and into the limo. Hannah and Quin came last. Seeing the crush in the car, Quin leaned in and told Jill to take off for Naomi's apartment. "Hannah and I will get a cab."

***

When Quin and Hannah reached the apartment, Ian was relaxing in the lounge alone.

"The women are with the girls upstairs in my old apartment. It was becoming embarrassing, so I came down here and left them to it. As a temporary measure, Naomi had bought a bag of teenager's clothes from the charity shop. They are all trying things on."

The bell rang. Hannah answered the door and Charlie walked in. "No tails, and I get the impression that the neighbours to number seventeen were pleased to get rid of the occupants.

"Nobody heard anything of the disturbance in the house and nobody saw the exodus of the girls," Charlie said. "Incidentally, where are they?"

Quin raised a thumb and jerked it upwards. "Up aloft, being refitted."

The papers, now sorted, were all arranged in some sort of order. Apart from the information about the grooming project there was little information that they could use immediately. There was, however, plenty that Gerald and a team of accountants and lawyers could get their teeth into.

In the meantime, within the Brussels house, there was a lot of giggling and chatter in Ian's now vacant apartment. By mutual agreement he had moved in with Naomi, so the six girls, along with Jill and Naomi, were all walking about in all stages of dress and undress. As each girl finished with the shower, they returned to the lounge where the pile of clothing was placed and sorted out something to wear.

Underwear they had, though the stack of panties and bras provided by Naomi soon disappeared as the girls discarded some of the coarser examples of East European origin they had been wearing.

Hannah came into the downstairs apartment, having been off collecting food for the girls. She carried a stack of pizza boxes. Quin picked up the phone and called upstairs to let them know. In seconds they could be heard rushing down the stairs.

They burst into the room, astonishing the men who realized that three were still in their underwear, the others, all dressed and looking quite normal. All grabbed the pizzas and, ignoring the men, started eating, still chattering. Two of the undressed girls were wriggling into jeans as they coped with slices of pizza with one hand, dragging up the jeans with the other. Jill appeared and forced tops onto the girls lacking them, saving the blushes of the men. The mini-skirt she had brought for the last thong-clad bottom was hardly worth the effort, though that was mainly because of the lack of effort on the part of the wearer, who was concentrating on eating.

Hanna explained that the girls had all been deprived of food for the past three days to focus their cooperation on being trained, which explained their enthusiastic concentration on their food.

All had been brought in from Russia, and all were recruited from rural areas to be trained as models. All spoke basic English. Ian spoke to them in Russian and discovered that they had been collected from the guest house they were in four days ago. The men who brought them to Brussels were not the people who had recruited them.

One of the girls mentioned that the men who collected them—the three men at the house—had raped them all during the journey, just to make sure that they understood who was in charge. It was only then that the girls realized that the modelling career they had signed-up for was a confidence trick to get control of them and force them into the porn industry.

They had no idea who controlled the men, or of the risks they had taken.

Naomi got in touch with the agency who dealt with the problems of distressed and homeless people. The response to the enquiry was not helpful. They discovered that the number of such cases was so huge the department was swamped and unable to cope.

Cass solved the problem in the interim, by offering them employment on the Sussex estate. All six girls accepted the offer.

The bodies in the sex house were never found, the police were not interested, since no official report was made. The anonymous call leading to the visit to the premises was presumed to have been a prank call, as there was no sign of any bodies, or of blood. The house was gutted with redesign and decoration in progress.

***

The action in London was well under way. The apartment leased by Grovich was repossessed by the owners under a high court writ.

In Brussels the apartment—in fact the entire building owned by Grovich—was condemned.

The architect responsible for the survey, having made his deposition on the subject, had been removed under a witness protection program to a place of safety. The police it seems were aware of the fact that people who opposed Grovich had a habit of disappearing.

Quin had no illusions about the arrest of Grovich. Lawyers would have him out in minutes. He was far more concerned with the fact that Grovich would be made to look bad in front of his own people.

Grovich was furious. He returned to Brussels to find his apartment gone, and the building flattened. There were legal reasons why he could not immediately rebuild. On the table in front of him was a demand for the accounting of his relationship with WOAD as well as the links currently suspected with smuggling drugs and arms under the cover of the food movements through the charity.

***

At the retreat the group met once more. Quin brought them up to date. "We have news that Grovich is back in the saddle once more. He is meeting with Ranala, Shahib and Noble today. Angelo has informed us that a coaster has been hired. A shipment is scheduled for Toulon. We have discussed matters with Angelo. We will be needed. It seems that the cargo will be escorted. After the last shipment he has laid on a fighter escort, A helicopter and a gunboat. So it seems that only place we can do this is like last time. On the quay!"

"He will be prepared after last time surely?" Charlie put in.

"This time the site is Toulon. The place is much more interesting from our point of view. There are no buildings occupied in the zone which is in process of being completely redeveloped. The ship comes in on Sunday and he has already squared the customs. The consignment will be signed off on the paperwork without physical examination. It seems it may be his last chance under the wing of WOAD. The charity is conducting its own enquiries, using independent consultants. What I suggest we do is move in before the handling crew arrive. We can then unload the cargo ourselves."

Hannah said, "That means that we will be breaking the law!"

Quin looked at her, eyebrow raised?

"I suppose this is the end justifying the means, again?"

"More or less. We will of course make sure that the legitimate goods go through regardless."

***

On the Riviera, Angelo Petrucci sat thinking. He was considering the implications of the scheme put forward by Hannah's friend for the cargo consigned to WOAD at Toulon. After considerable thought he lifted the telephone and rang the number given to him by Hannah.

***

Lorenzo Grimaldi sat with Francois Carriere and Albert Chung around the table on the veranda of his house on the Riviera coast. The blue Mediterranean was marked with white rips as the boats moved back and forth in the sunshine.

"So we are agreed? I will speak with Angelo. We will deal with this cargo ourselves. The drugs will split three ways. All the rest goes into our mutual fund."

Both the others nodded.

Carriere said, "I have arranged the reconstruction of the warehouse in Marseilles. The combination of quay and store will suit us well for future business."

Albert Chung nodded silently, agreeing with his partner. Then he looked up, eyes finding those of the other two men. "I have a proposition I think you should consider."

He paused assessing the mood of the others.

Grimaldi, having made his point, seemed pleased with himself. Carriere was more difficult to read. Always close mouthed, his face gave little away.

Chung continued, "We have a problem with the law enforcement agencies always. In this EU business we have advantages. The borders are down, but there are disadvantages. I propose we make the shipping legitimate!"

Neither of the other men made a comment. They waited to hear what he had to say.

"What I have in mind is, that by running a legitimate company we have a front that will stand up to investigation from police and customs. We actually invite them to advise on making things legitimate and make sure that we keep the company clean. Taking care to operate properly will make a legitimate profit for the company, so we will not lose money.

It means that we can operate the warehouse facility and use the quay with our own security to ensure there is no interference. I am aware that it will take time to set up, but I would also point out that we are operating a much bigger business than we have ever had before. We have got away with things so far because we were not big enough to be a problem. Now we are big enough to be noticed. If we play things properly, we will all win. We make sure that all transactions that we want to keep under the counter are conducted at sea for the time being. it means distribution will be needed from small landings as we have been doing up to now."

Carriere looked at Chung searchingly. "Is that your idea?"

Chung shrugged. "It is!"

Carriere looked at Grimaldi. "What do you think?"

Grimaldi looked thoughtful. As a man of action he was more inclined to knee-jerk reaction rather than considered planning. "You think this makes sense?" He said to Carriere, uncertainly.

Carriere was obviously surprised at the reaction. "Yes. I think it would make sense. But to work properly, I think one of us will have to go legit!

"Whoever runs the ships will need to concentrate on that only, and establish a clean public background. If it is worth doing, it looks like you will have to front the operation. I think it makes sense. In this partnership we are all equal. But you realize that to make this work, your share of our operation will have to be lodged in secret. You are going to have to live the life. I do believe that if we can make it work, we will be the biggest 'business' in France, maybe Europe. Your finance will need to come from a Cayman Island source."

Albert and Lorenzo looked at Carriere in astonishment. Albert had an idea. He had no thoughts on how it could be done, just the instinctive feeling that it would be the way to go. Francois Carriere had just put a little more thought into it, and, having attended business school for three years before the family business had failed, he had enough background education to realize that Albert's instincts were correct.

When he contacted Angelo, Francois told him that Albert was leaving the partnership to run a shipping agency and company, specializing in the Mediterranean and East-African waters. He also said that they would arrange the entire operation regarding Grovich's expected cargo.

***

In the retreat Quin turned to the others. "Scratch the Toulon operation. Our friends in the south have arranged everything in such a way as to keep the port and the ship clean. We can now concentrate of Grovich's Euro-dream."

***

At present in Tallin, Estonia, Grovich was feeling as angry as he usually was. His anger was now focussed on the group who were causing him the aggravation in England. Though he was not aware of any connection to his Brussels problems, he had the suspicion that there was in fact a link. His anger was concentrated on his former colleagues from the Board at WOAD. Due to his present suspension, he depended on the goodwill of Jer Shahib to keep him up to date on proceedings there. So far his current cargo of drugs was on line and making progress towards Toulon.

With two days to go before delivery he was confident he could satisfy his current customers, consisting of two of the biggest distributers in Europe. And the English customer was substantial. He anticipated a return of ten million on the cargo coming, and fully expected to have his old place in the community back by the time that particular problem had been solved.

Chapter twenty-four

The ground beneath his feet

In England with the removal of Grovich's base, Gerald Butler had managed to have all the people involved in the clear up from the Russian's side identified. Grovich avoided using local talent where he could. Most of the people identified were immigrants and Gerald immediately informed the authorities that these people were no longer in the employ of Grovich or his nominee's and should therefore be deported.

The subsequent period of assertion and denial trapped the people concerned in the legal net, forcing them to either stay or risk permanent branding as 'Undesirable Aliens.' It did mean that, in making the choice, Grovich had to decide whether to call them in or not.

For Quin, the time had come to take the decision they had put off up to now. He called the group together, hooked up with Ian and Naomi by internet and came right out with it.

"I have decided it is time we must something about Grovich. He is a madman. He has targeted Sheila and Sir Tony and also others of our group. We have been lucky so far but we cannot count on luck forever. Tony and Sheila are not here now because they would be vulnerable and are not, like us, professionals. In my mind the only way we can protect ourselves and them, is to remove Grovich from the scene. How do you feel about that?"

Hannah said, "I'm in!"

Charlie added his vote, and Jill was quick to agree.

"I am in favor, but I also realize that we may well be taking on the SVR, the overseas Russian Intelligence service. If that is the case we had better be damn sure that we are prepared for a long and lonely road."

Gerald walked in at that point. "Did I miss anything?" He said with a grin. He looked at the serious faces around him. "Ah, I see I have."

From Brussels,, Ian said, "If I read this correctly, Naomi should really relocate to the retreat while we get the situation sorted out."

Gerald looked at Quin. "Grovich?" He said quietly.

Quin nodded, "It's time!"

"We were expecting it. Though I must confess I was hoping we would embarrass him so much, the Russians would save us the trouble."

Quin called the group to order. "This has to be done right and clean. So I want you to get together and discuss ways and means. We will see what you come up with by tonight. After dinner we'll get together and take a look at your ideas."

The assembly split up and scattered through the complex preparing for the conference later that evening.

***

The dinner that evening was a lively occasion. The banter flew back and forth as the entire group had gathered including Sheila and Sir Tony, and Ian and Naomi.

Mary had excelled herself with the assistance of James and Molly Haddon, who had produced delicate pastries for dessert.

The entire party were seated enjoying coffee, some with cognac, some with other cordials. The room was alive with conversation which Quin was loath to interrupt. For a while he sat marvelling at the way the people interacted, Sir Tony, the aristocrat. Chatting happily with Robert Anderson, the maintenance man, both finding a common interest in the diseases of roses, and the qualities of different varieties of apple.

Gerald and Jill were not such a surprise. Both had a background of military training, but were also discussing a discovered enjoyment of classical music. Perhaps most surprising was the relationship that was developing between Charlie and Sheila. She was two years older. But Charlie, who he had regarded as being a lightweight intellectual, was discussing the merits of the Impressionists compared with the Post Impressionists and the Pre-Raphaelites. It was a side of Charlie that even Jill had not known about.

Almost reluctantly, Quin called the group to order.

"I hate to break up this party. I was sorely tempted to let it just carry on and talk about things tomorrow instead. Reality convinced me that the sooner we get on with things the better. I promise you all that, when this little exercise is over, we will be happy to entertain you all at the house where we can relax and get together without pressure.

Ian Bennet opened with, "The Department de la Surete/Securite Territorale otherwise known as the DST, (French FBI) are on the lookout for Grovich on charges of smuggling, extortion and suspected murder. The Belgians want him for offenses in relation to his building, and now also for illegal importation of under-age women for immoral purposes. Here he is wanted for tax evasion and suspected murder, though I do not think there is a case that his lawyers could not cope with here. What I am saying is, whatever we do, we have to make sure we do not get caught in the headlights when we are doing it. If we are going to shoot the bastard, it needs to be out of sight of all the agencies and spooks who abound in the areas where Grovich can be found." He sat down looking a little uncomfortable, but re-assured by Naomie who squeezed his hand and smiled at him.

Hannah spoke from her seat. "I think, ideally, we can work to place Grovich where his rivals/enemies can get to him. In dealing with Angelo and the Riviera mob, they made it clear that getting their hands on Grovich would be appreciated, especially by Angelo himself, for personal reasons. Otherwise my offer is still open. If you approve, I can drop out of sight and deal with him quietly, his associates Avo Ranala and Jer Shahib also."

Quin put in the fact that at present, with Grovich in Tallin under the protection of Ranala's men, it would be highly dangerous to get to him. "If we could lure him out of Estonia, tempt him, make an offer he could not refuse, perhaps."

From the back of the room Molly Haddon spoke. "I think if I might suggest it. I, I think I may have a way of bringing him out into view."

Cass lifted her hand. The murmur that started at Molly's words stopped. "What did you have in mind, Molly? Come forward where we can all see and hear you, please."

Shyly, Molly came forward, blushing. At 72, Molly looked and acted like an old age pensioner, your favorite granny. Dressed in stylish sensible clothes, she still looked as if an apron was missing from her attire. Her silver hair was tidy and she had the respect of the people around her, if only for her cooking abilities. What most were unaware of was that, when working before she married, she served in GCHQ. Since that time her abilities as a computer programmer and communications expert had been regularly called-upon until well after she officially retired from her Civil Service position. "I still play games on my laptop and IPad. As you probably are aware most banking in this day and age is done on or through the internet. I know a little about that. In fact I think I can claim to be an expert. If something went wrong with our target's bank accounts, I suggest he would want—no, need—to expose himself a little, to get things put right.

"Going through the paperwork we gathered from the various raids we have conducted, I have come across several points that I believe we can exploit. In fact I would go as far as to say, I can put a severe dent in his financial status."

Molly sat down. Calm now, she was confident in her own expertise, and flattered by the immediate reaction to her suggestion. It was clear that her suggestion had come out of the blue, and judging by the rise in conversation all around, a definite angle of attack which had not as yet been considered.

Quin allowed the conversation to continue for a while, before bringing the group back to the general subject at hand. The other suggestions all turned out to be variants of the ones already made, so Quin brought things to a close.

In close discussion with Molly, Quin decided to leave it with her to see if she could get a hook into Grovich's banking business. The resources of a pretty comprehensive computer setup at the retreat needed enhancement. The upgraded equipment, once obtained, could be swiftly integrated to give Molly the resources she needed.

Quin and Cass left Molly to organize her computer requirements and retired to their own quarters. As soon as Molly had the room to herself she turned on Skype and called an old colleague. Ken Mills was retired from his job at GCHQ. His wife had left him alone two years ago, dying quietly of a cancer which had been undiagnosed for far too long. Beth had been an old-fashioned girl when they got married and theirs had been a quiet marriage with one son who was the couple's delight. Ken and Beth had accepted their role in life and been content to live it out. Sadly, the death of Beth had not been planned for, as they expected to die as they had lived, together. Now Ken spent more and more time in the closed world of his computer, visited regularly by Michael, his son, and even more regularly by Jason his grandson. Both Michael and Jason shared his pre-occupation with computing and programming. When they were not with Ken physically, they were often with him in the network they maintained between them.

When Molly called, Ken was just thinking about wrapping things up for the night, but when he saw the caller he answered immediately. "Hi, Molly. What's new? How is the tea room doing?"

Molly said, "Ken, let's go dark!"

When you work in a place like GCHQ, you become well aware of how easy it is to hack into other people's computers. It was not surprising that, with so many experts on the site, the employees worked out how have private conversations. "Switching now!" Ken said. "So what is this all about Molly? Has James gone after the waitresses again?"

Molly laughed. "No, but the chef does have a cool butt."

"I told you, Molly. Whenever you feel like it, I have a place for you here." He laughed. Chatting up Molly had been a feature of their friendship for as long as he could recall.

"Ken, I need a little support here. We have a situation involving a Russian piece of rubbish, named Grovich. He is a zillionaire who is up to his elbows in just about any crime you can think of. At the moment he has targeted at least four of our friends, plus James and me. He is close with Putin and the Red Mafia. Currently he is hiding in Tallin with an Estonian crook, named Avo Ranala. We have managed to get him on the wanted list in Belgium, France and England, and we have wrecked two major drug deliveries, as they landed, destroying his distribution warehouse in France at the same time."

"Were you involved in that? I read about it, saw it on UTube, too. No mention of drugs though. So what do you need me for? I'm a bit shaky with a gun these days."

"I have decided to divert his assets." Molly's voice was quiet and even.

"Did I hear you correctly? Divert, you say?"

"Yes. Divert, shift them to where they will do the most good, and take them out of his control."

"You've thought about this?"

"Yep!"

"What would you like me to do?"

"Are you in?" Molly sounded a little uptight.

"Too right I am. I have been looking for a chance to screw one of those drug bastards for years. But I always thought I had too much to lose if it went wrong. Now Beth is gone I don't have the problem Are you thinking what I'm thinking? Using the porthole we used in the past?"

"It seems the best answer. I could not do it on my own. As you know it needs two sources to bring it off. Is your equipment up to it? If it isn't my people will supply anything you need, they have already agreed to update mine here."

Ken chuckled, "Molly, dear, Michael runs a software company and Jason, my grandson, is chasing his father in qualifications and researching for him already. I am state of the art. Let's get the show on the road. Which bank do we start with?"

"We'll start with our old friends, the Bank of Cayman, from there to the Union Bank, Cayman division. My new gear should be with me tomorrow, we can set up then." Molly kept contact with Ken on the laptop. She sighed contentedly, "Just like old times."

Chapter twenty-five

sowing the wind

Gerald Butler turned to Jill, smiling at her as she lay with her head on the pillow beside him still asleep. He was still trying to accept the fact that he was here, and she was here, and the world still turned. Things were starting up big time in the fight with Grovich, and ....What was that? He jerked his head up rolling out of bed sweeping the gun from the bedside table as he hit the floor. A swift glance told him that Jill, as expected, was already off the bed and on the floor on her side.

The bedroom door burst open. A big man with a shotgun stepped in, gun up firing at the empty bed.

Two shots simultaneously took him in the throat and smashed him back into his companion. Both Gerald and Jill stood and fired past the falling dead man, both bullets catching his companion in the chest. He was wearing a vest but the shots punched him back stretching him out on the floor beneath his dead partner. A third man dived to the side out of the way of his companions, but it did not save him from Jill's next two shots which took him in the neck and the head. There was a scurry of departing feet from the corridor outside the open front door of Gerald's apartment.

Gerald sighed and looked at the ruined bed. Then he looked at the naked figure of Jill, gun in hand, as she surveyed the mess.

"Guess we'll need to have the mess cleaned up." She said drily.

The man lying beneath the body of his dead companion stirred and groaned.

Gerald said to Jill, "Put some clothes on, Jill. You'll just get the poor man excited looking like that!"

"Does it do the same for you?" She said posing in a lewd manner for his benefit.

He growled, "Later. Let's get this mess cleared up first."

She went back into the bedroom and rescued her clothes from the chair by the dressing table where she had placed them.

Gerald anchored the survivor to his dead colleague and went in turn to find his own clothes.

Jill was on the telephone when he finished dressing. She put the phone down and said, "Do you want me to attend to that?" She nodded at his shoulder. He looked and was surprised to see blood oozing from three small wounds. "Well, I never did. D'you know? I did not feel that until you mentioned it. Now the bloody things sting like blazes."

Jill led him into the bathroom and took a close look at the three punctures caused by stray shotgun pellets. She took the TCP and some cotton wool from the cabinet. "No nosey neighbors, then?"

"Ouch! That hurt." Jill had found tweezers in the cupboard and had extracted one of the pellets. Gerald spoke again "The neighbors are away in Barbados for the month or so, thank goodness.

"The people downstairs will have heard little. The insulation in this building is good. You may have noticed. We get no traffic noise at all."

"There is a van on the way," Jill plucked another pellet out. "This one might hurt a bit. It's deeper." There was a pause as Jill dug deeper and Gerald sweated. Then with a sigh of relief she brought the pellet out and dropped in on the bathroom sink. Gerald relaxed and swore.

"Tut, tut. That's not good for a lady to hear." Jill said as she mopped the three wounds with the antiseptic.

Gerald nearly hit the roof as the liquid met the wounds. A pad of gauze, secured by sticking plaster, completed her ministrations.

"Charlie picked up the van from the lock-up and is nearly here already. So get dressed and we will be on our way. I thought we would go to Brighton. I know it's weekends they always talk about, and it is only Wednesday, but I thought we deserved a dirty night out at least after all our trials. We'll need a new bed anyway."

Changing the subject, Jill added, "Basement job, I suppose?"

"I guess. We'll let Joe Soap here help carry his mate." He dressed in tee-shirt and jeans before, lifting the eiderdown off the floor where it had ended up when they went to bed. It had a couple of pellet holes though not nearly as many as the sheets on the bed displayed.

They wrapped the shotgun man in the eiderdown and used the ruined sheets for the other dead man. The prisoner moaned about his sore chest but managed anyway. Gerald commented that he probably had broken ribs, but he got scant sympathy from his intended victims.

***

'Charlie rolled up as anticipated. With the bodies and the prisoner loaded in the transport to the retreat, Jill and Gerald went straight to the hotel. They had used his neighbor's Range-Rover for the drive down to Brighton where they checked in at the Majestic, taking a suite overlooking the channel waters.

After breakfast they hung the sign on the door and resumed matters interrupted by the shotgun the night before, only slightly handicapped by the bandaged shoulder.

***

Molly logged off-line with a yawn. Getting older meant she did not need the sleep she once did. But it also meant that she did not have the stamina which had once kept her going for 44 hours at a stretch, on more than one occasion in her past.

She said to Ken, "I've had it for now. Will midday tomorrow be all right with you?"

"I'll be here Molly. We're doing well. We'll aim to finish the job tomorrow. Goodnight. God bless!"

***

In Tallin, Grovich put the telephone back in its cradle. "Why is it I cannot get the people I hire to do the simplest of jobs?"

From the kitchen table in his home in Tallin, Avo Ranala smiled to himself and commiserated with his colleague. "Remember, Anton. It is the steady runner who wins the long distance race."

"My customers are still waiting for their latest deliveries. The goods have been in the distribution center for three days already. I have my people working on the next shipment."

Ranala shrugged. "You think you are unlucky. Someone had a warehouse fire near Marseilles. It burned for two days. They are still showing the mess on UTube."

Grovich looked at Ranala sitting stuffing himself at the table thinking, *Stupid pig, he will go soon.*

The phone rang again. Ranala picked it up. "It's for you!" He passed the phone to Grovich and left the table, his breakfast unfinished.

Grovich listened for a few moments. Then he called to Avo Ranala to turn the TV on.

The report on the fire in the South of France was on the news. There was some speculation at the unprecedented fury of the fire and suspicion that the inferno was because of some inflammatory materials illegally held in the warehouse / distribution premises. Other reports suggested that it was a depository for drug shipments and that the smoke from the fire was better than a solid heroin hit. The police were saying nothing, while awaiting reports from the fire service.

Grovich had gone white. He carefully replaced the telephone.

Avo said, "What was that all about?"

"Those bastards have burned down my distribution warehouse in Vitrolles. That was my warehouse on the TV. "He picked up the phone and dialled a number from memory. "Armand, did the shipment get through?"

"It certainly did, I anticipate the deliveries will be made during this next week."

"What happened with the warehouse at Vitrolles?" Grovich growled.

"What about it?"

"According to CNN it is in ruins! Are the trucks there, or are they still on the way?"

"They should be there yesterday. No, the day before. Oh my God!" Armand had switched his TV on. Grovich could hear it in the background. "They found the chassis of three trucks inside the building. They are investigating the possibility that the trucks caused the fire." The voice of Armand faded as he realized the implication of what he was saying. Grovich did not do failure. Armand put the phone down without waiting to hear what Grovich had to say. He turned and ran through his office to his car outside the door. He drove himself home and called his wife on the way to fetch the cases.

She said, "It is time? Meet you at the door!"

Armand had arranged his last minute rush as soon as he took on the work for Grovich. Aware that his employer had a cavalier attitude to employees, he had sworn he would not just stand and wait for the axe to fall. He would rather run and live, than stand and die. His wife, Charlotte, was part of the deal and agreed to be ready with the bags if the word was given.

At his house door he flung out of the car, stepped across the patio and jumped into the people carrier that he had obtained quietly. He was packed by his wife who was waiting with the engine running, her brunette wig and sunglasses, already in place for the trip to get the ferry at Marseilles. As he lay in the back seat on the journey he slipped into the Hawaiian shirt and the ponytail wig. The shades altered his face. The tan chinos completed the rig and he was ready to take the wheel when they stopped at the Walmart for bottled water and snacks.

***

In Tallin Grovich was incandescent. He was faced with the wrath of his customers. he had lost his distribution depot and network, and he had just discovered that his main bank account was empty. He had other accounts, but on the face of it he was no longer a millionaire, multi or otherwise.

The actual ramifications of this situation did not immediately occur to him. He turned to Avo Ranala, "Have your men make the hit on the known people in London."

Ranala said, "I have already sent a team to hit the lawyer and his woman. One survived. Unfortunately, so did the lawyer and his woman."

"So send more men this time!" Grovich gritted.

"No! I will not support your revenge any more. It costs men and money. I am not prepared to waste any more resources for your whims and fancies."

Grovich went purple. "How dare you!" As he stepped forward he found his arms gripped by two heavy hands.

Avo said, "You have managed to ruin yourself and your companies with this stupid vendetta against people that you still do not know. I will continue to support you, but not if you are going to continue this pointless exercise. Think about it!"

His arms were released The man behind him eased him through to the room he was occupying while he was a guest.

For the first time in the past few years Grovich actually sat down and contemplated his future.

Avo Ranala was thinking himself. Now that the situation had changed as it had, he was seriously considering just how much he needed the services of the Russian. With the links to the WOAD charity no longer of use, it was really of little use trying to resurrect what was now a lost cause. His feeling was to put the whole situation on hold and see just what Anton Grovich could come up with. If he turns out to have nothing to offer, then their ways would part. Business was business after all.

***

Back in the retreat Molly reported that the assets of the Grovich empire had been effectively dissipated.

She mentioned the fact that the services of her friend and ex-colleague, Ken Mills, had been invaluable in the task of stripping Grovich's assets. Since she understood the group planned to continue operations in a more formal manner in future, if he was agreeable, it might be worthwhile retaining his services. He has nothing else to do now he is on his own.

Cass smiled when she heard Molly's comment and suggestion. The Tea-room was still a preferred occupation apparently. "I will discuss this with Quin. Though if you wish to speak with him personally, by all means do. I really do not see a problem. You have the Tea-room to consider. I do realize that in these days of internet technology, where you are is almost irrelevant, provided there is signal, power and network, or something like that." Cass finished up with a smile.

Chapter twenty-six

Phoenix

Anton Grovich was now on the wanted list throughout Europe and within the United Kingdom. While not, as the FBI might have expressed it, on the top Most Wanted list, he nevertheless would be hunted actively wherever he was sighted.

His relationship with Avo Ranala covered his presence in Estonia, though travel elsewhere was more difficult and entailed false identity and a basic alteration in his facial make up. His identity had not been entirely obscured due to of those quirks of fate which beats the odds. In a restaurant in Geneva, a former victim, deliberately blinded by Grovich, heard a voice she would never forget. She found the owner of the voice with the help of her companion, who took a photograph with her cell phone.

Two weeks later Angelo Petrucci received the photograph from an unknown source. Within minutes Hannah Curtain's cell phone received two pictures. Side by side, they were marked *Old* and *New*. The information was passed to the Headquarters of the recently created, *Hunters Investigation Services.*

Based in Cannon Street in the city of London, the new addition to the Private Enquiry Agencies list specialized in finding people. It did not advertise any other activities.

The company set up by Gerald Butler was, as he stated at the time, a provocation to their former enemies. The company was chaired by Sir Anthony Merrick, and directed by Sheila LeBec and Robert Smith. A Brussels Office was directed by

Naomie and Ian Bennet. The other activities were run from the retreat by Quin Gilmore.

H.I.S (Hunters Investigation Services) was run with a staff of former investigators from police and security sources throughout the world.

Quin had the assistance of Hannah Curtain, Cass being in process of increasing the population and assuring legitimate succession. The arrival of the pair of photographs cleared up a mystery, unsolved since Grovich had moved to Estonia.

Avo Ranala was still active in that arena and was gradually building a bigger organization. Rachel Vishinski had appeared to replace the absent Hannah Curtain as assassin of choice in Europe.

At a meeting at Canonby House, Sheila and Charlie were discussing matters with Quin. Hannah came in with Cass who was showing the expected signs of her forthcoming motherhood.

"The blow-ups of the pictures are here. I don't think there is any doubt that this is Grovich. The experts have worked out the bone structure, they match. He was travelling under the name Vassily Borodin, described as a Marketing Director of shipping company, Occidental Cargoes, Geneva. It exists, but it is an agency. It does not run its own vehicles. It does own some containers and leases others as required."

"We will still need to do something about him." Cass put in.

Quin nodded. "You're right, of course. His active presence is a risk to us all. Especially since we know that Rachel Vishinski was employed by Grovich in the past and is probably working under his protection still. Hannah, did Angelo Petrucci have anything to add?"

"Not immediately. But after I fed him the Occidental Cargoes' identity, he was able to come up with more. It seems the shipping company specializes in importing antique artefacts. He is convinced the trade is dodgy. Probably drugs packed into or around the so-called artefacts. He will see what else he can find out. He is still looking for an opportunity to settle his debts with Grovich."

"Well, that's a start. We can run a trace on its operations from the office." Charlie looked at Sheila. "What about the Brussels office? They have records on all the normal European companies and I know that Switzerland has close links with their Euro-counterparts as far as security is concerned."

Sheila nodded. "I'll call Naomie. We can see what they come up with." She pulled out her cell and speed-dialled a number. Switched to loudspeaker, they could all hear Naomie when she answered. "Hi, Sheila. What can I do for you this fine spring morning?"

Naomie, we are at Canonby discussing a company called Occidental Cargoes. It seems our old enemy Grovich is working with them under the name, Vassily Borodin. We would like any information you can gather. Angelo Petrucci reckons he is still into drugs."

"I'll get onto it. Why not give Molly a shout. She seems pretty good with the on-line investigations. Perhaps she can find out a few things from her viewpoint." Naomie hesitated. "Oops. I've just realized Molly is back at the Tea-room."

Sheila laughed. "She is still on the books. But we do have her pal, Ken Mills, on tap we'll give him a try. I cannot believe we had not already thought of that." She looked around the others. "Anything else?"

Cass called out, "Any news, Naomie?"

Naomie laughed. "Wow, Cass you are keen. No news. How's the baby?"

"All seems okay, but I'm getting heaveee! I'll see you next week. Bye!"

"Bye all. I'll get back to you, Sheila."

***

"It's a holding company, called Phoenix." Ken Mills reported. Occidental Cargoes is a trading title only. Rachel Vishinski is listed as Company Secretary. Vassily Borodin is Managing Director. But the company is backed by Tallin commerce. That is Avo Ranala to you."

"Have you any idea about banking, finance, etc.?" Cass asked.

"I'll get back to you." Ken said, "By the way, thanks for calling. It's good to be needed."

Cass said, "Look, Ken. If you would feel happy about it, you would be welcome either here at Canonby, or, if you would rather be there, at the retreat with Robert. All the equipment is there and here. Think about it and let me know."

Cass passed the information on to Naomie in Brussels, then had a long conversation with Hannah about the Phoenix connection.

"I'm fairly certain, if Grovich is financed by Ranala, he will be hands on in the Phoenix business. It seems pretty certain that his Russian contacts have dried up. It is said that Putin does not do failure and, in the eyes of the world, Grovich has failed disastrously. Tell me, Hannah, what do you really think about this Rachel Vishinski woman?"

Hannah smoothed her skirt. She had ditched the trousers since she started working in the office with other people. The jeans and chino's were kept for outside work now. "Rachel Vishinski is a cruel vindictive killer, a suitable companion for a man like Grovich. She was KGB and attached to the GRU during Afghanistan. I am now referring to the current Afghan conflict in which the Russians claim no official part, just as they claim no part in the Ukraine conflict or the Georgian. Her work in Afghanistan made her feared by the Mujahedeen, and all of the men who worked with her. Ruthless, merciless, I cannot really find the correct words to describe Rachel Vishinski. Just do not let yourself be caught by her."

Cass shivered at this description. "Whoa! She sounds truly bad. So how do we get that one?"

Hannah smiled grimly. "We don't. I will! She will come after me. I invented the role she thinks she is playing. The 'angel of death' is the mantle she currently wears. The problem with that sort of title, especially when you are a successful assassin; is you begin to believe it. That is the weak point that can get you killed."

"Is that why you gave up? Joined us, I mean." Cass said softly.

Hannah looked hard at Cass for a moment, then her gaze softened. "Partly," she admitted. "But mainly because of something else." She stopped, hesitating.

Cass looked at her keenly. "A man?"

Hannah smiled. "Funny you should say that. It was not a man per se. I saw Jill with Gerald, and Charlie with Sheila. I suddenly realized that I was in danger of dying without knowing a true relationship. How about that?" She looked at Cass defiantly, daring her to laugh.

Cass looked back thinking how incredibly lonely life must have been for the woman in front of her. "Now there is someone?"

Hannah nodded, "He doesn't know of course."

"Why don't you tell him?"

"He's married!"

Cass nodded. "I see. I know him, of course, and I should say I know him better than you do."

"What do you mean, you know him?"

"There is only one married man who would qualify since you arrived in the group. Only one that you have worked with. I'm pretty sure that Quin would not qualify, as he is in many ways too much like you. It's Sir Tony?"

Hannah went white. "Is it that obvious?"

"No, I happen to be a good detective. Knowing that there was someone gave me the clue. I also noticed that Sir Tony was aware of you. I can tell you that his marriage is loveless and his wife has a woman lover."

Hannah looked at Cass. "You know this?"

"They married for convenience, strictly business. Only recently has Marion, his wife, become completely honest with him. They are nearer to being friends now than they ever have been. She has even offered to divorce if he wishes, without opposition. That is the latest information I have. Finally, I believe he is interested in you because I noticed, when you were with him, he made no passes at you. Nor did he ignore you. In my book, he is interested."

Hannah was stunned. This was not a situation she was accustomed to.

Cass spoke again, "Speak to Sheila. She knows him better than anyone else."

***

In the H.I.S London office, the general office was busy with several of the agents working at their computers. In the inner sanctum Sheila was talking to someone on the phone. As soon as Hannah made herself known she ended her call and greeted her with a smile.

"I have just been on the phone to Cass. Two things. What she told you is absolutely true, and I agree with the assessment of Tony's interest."

Hannah's initial reaction was anger, until she realized that these interfering people were acting like friends. Their interference was for her, not against. The heat disappeared. She looked at Sheila and her shoulders dropped. She looked absolutely depressed.

Sheila pressed the intercom button. "Come in." She said quietly and rose to her feet. "Back in a second," and left the room.

Sir Tony walked in from the inner office, and saw Hannah sitting looking absolutely depressed. He didn't hesitate. He walked over and lifted the startled woman to her to her feet and into his arms, holding her close. It just seemed so unconscious, so natural. She lifted her face and he kissed her.

For the first time in her life Hannah Curtain relaxed, and let her defenses down with a man.

"Are you all right?" Tony asked anxiously, after a mutually enjoyable few moments.

Hannah leaned back and looked up into his face. "I feel better now. Thank you."

Tony made to release her. But she tightened her grip round his neck. "Not yet."

Tony held her close once more and started talking. "Hannah, the day we met I was, for the first time in my life, lost. I wanted you. Love at first sight? Call it what you will. I was hopelessly gone. I am married but not in love with my wife. Nor does she love me. She has offered to divorce me, but suggested we live our own lives for a while and decide later. I did have a mistress but since we met I have dropped the relationship. I dropped it, despite having no hope or expectations of getting to know you better. If this moment means you feel the same, I'm happy to do whatever you ask, just to allow us to be together."

"Stop talking." Hannah said and kissed him.

In the other office Sheila, who was listening on the open connection at her secretary's desk, lifted her hand, thumb raised. The staff let out their collective breath, The smiles reflected their reaction to the news that Sir Tony, as he was known in the office, had found someone at last.

***

The road was clear ahead of the speeding Mercedes convertible. Vassily Borodin smiled to himself as Rachel Vishinski drove smoothly keeping within inches of the white centre line. At the speed they were maintaining, they should soon be in touch with the two truck-trailers they were expecting.

One of the vehicles came into view. The Mercedes swiftly caught up and, slowing as they passed, signalled the driver to pull over and stop on the hard shoulder.

The container on the trailer was marked Occidental Cargos, the logo of the company Borodin managed. The driver smiled as he recognized Borodin. He opened the door and climbed down, stretching his arms and easing his back. "Good day, sir, and Miss. What brings you right out here today?"

They all walked over to the grass verge beside the ditch alongside the road. Rachel shot him between the eyes. As the driver fell into the ditch she replaced her pistol and turned back to the truck. Borodin took the Mercedes and led the truck to the next junction where he turned into the side road. The barn was nearly one kilometre along the road and off by itself. With doors opened ready, Rachel drove the entire rig into the barn and switched off.

She helped Borodin close the doors and lock them. They left in the Mercedes, swiftly making their way back to the main road once more.

The second truck-trailer was parked at an overnight truck stop. The driver was checked in to the roadside motel. When the Mercedes arrived it did so with minimal fuss, parking beyond the row of heavy vehicles out of sight of the café and accommodation.

In the motel the driver called his colleague, surprised that he had not already arrived at the truck-stop. He could hear the phone ringing out, but was unaware that the phone was still in the pocket of his friend, unheard by the owner.

The driver rang his manager. Borodin answered. "Yes. What is it. "He sounded impatient.

"Sir, my friend, Francois, is not answering his cell phone, and the truck has not arrived at the night stop."

"Where are you now?"

The driver said, "I have a room at the motel for us both."

"What number?"

"Seventeen. Why do you need to know?"

"I may need to come there, idiot."

"Ah, I see. Do you think there is something wrong?"

"Possibly." Borodin rang off, now standing looking at room 17 at the motel.

He knocked at the door. When it opened he shot the driver in the heart. He lifted his phone once more. "Rachel, my dear, please depart. The ends have been tied up."

Returning to the Mercedes, he followed the departing truck back up the road to the barn, where they parked the second truck. At the trucks Anton Grovich, aka Vassily Borodin, greeted Rachel with a smile. "This should make it possible to get rid of that peasant, Ranala." He climbed into the cab of one the trucks, joining Rachel who was seated still.

He nodded at the bed behind the seats, and followed her through the gap stripping off his clothing as he went. Rachel was also stripping, as they celebrated their latest exploit in their own way.

***

Grovich spoke on his cell phone, his rapid words reminiscent of the old Grovich. Rachel listened and approved.

He finished his call, turned to Rachel and said, "It's time Avo Ranala retired." Rachel looked up with interest. Grovich saw the interest and slowly nodded. "Yes. I think you should make plans to that end. This consignment is sufficient to put me back on my feet. Patrick Romande is arranging to pick up as we speak."

Rachel spoke for the first time. "I do not trust that man."

"My dear, you will be here when the moment comes. There are the weapons you may need in the cargo of the other truck." He tossed over the keys, "Perhaps it might be best for you to sort them out now, before the party starts."

Chapter twenty-seven

End Game

The truck arrived at the barn, preceded by the Toyota, long cab pick-up. Six men came out of the pick-up, armed and wary. They stationed themselves around the area while the truck reversed up to the barn doors. A limousine drew up behind the truck and Patrick Romande stepped out. A dapper man, dressed in dinner jacket with black tie, he wrinkled his nose at the soggy ground beneath his feet. Anton Grovich strode through the now open barn doors and met him with a smile.

"You have the money?" He asked.

"You have the goods?"

"Of course. The truck can be unloaded by your men as soon as the money is on the table."

Romande gestured to one of the men accompanying him. The man came forward and laid a case on the bonnet of the limo. He unsnapped the lid and exhibited the packed wads of money filling the case to the brim.

Grovich stood aside and waved the men in to start on the transfer.

The two principles stood and watched as the transfer took place. The second truck was opened and the balance of the consignment was transferred.

Romande was looking around all the time, not trusting the apparent lack of support for Grovich. He became more and more agitated as the last few bags of product were transferred.

Finally, he waved to the man with the bag. "Put it in the car!"

The man was sweating. He started to close the bag, lowering the lid.

Grovich said quietly, "No!" The man looked at his boss helplessly. Romande shrugged and lifted the automatic he had in his hand. From the darkness there was a quiet cough. Romande looked down at his shirtfront. A hole had appeared black against the white material. Grovich stepped forward and took the case, from the sweating man. Romande folded and sat down on the ground as Grovich went into the barn. The gunmen with Romande realized that something was wrong, and started firing at the barn. From the woods came the quiet shots taking four men before they realized they were under fire themselves.

The survivors ran looking for cover and dropped before they could find it. The only member of Romande's party still standing was the unhappy man who had brought the case.

Rachel appeared from the woods, her rifle in her hands. She ignored the trembling man and called Grovich.

The Mercedes started up and appeared from behind the barn. Rachel signalled the survivor to get into the car. She followed him. Grovich drove off leaving the empty trucks and the full truck beside the limousine and the scattered bodies where they lay.

***

Avo Ranala was annoyed. "Where has Grovich gone now?"

His secretary said, "Mr Borodin reported following the double shipment south to the rendezvous two days ago. There have been no updates from the Director or either of the drivers. I have called their cell numbers but they seem to have disappeared completely. Canelli managed to trace the trucks.

He said he would rather talk directly to you this afternoon, when he has sorted everything out. He will give me no further information."

"Get him on the phone in my office. Now!"

White faced, she turned to her phone and started punching numbers. She had never seen her boss so angry.

There was no answer from Canelli's cell so she rang the number she had for Canelli's number two, Alonzo. He answered "Pronto!"

"Thank god, you are there."

"What is it? I am busy." Alonzo said impatiently.

"Avo Ranala wants to talk to Canelli. Now! He is on fire!"

"Shit!" Alonzo said. "We are just clearing up the fucking mess left by your man, Borodin, and his girlfriend."

"What about the cargo?"

"It is here. Okay. I ask Canelli to call now." Alonzo rang off.

Five minutes passed. The phone rang. "Ranala?" The impatient voice of Canelli rasped.

"Hold one," The harassed secretary replied. She switched the call through to her boss and sat back, flipping the switch as she did so. With the volume turned down she listened to their conversation, as the recorder taped everything said.

Avo Ranala made up his mind. Grovich had gone too far this time. There was no doubt in his mind that the massacre in the French barn was the work of Grovich and that bitch, Vishinski. The fact that the drugs were safe, retrieved by Canelli to whom they were consigned in the first place was not enough. He would lose money paying for the clear up. Canelli had made it quite clear. Though he would still be in profit, it was an expense he did not need. He called a personal number. "Radick, I have work for you."

"I am busy. I still have the new loop line to complete to Waterloo station. What is it?" Radick was a model railway enthusiast and he was integrating the Eurotunnel line into his system.

"Vassily Borodin, aka, Anton Grovich, and his girlfriend, Rachel Vishinski. Remove them both."

"Ha, Rachel Vishinski, that will cost more, she is pretty good."

"No matter. Do it as soon as possible!"

"Okay, okay. I finish Waterloo later. Where are they, these two lovebirds, hey?"

"How the hell do I know. They were last seen in Southern France. My guess will be Paris. But that is just a guess. Ask your contacts." Ranala slammed the phone down and called his secretary in.

"Call my house. I will be home in twenty minutes. Tell Greta to be ready for me." He leered at her. "You could come and join us if you wish."

She shuddered and shook her head. "I think not, sir." She waited tensely, until Ranala left laughing at his joke.

***

Astrid Colbert was an extremely accomplished actress, as well as being a spy for the Serious Crime Investigation division of the Euro-co-operative crime unit. Her position here was seriously important and had taken time and effort to establish. The intelligence she gathered was building a picture of some of the most wanted criminals within the Union.

Soon they would delete Ranala from the list and at the same time, if Ranala did not get there first, Grovich and Vishinski. It was her current role and she played it straight. Reflectively she put her hand up her skirt and rubbed a place on her inner thigh where the holster of her .22 automatic rubbed. She had been tempted to shoot her boss on several occasions. *Another time*, she thought, *another time.*

***

Rachel Vishinski adjusted her raven wig. The flowing hair dropped to her shoulders and framed her rather broad-cheeked face making it look narrower, her grey eyes, behind the brown inserts searching everywhere for the signs that someone was home. It had been annoying seeing Ian Bennet at the hotel when she had checked in. She was hoping the surprise she had left for him would keep him out of the way. She did not think she had been identified anyway.

Quin Gilmore saw the dark haired woman checking in from his seat in the lobby. He almost missed it. As a child Rachel Vishinski had been trained as a gymnast. An accident had robbed her of her chance of fame. It had left her with a slight flaw in the former smooth flow of her walk, almost a twitch in her right leg as she stepped forward. Quin saw this as the dark haired woman turned and walked to the elevators. *Surely not,* he thought. Making his mind up he called Ian on his cell. "I think you have been recognized by Rachel Vishinski, Now black long hair and brown eyes. Watch your back."

Ian, who was entering his room, left the door open and, from behind the door, started a conversation with a fictitious person in the bathroom. Rachel, following down the corridor, hooked a small package to the door handle as she passed, following the porter carrying her bag.

When she passed, Ian stepped round the door and examined the small object attached to the door. In his room he cut the corner from one of the laminated brochures left by the hotel for the guests information. Back at the door he carefully inserted the plastic into the gap on the trembler mechanism on the bomb, rendering it safe. He then removed the bomb.

Rachel was unaware of these events now having driven to the Ranala house, her car parked in the driveway of a neighboring house.

The Ferrari driven by Ranala arrived with a flourish, driving directly into the opened garage. the door promptly closing behind it.

Rachel left her car and walked up the drive to the Ranala house. She rang the bell, her other hand round the grip of the suppressed Glock automatic.

A maid answered the door. Rachel said pleasantly, "Mr Ranala, I was asked to join him." The maid sniffed, "He is in the garage," she opened the door and let Rachel in. "Through there." The maid pointed at a door partly open, through which came scuffling sounds. She obviously did not approve of what was going on in there, but Rachel thought was obviously watching. She stepped over to the door. The red Ferrari was there, another car on the far side. Across the bonnet of the red car a woman was sprawled, skirt round her waist, legs wrapped around Ranala, whose bare bottom was rising and falling, pumping away at his task.

Rachel shot the maid and stepped through into the garage. She put two bullets into the fuel tank of the car before Ranala noticed her. He stopped what he was doing as Rachel took off the wig.

"Shit!" he said. Rachel shot him in the stomach, and put a second bullet in the woman's head.

Ranala fell across the dead woman. Rachel took out a book of matches and struck the entire book, then dropped it into the growing pool of petrol. She stepped back through the open door and closed it behind her. The dead maid lay on the floor staring with dead eyes at her killer. Rachel replaced the wig and walked out of the front door, back to her car. She picked up her car from Nice Airport, and drove to Besancourt to join Anton with her news.

***

Hannah Curtain rose from the ground in the garden of the hotel bungalow complex in Besancourt. The process avoided the rain-laden leaves of the plants all around her. The area was light and shadow, the plant life moving the leaves and branches flirting with the wind and rain, creating shifting patterns throughout the night gardens. When Hannah moved she became part of the pattern flitting from shade to shade, her dark striped face difficult to separate from the background she had chosen.

The patio door on the closest bungalow opened and closed in a smooth, swift, movement. The print of soft shoes appeared briefly in the wet surface of the patio, the footprints showing briefly across the stone slabs to disappear into the garden foliage. In seconds the rain wiped out the signs of Rachel Vishinski's passing.

Hannah clapped her hands silently, acknowledging the acuity of the Russian assassin. She waited. With ears and eyes unfocused, she depended on the sound and sights of the night to give her warning of the approach of her opponent, if and when she came near.

Her patience was rewarded. The rustle of an accidental contact with the leaves of a nearby bush, gave her direction. She refused to concentrate on the sound, aware that it could be a diversion.

It nearly caught her out. The light footfall had her rolling to her right, knife out and poised, the blade scoring Rachel's arm as it drove her blade into the ground, not her stomach. Hannah lifted her blade across Rachel's exposed chest. Rachel twitched to one side, the blade cutting her shoulder instead, drawing blood.

Rachel back-flipped and raced back to the bungalow followed by Hannah. As she flung open the door, Hannah threw her knife.

Inside the room Grovich leapt to his feet. Rachel stood bleeding, blocking the doorway for a moment. She spoke. "That bitch Hannaaaaa..." then collapsed to the ground, Hannah's knife clearly visible in her back. Grovich fired at the vague figure visible out by the bushes. He realized that he had missed. The figure disappeared.

He crouched beside the collapsed figure. "Rachel" he said, disappointment clear in his voice. He wrenched the knife from her back and wiped the bloody blade on her clothes. He shouted at the night outside. "I'll let you have this back one day, bitch."

***

Back from Tallin, Quin and Ian were stunned to hear of the demise of Rachel Vishinski. Hannah had been in touch. She was keeping Grovich in view, having reported that he had gathered a group of thugs around him, and appeared ready to go back in business on his own.

Angelo had reported that a man named Canelli had apparently got hold of the latest cargo of drugs, and that Borodin had ordered the Occidental Cargoes company to clean up the recovered container, truck-trailer combinations, now the police had finished with them, and get the business back into proper operation. He also reported that rumor had it that Patrick Romande, and at least six of his men had been found dead. His accountant had also disappeared, and apparently joined Borodin in the Phoenix Operation.

Presumably, the assets of Patrick Romande had accompanied him to his new position.

Hannah Curtain had not returned from Europe. She had called Sir Tony, mentioned unfinished business, promising to return soon.

***

Angelo Petrucci got the call at three in the morning. "Angelo, it is Hannah. An absent friend will be visiting your colleague Lorenzo this morning to confirm a deal in imports. It entails using the shipping company. I had the impression that the shipping company was to remain clean, at least until its reputation was established?"

Angelo was now fully awake, his mind working. "Hannah, I will arrange this. I depend on you looking after business if I don't quite complete things?"

"You have my word!"

Angelo wasted no time. He was on the phone to Arthur Chung and Franco Carriere within minutes. In short terse sentences he told them what was happening. It was a situation that, months ago, would not have raised an eyebrow among them. With the establishment of the shipping company and the agreed intent to keep it clean, the attitude of the two, Chung and Carriere, had changed when they realized that profit without the risks entailed with law breaking, was not for mugs alone.

Both were angry, when they realized that Lorenzo was arranging the deal without consulting them.

Angelo told them a little about Grovich and the death of his wife and child. Then he told them he would take care of Grovich, but Lorenzo would be their business. To his relief they agreed. A rendezvous was arranged for the following day. Angelo prepared to deal with Grovich.

Sabine who had been listening also quietly made plans. Her automatic shotgun was still in good order.

Chapter twenty-eight

Finale

Lorenzo Grimaldi had a good feeling about this meeting. His association with the others had meant a reasonable return from the business. But he was not really committed like the others. This stupid business of the shipping company was just a waste of time. What Borodin was suggesting would give him the lead in the group and he could stop all this nonsense with the shipping company right now. The meeting was to take place in the Casino in Monaco. A private room that would not be targeted as a hotel venue might be. He was there in advance to make sure all was in place when the meeting started. What he was not aware of was that there was a snooper system installed in all rooms of the Casino. Angelo was aware of this. Sabine worked at the Casino and because of that he was able to get access to the system for the room. Arthur Chung and Franco Carriere sat and listened to the discussion between their partner and Vassily Borodin, detailing the abuse of their agreement to maintain the lawful operation of shipping company, and the suggested subordination of their place in the partnership, or their elimination, if that was unacceptable.

Angelo looked at the two men. "Well, what are you going to do about it?"

Arthur Chung brought out a Glock automatic. Franco cocked a Walther PPK. Angelo had a knife. Chung screwed a silencer onto his weapon. "Let's go," he said.

The two men at the door of the room moved to intercept them. Chung shot them both. The three men removed the bodies through the private side entrance, placing them in the people carrier sitting waiting beside the building.

The three then returned to the private room door. They exchanged looks. Then Franco opened the door and stepped in, followed by Chung and Angelo. The two men looked up in surprise. The single bodyguard each man had with him dropped silently from bullets from Chung's Glock.

Angelo said, "Anton Grovich, I presume."

Grovich said, "I am Vassily Borodin. Who is this Grovich you speak of." Angelo did not hesitate the knife flashed. "You had my wife and daughter murdered."

Grovich turned as the knife was thrust at him. His vest turned the blade slicing through his sleeve and into his arm. He reared to his feet flinging Angelo at the other two men. Lorenzo tried to get past his partners but found himself at the receiving end of the PPK of Franco Carriere. Rammed up against his body the report was muffled. Lorenzo swore as he crumpled to the floor.

Grovich had made it through the door which he slammed in Angelo's face. By the time Angelo got out of the building the people carrier was away.

***

Hannah Curtain watched the Nissan as it drove off making for the high mountain road to Menton and the Italian border. She was on a motorcycle and she was not taking prisoners. Taking the middle level she gained on the Nissan, which suffered from the fact that the driver had a deep knife wound in his right arm, and he was literally running for his life.

She was ahead of the Nissan at Caroles. Guessing he would make for the Autoroute at that point, she found a spot which would allow her room to use the rifle strapped to the motorcycle. The place was just before a bend with a drop-off of perhaps 200 feet beyond.

She parked the bike, and settled down in between two rocks overlooking the climb up to the corner. Checking the rifle she waited.

Five minutes later she had her guess confirmed. The Nissan was coming up the hill toward her position. As the car passed she shot out the right-front tire. The Nissan careered across the road toward the cliff face then back across to the low wall overlooking the drop-off. It smashed through the wall and stopped teetering balanced on the edge.

Hannah ran across. Grovich was groping for the seatbelt lock. Every time he moved the vehicle moved on its pivot point. Hannah knocked on the window. Grovich turned hope in his face, thinking help had arrived. When Hannah knew he recognized her, she leaned on the front wing, just a little. It was enough. As Grovich frantically struggled, the vehicle over-balanced, and bounced and crashed its way down the near vertical slope to come to rest in a crushed heap half on the road below. Unlike in the movies it did not burst into flames. Nor did anyone crawl out. Hannah climbed back onto the motor bike and tooled down the hill, turning off onto the side road where the Nissan had ended up.

The two bodies in the back were sort of mashed into the bodywork. Grovich was fairly intact apart from his rather squashed head which had hit the tarmac from the look of things. Hannah reached in and checked for a pulse. Reassured there was none. She waved to a passing car calling out for them to tell the police. She climbed onto the motor bike and rode off, back to Monaco.

***

Angelo called Quin on his cell phone. The message was short and final. "Grovich suffered a single car accident on the Riviera, last night. No survivors. Inform Hannah."

Hannah arrived in London the same evening, late. She joined Sir Anthony in his suite at Grosvenor House in Park Lane.

As she walked through the door she said, "The answer is yes, yes, yes!"

***

In Canonby the Lady of the Manor looked across at her Lord of the Manor. "Who was that?"

"That was Angelo, the Grovich matter has been settled."

She looked at Quin, her husband. Then said, "I hope he suffered something of the pain he inflicted on others.

The End

www.ingramcontent.com/pod-product-compliance
Lightning Source LLC
Chambersburg PA
CBHW051526260626
47170CB00003B/811